The Tomb of the Gods

(Matt Drake #4)

David Leadbeater

Copyright © 2013 by David Leadbeater

All rights reserved. No part of this publication may be reproduced, distributed, or transmitted in any form or by any means, including photocopying, recording, or other electronic or mechanical methods, without the prior written permission of the publisher/author except in the case of brief quotations embodied in critical reviews and certain other non-commercial uses permitted by copyright law.

All characters in this book are fictitious, and any resemblance to actual persons living or dead is purely coincidental.

ISBN: 1482545195
ISBN-13: 978-1482545197

Books by David Leadbeater:

The Bones of Odin (Matt Drake #1)

The Blood King Conspiracy (Matt Drake #2)

The Gates of Hell (Matt Drake #3)

The Tomb of the Gods (Matt Drake #4)

Chosen

Walking with Ghosts (a short story)

Connect with the author on Twitter:

@dleadbeater2011

Visit the author's website:

www.davidleadbeaternovels.com

Follow the author's Blog

www.davidleadbeaternovels.blogspot.co.uk/

All helpful, genuine comments are welcome. I would love to hear from you.
davidleadbeater2011@hotmail.co.uk

ACKNOWLEDGEMENTS

For invaluable help on this action-packed journey I'd like to take a few minutes to thank some fantastic people:

First and foremost, my wife Erica, for her absolute understanding and unflinching support.

My parents for their enthusiasm, encouragement and help.

Amy Eye of The Eyes for Editing – for her top-class editing work and for putting up with all of my many urgent requests.

Martha Bourke – author of The Jaguar Sun series – for a wealth of invaluable information that helped to get me started on this ever-winding road.

Andy Brown – of ClickedTwice Design – for designing the awesome covers.

And to every single person who has bought a Matt Drake adventure and loved it – the journey has only just begun!

I would also like to acknowledge the classic poem – The Charge of the Light Brigade, by Alfred, Lord Tennyson, which inspired the climatic scene of this series.

PART 1

What makes a hero. . .

ONE

Beyond the tiny airplane window, a bruised sky reflected the state of his soul.

He cast his gaze around the cabin. Pretty stewardesses in red skirts and white blouses dished out microwaved food and offered passengers drinks. The aromatic smells of cooked meats and vegetables drifted through the air. Couples and their kids chatted animatedly, but not as much as they had a week or two ago. This was the plane's return journey. The one taking them all back home.

To London.

Drake moved his head slightly back toward the window. His face betrayed nothing, but his mind flicked over recent events faster than it could assimilate the data. After a few minutes, he closed his eyes, letting out a sigh of frustration. He needed to slow down. He needed to take stock. A twelve-hour plane ride should give him time to do that.

Two days had passed since the Blood King's defeat beneath Diamond Head. Since then, Drake and his friends had been flown to the CIA's office in Los Angeles for a full debriefing and then promptly been ushered into a meeting with Jonathan Gates, the US Secretary of Defense. There, Gates told them the shadowy operative Russell Cayman, the man who had taken over Torsten Dahl's archaeological exploration of the first tomb of the gods in Iceland, had invited all of them—including Gates himself—to an explanatory discussion in a neutral building in L.A. At this meeting, he told Gates, he would reveal his reason for usurping Dahl and furnish them with some details of the group he worked for.

The Swede, Dahl, was already en route, flying in from Iceland.

At first suspicious, they'd all been won over when Cayman agreed that the Secretary of Defense and his entourage of bodyguards could accompany them, no questions asked.

Hayden was optimistic. "Maybe Cayman isn't such a bad guy after all," she had said. They were all working on the location of the third tomb of the gods, but the map was beyond ancient, slightly eroded, and in need of translation. She thought that a full-disclosure chat with Cayman would further their joint goals faster than a hundred academics.

Drake was torn between wanting to meet Cayman, the man they were sure was tied to Wells somewhere down the line and thus tied to Alyson's murder, and the need to travel quickly to Wells's flat in London to search for something only he might find.

A clue as to what the hell Wells had been involved in. And why.

Wells, at heart, had been an SAS officer and a patriot. Drake had always known that. Beyond everything, Wells put his country first.

For him to know about Alyson's death and not tell me…
What would make a man like Wells do that?

Cayman might know. But the flat in London—*that's* where the real evidence should lie. So Drake, along with Mai and Alicia, settled on a journey to London that they hoped led to the clues to a real answer. Drake asked Ben to accompany him, and the young man had deliberated hard, but elected to stay close to his girlfriend. Ben had been fighting for her for some months now and wasn't about to let her drift away. Karin stayed with her brother, her elation at beating the Blood King and the seven-layered trap system before uncovering a second tomb of the gods, had been badly tempered when her new friend Komodo had been immediately sent back to his Delta base, destination unknown.

Drake drifted back to the present and checked his watch. In three hours, they would land at Heathrow. Wells's flat was on the outskirts of Mayfair, just off Park Lane and Piccadilly. An easy tube journey from Heathrow. Once they landed, Drake, Mai and Alicia were prepared to hit the ground running. Mai's infractions with her bosses at the agency had been forgiven—the Japanese had seen the importance of finding the third Tomb of the Gods and the hinted-at doomsday weapon it may contain. She'd been given full reign to deal with the situation however she saw fit. Agents were at her disposal. Alicia remained part of Drake's unofficial team, a team that had been evolving since they had first met Jonathan Gates back in Washington DC, Drake had realized.

A stewardess leaned over him. He refused the snack. His eyes lingered on the shots: the whisky, the vodka, the quick cure. Very slowly, he shook his head. When the stewardess pressed the sale, mistaking raw need for playfulness, he closed his eyes and waited until she went away.

Behind his eyes, those eternally sad eyes, he saw them both how he liked to remember them. Beautiful and brimming with life and love and happiness. Alyson had always been like that. With Kennedy, the contentment had just started to shine through when. . .

...when. . .

I miss you both so much.

He had moved on. To a degree, anyway. To drink their memories away was to sully them. To forget the happy times they shared was to waste them. And an ex-SAS soldier was stronger than that. Deep inside him was a core of pure steel.

He hardened himself now. There was a promise of tough work ahead. Not only for him, but for Hayden back in L.A. She would be meeting Cayman soon, and then the shit might really hit the fan. He considered giving Ben a call on the Satphone, trading a joke or two about his band who had hit the limelight at last (without him), and maybe firing off a few old Dinorock quotes. But then, Alicia caught his eye from across the aisle.

"Fucksake, Drake," she whispered. "Stop shutting us out. We're here to bloody help you."

"The least you could do," Drake said. "Considering. . ."

"Considering what? The only thing I consider is the size of—"

"*Considering*. . . that you two lied to me for seven years."

"I hadn't *seen* you for seven years. I went rogue, remember? And I only heard about it a couple of years ago, Drake. Just like Mai. I guess we both thought it had gone way past the time to tell you."

"So you made the choice for me."

"We didn't know anything! Well, nothing beyond the fact that Alyson didn't die in an accident and that Wells had knowledge of it."

Drake frowned. "But how could you know I'd moved on?"

"Don't be so naïve. I knew where you were and what you were doing. So did Mai, I'm sure. The world's a smaller place with Facebook and Twitter around. And before those two, there was still the web, and boyfriends who knew how to use it."

Drake sat back. Deep down, he knew that what she said made sense. Time moved by quickly, and to send a man back to the worst place in his life after five years of healing could have been more of a curse than a blessing.

The seat belt sign clicked on. The plane began to descend.

Drake met Alicia's crazy blue-eyed gaze. "The investigation will be even harder," he said, "now that we know Wells wasn't controlled by the British government, but by some greater secret organization. Now that we know he wasn't the man he pretended to be."

Alicia buckled up. "Oh, I'm pretty sure he was a perv, Drake. But I guess his being dead doesn't help us much."

Drake stared, a little amused despite himself. "I guess not."

*****

Once through passport control and past the luggage carousels, Drake headed immediately for the depths of the underground. Tired old escalators groaned as they descended, taking them past dozens of picture frames, all inlaid with advertisements of the latest shows and movies and expo's. *Walking With Dinosaurs*. *The Hobbit*. Eurogamer. Once at the bottom, a spider web of signs seemed perfectly designed to confuse newcomers. Drake, Mai and Alicia spent a few minutes deciding which line to take and then which direction to go. Hordes of Londoners and tourists of every color and race flowed past them without checking. A busker strummed a jaunty tune at a nearby junction.

"Piccadilly line," Alicia finally said. "Takes us all the way to Green Park. Isn't Wells's place just off that?"

"On the other side of Piccadilly," Drake said. He slipped his mobile back into his pocket and worked out the time difference back in L.A. Only about seven a.m. in the land of sunshine and celluloid. Hayden and her CIA colleagues were due to meet Dahl off the plane at nine a.m. and then proceed to meet with Cayman at ten. Drake's suspicions of the shady DIA operative deepened with every mile he traveled. He didn't just fear for Ben; he feared even for the highly capable people like Hayden and Kinimaka. And Dahl. What was his Swedish friend about to walk into?

Who was Russell Cayman? And just how far up the food chain did his bosses make their, no doubt, sumptuous and immoral nests?

So far up, Drake thought. *They were beings of mist and shadow, fleeting like ghosts. The power behind the power.*

They found the right station and waited behind the yellow lines for their tube. Mai drifted to his right, Alicia to his left, unconsciously putting a barrier between them. Alicia stepped forward as the tube whistled past.

"Shag it, it's packed out. If I get groped on this thing, some bastard's getting off minus a set of balls." She paused. "Unless he looks like Boreanaz. Then. . .we'll talk."

"Or Belmonte?" Mai said, her soft, sweet voice belying the venom intended. "I'm surprised you didn't stay in L.A., Myles. You knew your old lover was arriving with Dahl, didn't you?"

"Been there," Alicia said. "Banged that. I've had better."

"Oh, hundreds I'm sure."

"Bloody hell." Drake exploded. "If I'd known it'd be this hard with you two, I'd have bloody well come alone."

The train rattled through the darkness, the bright windows

illuminating pipes that twisted and snaked their way along the tunnel walls. As he studied his fellow travelers, Drake was amused to see how many of them stole glances at each other when they assumed they weren't being watched. And the traditional open paper was long gone now, replaced by Android phones and Amazon Kindles.

Green Park arrived quickly. They exited the tube station and found themselves on a busy London street near the sprawling Ritz hotel. Drake zoned out for a few minutes when a black Bugatti Veyron took the right turn at the lights to head down the side of the famous landmark.

"Earth to Drake," Alicia murmured. "It has four wheels, a bonnet, and a windscreen. It's just a car."

Drake glared. "Don't push it, Alicia. I still haven't forgiven you for shooting up that Shelby Cobra."

"You mean the one with the bad guy in the boot?"

"You could have easily shot him and missed the car, Alicia. I'm not that stupid."

Mai spoke up as they crossed the road. "Or maybe she's not as good as you think she is, Matt."

"Fuck off, tiny sprite." Alicia strode ahead, aiming for the street where Drake indicated Wells's flat was situated. After a few minutes' walk, they paused outside a nondescript three-story building built of grey stone, cast-iron gutters and thick, darkened windows.

"Guess I'm not so bad after all." Alicia raised an eyebrow at Mai. "This is the place. I only came here once, maybe seven or eight years ago. But this is definitely Wells's home."

Drake checked the address he'd been given. "Yep."

They started up the steps.

"We'd best be quick," Mai said quietly. "A pack of bruisers

has been following us since we entered this street. They're hanging back for now. Probably just guards hired to watch Wells's place. They'll take their time checking us out or they'll be on us in minutes, depending on orders. My guess is the former. We could be anybody, after all. *Keep going.*" She hissed as Alicia faltered.

Matt Drake knew better than to look back. He'd been looking back and staying purposely stagnant for seven years.

It was time to move forward and fully embrace the power and the violence and the tremendous skill he had been born to utilize.

He could be a force of nature. A savior of worlds. Deep down, he'd always known it. The time was coming when he'd have to prove it.

TWO

Hayden Jaye tuned out the conversation around her for a few moments. Ever since Dmitry Kovalenko ordered the attack on the CIA safe house, killing most of her team and taking her hostage, events had unfolded with such crazy rapidity that she'd barely had a moment to take stock. Even the weeks convalescing after the first knife wound had passed in a blur as she tried to piece together all that had happened and what the Blood King's next move might be.

But now, healing slowly from the second knife wound—a wound that hurt less and healed faster with the intimate knowledge that Ed Boudreau was dead—she had consciously been taking as many spare moments as she could to sort out her feelings for Ben Blake.

He was too young for her. He was too immature for her. At a professional and career level, they were poles apart. If it were a business decision, it would be easy.

Hayden wondered if the spirit of old James Jaye was still riding her back, forcing her nose to the ground so she couldn't see straight. But it didn't feel that way. Her heart was telling her the relationship was wrong, not her mind. *But what was the problem?* Could she let something that had, at first, felt so right dissipate without a fight?

And here she was, about to meet not only the famous

Torsten Dahl but also Daniel Belmonte—one of her old flames—whilst Ben and his sister waited back at the HQ, ready to process any information Dahl might bring with him. The big Swede had been toiling persistently inside the Icelandic tomb for weeks upon weeks and had actually stepped up operations when Cayman appeared and took charge. But Dahl had kept many secrets to himself, and Hayden believed, had even managed to place a trusted man on the inside.

As for Belmonte, it seemed Gates had been so impressed with his clandestine burglary at Kew Gardens that he had instantly decided Belmonte's special skillset might prove of further value before this increasingly desperate operation ended.

Belmonte, ostracized for years, had jumped at the chance to return to the government fold, albeit under the directions of a different country. He had even offered the additional help of his protégé, a woman known only as Emma.

As the passengers began filtering through, Hayden again put her life on hold. At this rate, the friggin' pause button would be worn out before she got the analysis down.

Maybe she analyzed her problems too closely.

In any case, she walked forward with a genuine smile when the Swede, Dahl, strode toward them.

"Torsten." She stretched out a hand, then felt herself grabbed and given a friendly hug.

"Hayden!" Dahl cried warmly. "It is so good to see you again. The wrong circumstances, I'm sure, but good nevertheless."

Hayden let herself be held just for a moment, basking in the security offered by the big, kind Swedish Special Forces officer. The sanctuary she sought was the sanctuary her father had once given her. That ultimate feeling of safety and the deep knowledge that if she ever started to hurt, she could always find a refuge.

And now, she knew why she couldn't stay with Ben Blake. No matter how hard he tried, he could never offer her that.

Hayden pulled away, smiling. "To hell with the bullshit circumstance. It's great to see you." She waved Kinimaka aside. "Over here is Jonathan Gates, the US Secretary of Defense."

Whilst the pair shook hands, Hayden assessed their surroundings. She had men positioned at every egress point and scattered around the room. Despite Cayman's assurances and his insistence that even the Secretary of Defense and his plethora of secret service agents was welcome to accompany them to this meeting, her shit-radar remained on full alert.

"We should get going soon," she said. "The meeting's in forty-five minutes. We don't wanna give this shitheel any excuse."

"Agreed." Dahl nodded. "I have met said shitheel, and must say I can't disagree with your statement."

Dahl's rhetoric was already jarring her. She suddenly understood why Drake teased him endlessly. It wasn't through spite; it was simply a way of coping. And, Dahl, in his way, understood that.

"And meet Mano Kinimaka, my partner." Hayden stepped aside as the big Hawaiian now came forward, offering a gruff hello.

And then her heart leapt as a familiar face threaded through the crowd. Daniel Belmonte, the master thief, her ex-lover, the Englishman every woman wanted to hate, but always ended up wanting more than they bargained for.

Alongside him walked a thin blond girl, hair curled into tight ringlets. Big blue eyes rounded off the archetypal likeness of the pretty blonde, but Hayden knew that if this woman accompanied Belmonte to a live job, being pretty would be the least of her attributes.

"Daniel," she said with forced neutrality. "Thanks for coming."

"How could I resist?" His eyes sparkled, then went blank. "But no, seriously. I couldn't resist. I was ordered to come here."

"Huh?" Hayden frowned. "But who—"

"Gates. Jonathan Gates." The Secretary of Defense came alongside her. "Pleased you accepted my invitation."

"Well when I say *ordered,*" Belmonte turned his voice down to a whisper. "You know I've always used the term loosely, don't you?"

Hayden took a deep breath. This was going to be a long day.

Gates turned and led them outside to a waiting limo. The hot L.A. air struck them as soon as they were out of the building and a dusty wind swept along the road. Hayden took a second to introduce herself to Belmonte's friend, not wanting to exclude anyone, and learned her name was Emma, and that she was Belmonte's charge and responsibility, not to mention his apprentice.

In what? Hayden wondered. Was Belmonte blasé enough to want a thief's life for such a young girl?

When the limo moved away from the curb, Dahl began talking.

"Excuse my manners. I know introductions haven't yet been completed, but I have information that I must impart." He nodded at the secretary. "It has been a long flight. I was hoping Drake would be here, but I guess he felt he should be in London, yes?"

Hayden nodded. "Right. He's following up the Wells lead."

"Hmm. Well, good luck to him. But now. . .as regards the eight pieces of Odin. Do you remember them?"

"Eight?" Belmonte immediately interrupted. "I think you mean nine, don't you?"

"No. I mean eight. The ninth piece, the Shield, was lost in Eyjafjallajokull."

"That's easy for you to say."

Dahl blinked. "I once said that to Drake. It wasn't funny then, either. Now please shut the fuck up and let me talk." Dahl moved in his seat, the leather creaking loudly. "The remaining eight pieces of Odin were transported to the Swedish Museum of National Antiquities in Stockholm to be assessed and carefully guarded before a decision could be made as to their final destination. All standard procedure."

"I'm aware of all that." Gates flicked his gaze between the Swede and the road ahead. The road that led to Russell Cayman. Hayden wondered what percentage of Gates' brilliant mind was focused on the job. He'd barely begun to grieve for his murdered wife.

"Good." Dahl looked around the limo. "Then is anyone aware that all eight pieces were removed by the American government a few days ago and transported to a military base in Stuttgart, Germany?"

Gates snapped his head around. Hayden felt her mouth go dry. *"What?"*

"How on earth could the American government authorize the removal of Norse artifacts from Scandinavian soil?" Belmonte wondered.

"Because someone. . ." Dahl's voice dropped even though he was among friends in the limo. "A very powerful someone in the Swedish government allowed them to. The same someone—I'm guessing—who gave them control of my exploration."

Gates shook his head. "I've heard nothing of this. If the order came from Cayman, then I don't think it came directly from the US government."

The big Swede stared. "You've lost me there, sir. Isn't Cayman DIA? A man from the special weapons division? Does he not work for a US agency?"

Gates pursed his lips. "We're about to find out, Dahl. My philosophy for getting by on the Hill has always been a simple one—*don't trust the bastards.*"

Dahl was momentarily silent. "The good news is that I managed to place one of my trusted men onto the exploration team before I left Iceland. He is nothing more than an ancient language specialist, but. . ." Dahl paused, purposely waiting so he could gauge who was the brightest in the car.

The limo slipped off the 405 onto the I10 and headed toward Santa Monica. Gates and Hayden were the first to speak up. "The whorls? They're the key?" Hayden said. "So the key to everything is deciphering the language that was written by the ancients? By the gods?"

"Isn't it always?" Dahl said with a smile.

Gates frowned. "So you're staking everything on a guess – that the gods recorded their intentions—from the map that shows the location of tomb three to the method of starting and stopping the doomsday device? Forgive me, Dahl, but that's one big-ass wager."

Hayden felt a pang in her heart when she immediately hit on what Kennedy Moore would have said. "Pussies don't last long in Vegas, baby."

Even Kinimaka cringed. Hayden quickly addressed her

boss. "What I mean is—the wager's informed enough to warrant the pay-off, sir." She turned to Dahl with an earnest appeal in her eyes. "Isn't it?"

"Exactly." Dahl managed to remain deadpan. "Well said."

"Your man." Gates was clearly thinking hard. "He could translate all this stuff and give us the heads up before Cayman's guys?"

"He is capable of that, sir."

"Excellent." Gates nodded. "Then we may have an ace in the hole."

"We may have more than one." Dahl smiled. "I bring more than one gift. I am Swedish, after all. This"—he pulled out a cell phone and clicked a few buttons—"is a photograph of the map I found in the tomb of the gods." He glanced at Hayden. "Is Ben still helping you?"

"Sure."

"Give me his mobile number, Hayden. He deserves a chance to decipher this too."

*****

Ben Blake smiled to himself as his sister, Karin, fended of the advances of the second geek of the day. Before she had left for her meeting, Hayden made sure that the pair were not only safe, but also in a position to help out at a moment's notice. Thus, she had ensconced them in a little room crammed with other uber-geeks in one of the Los Angeles CIA buildings. At first, Ben had rebelled, citing that he had stayed behind to help Hayden, not to be hidden inside the citadel of geekdom. Drake would never have left him marooned amidst so much angst and acne. But Karin had talked him into it, exerting her hard-hitting sisterly love, and now she was bearing the brunt of ninety percent of the churning hormones in the room.

Payback.

"Have they never seen a girl before?" Karin leaned over and whispered in his ear.

"Not one they could physically talk to." Ben grinned widely. "It'll be interesting when I have to step out and use the men's room."

"*Do not* leave me alone in here." Karin hissed. "Unless you wanna see a roomful of virgins singing soprano."

"Oooh, sis." Ben laughed. "What would Dad say?"

Karin pointed at his cell phone. "Ask him. That's him ringing now."

Ben chatted a little with his father before a message pinged up on the computer screen in front of them. Karin reached out to click the mouse, and Ben swatted at her hand.

"Mine," he whispered. "Could be from Hayden."

"Like I wanna see what you two mail each other."

Ben quickly ended the call. "Well, I'll say this, sis. There's no way it's as dirty as the stuff Komodo and you have been texting each other. Or is it called *sexting* now?"

"Shut up."

"Yeah, that's it. *Sexting.*"

Ben clicked on the message and was pleased to see it came from Torsten Dahl, and that it consisted of several attachments, each a picture of the map the Swede had discovered in the first tomb of the gods.

Karin mumbled about her contact with Komodo being curtailed for a while because of a *friggin' mission,* whilst Ben looked at the map from the various angles.

"We need to figure out where the third tomb is," Ben said seriously. "And fast."

Another geek made his move on Karin.

"*Piss off!*"

Ben's sister stood up, shook her hair out, and addressed the room. "Get this. I'm not one of you. I don't think like you. I do have a large brain, but it does not focus around penis. I don't heart nerds. I heart soldiers. I'm not a secretary. I'm a friggin' black belt. So unless you're severely into S&M, I suggest you stay the fuck out of my way."

Karin sat back down and sighed. "Okay, Ben. Now we can focus. Let's find that third bloody tomb."

*****

The limo stopped outside a high, nondescript building far enough away from Santa Monica beach that they couldn't even smell the sea, let alone see it. Gates's three-man secret service patrol exited first, closely followed by Hayden, Kinimaka and Torsten Dahl. Hayden saw Belmonte place a restraining hand on Emma's knee as she made to follow and watched as the British thief waited for Gates to receive the all clear.

Hayden walked up to Gates as he came around the back of the limo. The street was quiet. Only a few cars cruised its length, and the sidewalks were relatively deserted. They were far from the shopping district and most of the office workers were already chained to their eight-to-fives.

"Any more contact from Cayman?" Hayden asked quietly.

"Nothing. But Cayman's a man of principal. We all agreed the time and place. He'll be there."

Hayden looked up. A forest of tall buildings filled her gaze. She glanced at the secret service agents and received a faint nod in return.

"All right," she said. "Let's go."

As they walked, Hayden thought back over what Cayman had said to her. He'd called out of the blue the day after they brought the Blood King up from the depths of the Diamond Head volcano. At first, she'd been highly suspicious, listening without comment as he explained that he would reveal what he knew about the ancient language of the gods and the map Dahl had discovered in the Icelandic tomb. He'd said he wanted to tell her who he worked for and what he knew about the doomsday device. He was a good speaker. Even then, he was starting to make sense. He told her that he'd invited Torsten Dahl to the meeting, as a peace-making gesture. And then he told her that he'd also invited her boss, the Secretary of Defense, along with the secret service.

Hayden was impressed and convinced.

Maybe Cayman was working deep undercover for the DIA, or even the CIA, and wanted them on board. Their actions so far certainly deserved some kind of recognition.

Dahl walked alongside her. "I sent the pictures to Ben. We need his intellect, my dear, so please tell me you haven't shagged all his brains out yet?"

Hayden coughed. "C'mon, Dahl. Let's focus, shall we? Gates might suddenly love this guy Cayman, but we both know that his judgment may be impaired."

"I did wonder. Why not take a leave of absence?"

"He wants to see this through. For his wife as much as himself, I guess. And he's very good at what he does."

"And you, Hayden. What do you think of Cayman?"

They entered the lobby. A man wearing a smart suit sat behind the desk opposite, looking surprised at the sudden influx of people into his building.

Hayden let the secret service take the lead. "Cayman? Well, he talks a good game. But then—" She smiled. "Don't we all?"

"The man's lower than dirt," Dahl said. "I've met him."

Kinimaka made a point of getting her attention. "We're going up, boss," he said, indicating the elevators ahead. "You ready?"

Hayden nodded and gave Dahl a look. The big Swede nodded his readiness. Belmonte and Emma were busy surveying the room and its CCTV cameras, as well as the windows, doors, air vents, and any other means of ingress.

"Let's use the elevators," Hayden said to him with a grimace. "So much easier."

"You would think so, Miss Jaye," Emma said in a reflective tone, "but they're chiefly just another way of controlling and surveying the masses."

Hayden now remembered the most annoying thing about Belmonte. He was a massive conspiracy theorist. Clearly, he'd passed along much of what he believed in.

"Let's try them anyway."

The large group moved toward the nearest elevator. The secret service insisted on checking it out and then made noises indicating that only the Secretary and themselves should travel on the first one. Hayden acquiesced to keep the peace and filed into a second elevator. Kinimaka jabbed the button for the top floor.

They traveled up in silence. Weapons were checked. Belmonte pointed out the location of a cleverly hidden camera. Emma stood on tiptoe to plaster chewing gum over it.

"Always let them know they can't beat you," she said with a cheeky little smile.

Belmonte smiled happily as if to say *that's my girl*. Hayden kept her gaze firmly on the flashing floor numbers, trying hard not to think about the weeks she had spent with the British super-thief.

But, truth be told, they were good weeks. Hard to forget.

The elevator slowed. The doors slid open. Hayden stepped out and saw Gates with his secret service guard just ahead of them. She peered around the room. Kinimaka padded to her side, voicing a few choice expletives of surprise.

The entire top floor of the building spread out before them, unfurnished and empty apart from two men clad in combat gear and full-face helmets walking toward them, guns held loosely at their sides.

Gates was just turning toward her, his face puzzled, when fire and fury erupted around him.

THREE

Drake broke into Wells's apartment and then stood back whilst Mai moved in to disable the alarm. They were prepared for the men following them to make a move, but nothing had happened. In less than a minute, they had free reign. Drake remained motionless for a while, studying the layout of the place. A short hallway led to a living room beyond which sat a kitchen and a bedroom. The living room was furnished in a Spartan manner. Nothing existed that didn't have purpose. There was no sign of a woman's touch. All the colors were dark, making the corners hard to distinguish—a mirror to the apartment owner's soul.

Alicia remained outside the door, using a well-positioned set of hallway windows to her advantage, and set about cataloguing their potential enemies in the street below.

Drake waved Mai into the bedroom, whilst he took the living room. The irony of the Japanese agent finally making it into Wells's bedroom after the man was dead was not lost on either of them and they shared a somber look. Mai would be going through more than a few inner torments, Drake thought, since it was she who pulled the trigger.

He would have put money on it being Alicia. But then, that girl had never failed to surprise him.

A large oak table dominated the back of the living room.

The only item standing on its polished surface was a framed photograph. The picture showed Wells and a few of his army pals, arms over each other's shoulders, most likely at the end of some secret operation or other. *An operation for the British government?* Drake wondered. *Or for this secret group he and Cayman worked for?*

Drake moved on. The front of the living room held a two-seater leather sofa and a forty-inch TV. A drinks cabinet was well stocked. Drake resisted the urge to investigate. He rummaged through another cabinet, but found it to be nothing more than a tasteful frontage for a DVD/CD rack. One by one he checked every case for hidden contents. As he worked, he listened to Mai poking around the bedroom.

He heard her walking toward him. "Find anything?"

"A set of unusual DVD's. Some erotic art books from Japan. A signed picture of Kylie Minogue. Nothing unusual."

Drake raised an eyebrow. "You think?"

"For Wells, I meant. Now, have you checked *that?*"

He guessed to where she was pointing. "Boot it up, Mai. We should check but my feeling is Wells always remained old-school. If there's something here, it won't be on his PC."

Mai pressed a button and the big machine started clicking and whirring. "This place," she said, "has already been picked over. By a pro. Can you tell?"

Drake took a second look around. "Not really. No."

"Little things," Mai said in her quiet, unassuming voice. "Mainly, the faint scent of a woman's perfume in the bedroom."

"You said it was a pro."

"She was," Mai said with half a smile. "But even a pro adheres to the ritual of cleanliness, Matt. Besides, it's so faint most wouldn't have caught the scent."

Drake gave up on the DVD/CD cabinet and walked over to her. Carefully, he gave her thick lustrous hair a sniff.

"Be careful," Mai told him. "I keep a small poison-tipped needle back there."

"Yet another reason not to date a spy." But she smelled good. Vaguely of aniseed and vanilla. As he leaned forward he noticed a framed picture hanging on the wall, a photograph of a coyote standing in the foreground of a stark wilderness, snow and the barren sticks of dead, frozen trees all around. He was about to head over for a look when Mai pointed past him. "Wells has a PlayStation too. Do you think—"

Drake snapped back to the present. "No need to check, Miss Shiranu. He definitely owned that game."

"Wells was a lonely man. Just look around. He had no one who cared for him. No one special in his life."

"Men who keep secrets are always lonely," Drake said. "And men who also betray their friends die alone."

Mai bent over as the screen flicked into life. "So we're looking for anything that might lead us to *who* he worked for and how he knew Cayman."

"And for what he knew about Alyson's death, if anything. What I need to know is who gave the order and who executed it."

As he said the words, Drake felt the blood run hot through his veins. Someone had ordered the murder of his wife and his unborn baby. If one thing was certain in this entire world, it was the fact that all those involved would die for their sins.

Mai clicked a few icons. "Look at this," she said, surprise tingeing her voice. "Wells had a Twitter ID, a Facebook profile, and was a member of Goodreads. I think this proves that you were wrong, Matt. He wasn't *old school* at all."

Drake clicked onto 'history.' The last entry, dated the night before Wells had flown out to Miami, was a single line. One link to one site.

Hotmail. Password change.

Alicia popped her head around the door at that moment and told them, in characteristic style, to hurry the fuck up. The arseholes outside wouldn't stand around playing with their dicks forever.

"I have a crazy idea." Drake pushed past Mai and started skimming the mouse across a plush pad. "We were always taught to leave messages where they couldn't be found." He clicked onto Hotmail. "Except by the person who shared the account."

Mai glanced sideways at him as he hovered over the password box. "You know what it is?"

"If Wells had something to hide and wanted *us* to find it. . ." Drake bit his lip. "Then this is how he would do it. If not, well, we've lost nothing."

He typed a password slowly. Mai's eyes opened wide. "*Maitime? Really?*"

"What else could it be?"

The screen flicked onto the Hotmail website. Drake clicked the 'Drafts' folder and paused as three messages popped up, each one highlighted in bold to show they hadn't been viewed.

"They should be close copies of emails Wells sent to. . ." He paused. "A man called Andrew Black." Drake scrolled down the body of each email. "Nothing more than a simple message," he said with a tinge of disappointment. "*Sending latest version by snail mail, my friend. Needless to say, I know, but for all our sakes—keep it safe. Will be in touch when back.*"

"Hmm." Mai pointed to snatch of email where Andrew Black had responded. "*Getting some Mai time, my old friend?*"

"*Hopes are high, as ever.*" Wells had responded.

Drake clicked through Wells's online directory. An address was listed for an Andrew Black at nearby Sevenoaks in Kent. "We should follow this through. If Wells was shipping something to an old friend before leaving the country, it would be of huge importance to him."

Mai nodded and was about to respond when Alicia stuck her head through the front door. "Time to stop fannying around, people. The thugs just got reinforced."

"We're coming." Drake shut the PC down. "How many are there?"

"Enough so that we may have to fight our way out of London." Alicia grinned. "Just the way I like it."

FOUR

Hayden instinctively ducked as the row of windows to her right exploded. Shattered glass burst across the room in a deadly wave. The two black-clad combatants walking toward them ducked and started to open fire. If the onslaught was designed to numb their senses and slow their reactions, it served its purpose. The whole team was crawling and scrambling across the polished floor, glass showering them and bullets impacting the walls behind them. One of Gates's secret service men had managed to stay between his boss and the destruction. His body danced for the last time as it was riddled with bullets and he fell backward on top of Gates.

Hayden rolled onto her good hip, grimacing as pain shot through her wounded side, and slipped her gun out. Before she could aim, she heard the loud report of gunfire and glanced across to see Dahl already shooting. Belmonte was on his knees behind Dahl.

Hayden saw one of the combatants spin around as a bullet took him in the shoulder. She fired at the other, creeping forward as she did so. Her bullet struck his helmet, flipping him backward. Dahl fired again, but another of Gates's secret service agents cried out.

Blood sprayed from his neck, showering Hayden.

The CIA agent loosed more bullets. Both combatants were now down. Belmonte was screaming.

Was he hit? Hayden wondered. Gates was barely moving, but then his last surviving bodyguard was pinning him tightly to the ground.

"Evac!" the guard shouted. "It's a fuckin' ambush!"

Even now, Hayden could hardly believe her eyes. Had Russell Cayman, a DIA agent, just tried to take out a US senator? Where was the psycho getting his orders? Or was this some other kind of terrorist plot? Either way, they were screwed.

A high, keening sound preceded the impact of something big against the side of the building. Hayden suddenly realized this was far from over and hit the deck.

"Cover!"

A huge explosion shook the building to its very core. Behind them, the elevator shaft groaned and shuddered. Hayden saw the elevator buckle out of shape. In another second, it shook and seemed to hang at a precarious angle.

"No way out," she whispered.

"Yes!" Belmonte suddenly shouted. "Yes there is. There's a freight elevator on the other side of the building." He pointed across the expanse of the devastated room. "Across there."

He stood up, Emma cradled in his arms.

Tears shone in the thief's eyes.

Hayden gasped. "Is she? Is she. . ."

"Dead," Belmonte said quietly. "Yes, she is."

Gates threw his bodyguard off. Dahl gauged the ground they'd have to cover to make the freight elevator. "Run the gauntlet," he said. "It's the only way. And quickly."

"Do it!" In close formation they ran, Hayden, Kinimaka and

Dahl on the outside, guns drawn and aimed at the shattered windows. Gates, Belmonte with Emma in his arms, and the last secret service agent on the inside. As they passed by the windows, a great flash preceded the launch of another rocket. This one impacted where they had been a few moments before, destroying the elevator shaft.

They all managed to keep their feet, scrambling and struggling on. A barrage of gunfire blasted through the holes in the side of the building and they found themselves actually running a gauntlet of hot lead. Hayden felt something flash by her temple like a heated breath of air and another rip apart the hem of her jacket. Dahl grunted as something nicked an arm, but still managed a crazy laugh.

"Move!" he shouted.

"Who the hell are these people?" Hayden yelled.

Bullets zinged around them, a forest of whistling death. A third rocket exploded against the side of the building and something inside its structure suddenly lurched. Hayden crabbed sideways for a second. The last secret service agent caught a round in the thigh and collapsed in their wake. Dahl reacted instantly, grabbed him, and hauled him through the destruction.

Hayden ran beyond the edge of the last window. The rest of the team sprinted behind her, reaching safety without any more casualties. Gates reached out to press the elevator's call button, but paused in uncertainty.

"Call it," Dahl said. "But we're going down the stairs."

"And quick," Hayden said. "Even Cayman's plan B has a back-up plan, it seems. If Cayman's behind this."

"Too convenient not to be," Gates muttered. "Boy, does he have a god complex. I'll see his ass burn in jail for this."

"Those bloody alarms are pissing me off," Belmonte said. Hayden guessed he wasn't used to hearing them.

"No. It means people will be evacuating," Dahl told him. "A good thing."

"I don't get it. Cayman's American government," Hayden said. "Like us. CIA. DIA. Doesn't matter what agency you belong too, we all serve the same boss."

Gates eyed her. "I'm guessing not."

More gunfire erupted behind them, the walls getting shot to crumbling confetti.

"You think those crazy rumors about an elite group *directing* the world governments are true?"

"I'm betting my career on it. And my life too, it seems." Gates looked back at the dead agents. "There has been too much death around me lately."

"Maybe you should take a break." Hayden followed Dahl as he pushed through the exit door and began to head down the concrete staircase. At that moment, from the room behind her, came a deep roaring blast, the kind of noise that doesn't just frighten a person, it evokes a feeling of such intense terror it might stop a heart between beats.

"Bomb!" Dahl cried. "Oh God, run!"

They ran for their lives. The deep, ominous sound of girders shattering and load-bearing walls collapsing stung their ears. A terrible rumble preceded the ceiling collapsing behind them, and just for a second, for one mortal heart-stopping instant, Hayden saw the entire room begin to tilt and shift.

The skyline was moving. *The entire top floor of the building was shearing off!*

They pounded down the stairs. Gates tripped and began to

roll, but Dahl twisted in mid-flight, scooped the US Senator up and flung him over a shoulder without losing more than a stride.

A supersonic mass of glass, concrete, brick and plaster exploded in all directions, shattering the windows of surrounding skyscrapers and blasting debris across the entire block. A deadly heap of shale slid away from what was left of the top floor and plummeted to the ground, trailing dust and shards and chunks of wreckage. The heap shattered against the parking lot below, sending out a plume of crushed rubble. Tiny fragments of waste fluttered away in the wind.

Hayden heard it all. They all heard it. The roar of the explosion and its aftermath was like a charging dinosaur on their heels. Smoke billowed around them and it was all they could do to see the way ahead. Shards of the wreckage, compressed by the collapse of the roof and then sent ballistic by the explosion, speared past faster than bullets.

Belmonte almost dropped Emma's dangling body, but caught it and went headlong for half a flight of stairs before arresting his fall. They raced down the stairs without pause, without feeling even a hint of fatigue until they reached the lobby.

Dahl took a moment. "Everyone alright?"

The agent he had saved groaned.

Belmonte glared at him. "Fuck off, you toffee-nosed twat."

Dahl let it go. He surveyed the parking lot and roads outside the lobby, then turned to Hayden. "His men will be out there."

"I know. But there's no other way."

Dahl spared a dispassionate glance for Belmonte. "If they give chase, you'll need to leave her behind. Or die with her."

The Swede stepped through what was left of the front doors. A thin cloud of dust swirled around them as they moved carefully into the parking lot. Hayden glared, practically stripping the paint off cars and the facades off buildings, such was the intensity of her appraisal. Kinimaka, as ever, walked beside her and Torsten Dahl positioned himself out front—the target man, as always. Civilians stood outside, coughing and staring, dumbstruck. Ambulances wailed and flashing cop cars were arriving on scene.

Dahl suddenly pointed. *"There!"* He made a beeline for the nearest car, a family-sized Chevy.

Hayden saw hordes of men piling out of three black sedans parked at the curb. Fear slammed down her throat like a clenched fist. These guys were here to finish them off. Cayman had absolutely no intentions of letting them leave this place alive.

Kinimaka smashed his way into the big Chevy. "We gotta run!" he shouted. "Come on!"

In another minute, Kinimaka was revving the engine, making it roar and then slewing the car across the grass median and out into the road. Hayden checked her gun and gave her backup to Dahl. She watched as he checked the mag, face hard as Icelandic rock.

"They'll come after us."

Kinimaka floored the accelerator, speeding into a light traffic and making sure his own gun was ready as the three big cars with their murderous passengers began to give chase.

Straight toward downtown L.A., Beverly Hills, and, ultimately, Hollywood.

FIVE

Drake stepped out of the apartment first and walked down the short set of steps that led to the street as darkness began to send its inky tendrils across the southern skies. The sound of traffic and the hubbub coming from the underground station could clearly be heard a few hundred feet away.

Walking down the pavements on either side of the exclusive street were youths brandishing an assortment of weapons, among them baseball bats and tire irons. Several more youths advanced down the middle of the road.

Mai stopped at his left shoulder, Alicia at his right. The Englishwoman gave a happy laugh. "Some sparring practice. It's been a while." She spared a glance for Drake and Mai. "Don't hurt 'em too bad, ladies."

More cars suddenly slewed around the corner and came to a screeching halt halfway up the road. Doors were flung open and more youths leapt out, weapons in hand, their harsh grunts of challenge little more than caveman bravado.

Mai smiled at Drake. "And now they give us an easy way out."

"Amateurs tend to do that." Drake watched her glide away and then faced the half dozen rough-looking kids stalking toward him. "You need to stop," he said to them forcefully. "Whatever they're paying you ain't worth a beating."

Two of them actually stopped, but more out of bewilderment than prudence. Drake high-kicked the first and stole his bat, used it to catch the swing of the second and slid into the man when his heavy swing made him overreach. Drake heaved him over a shoulder, straight into a third assailant and, by then, the remaining three were wide-eyed. One found some daring and came in swinging. Drake used him as an example. He caught the tire iron, gripped it hard, and sent it slamming back into the youth's face. Blood from a broken nose sprayed everywhere. He fell down, crying.

To his left and right, Mai and Alicia were dealing out similar lessons. Drake moved next to one of the still-running cars. He heard the youth inside calling for more reinforcements and thought the next bunch might not be so inadequate. He picked up a bat and jumped into the passenger seat.

"Who ya ringing?" He jammed the end of the bat against the youth's cheek, mashing him up against the window.

"Percy." The youth gasped. "Don' hurt me, man. I ain't done nothin' to you."

"That call"—Drake nodded at the discarded mobile—"did more hurt to us than all these kids put together. Get out of the damn car. Now."

The youth was gone in a second to be replaced quickly by Mai. "Shall we go?" she asked, flexing her fist.

Drake stared at her. "Aye up. One of 'em clock you one?"

She made a face. "Splinter"

Alicia leapt across the hood and then climbed onto Mai's lap. "Stop chatting up the help, Drake. Let's get the fuck outta here."

Drake reversed quickly, swinging the car backward around

the corner and out into the flow of traffic. There was just enough space for him to make sure they weren't going to rear-end anyone. He jammed the accelerator down hard just as two silver-colored BMWs cut across the car behind them, provoking a flurry of screeched tires and blared horns.

Drake saw the men in the rearview. "They're behind us."

Alicia seemed happy enough perched on Mai's knee. "Haven't done this since I was a kid."

"They're behind us, Alicia. And they won't just have sledge-hammer shafts and baseball bats this time."

Mai shifted uncomfortably. "You, a kid?" She shook her head. "I don't believe it."

"Did you two hear what I just—?"

"I heard you banging on, Drake." Alicia turned a stare on him. "Probably best to leave it there, eh?"

"Still a kid." He grumbled. "Always a kid."

"If it helps me cope. . .then yes. Always."

He drove. Piccadilly hummed this time of night, crawling along with cars, buses and cabs, the pavements thronged with crowds of people. But still, Drake managed to weave his way forward at some pace, fast enough so that their pursuers couldn't stop and chase them on foot, but still keeping under a reckless pace. The lights were kind to them. Even a big red open-top, double-decker bus, thronged with tourists, moved aside so they could pass. Drake began to wonder if there was a siren on top of the car.

But their relentless pursuers kept pace. They passed the bottom end of Bond Street and Fortnum and Mason, the Royal Academy and Le Meridien.

"You know where we're headed?" Alicia twisted around to look behind them and then back to the front. "Picca-fuckin-dilly Circus. Well done, Drakey. You led us to the biggest bottleneck in the country."

Drake knew she was right. But plan B was already streaming through his subconscious. "Sometimes, Myles." He sighed. "You make a silly metaphor sound plausible— you know, the dumb blonde?"

Alicia squirmed. "Bollocks."

Mai grunted. "Please stop grinding your bony arse into my thighs."

That gave Alicia a moment's pause. "Never heard that before." She confessed. "It's normally the opposite. And *bony?* I'd go more with sexy, full and round."

Drake stole sidelong glances, but when the bottleneck of Piccadilly Circus loomed ahead, he quickly threw the car to the left and pulled up to the curb. "Quick. Foot traffic here is in the thousands. We'll lose them among the herd."

They leapt out, hurrying along the pavement and quickly joining the throng. The London air hit them with a sharp bite. Hundreds of heads and bodies bobbed all around them. Drake made for the corner of the circus and cut along the frontage of The Sting. Bright lights and clothes-store music assaulted his eyes and ears for a second, washing out of the open doors and surrounding him. Then he was past, joining another crowd waiting to cross the road to the small island that separated Regent Street from Glasshouse Street.

"Nip up Glasshouse," Alicia motioned briefly. "We'll be able to cut through Soho and use the Leicester Square tube. I'll Google car rental outlets."

Drake nodded appreciatively. "Sounds good."

They crossed the road amidst the mass of tourists, locals and day-trippers as the bright lights of the Piccadilly Circus big screens flashed above them. There was a single moment of loosening up, when Drake's mind flitted away from their pursuers and refocused on what they might discover about Wells when they tracked his friend, Andrew Black, down to Sevenoaks, and then, from deep in the heart of Piccadilly Circus the unmistakable sound of a gunshot rang out.

Many people paused, their faces frozen in fright. Even now, unable to believe their eyes, they didn't react, just listened, awaiting that second shot that would confirm what they dreaded and possibly end their lives.

But Drake, Alicia and Mai reacted in an instant. Drake said, "There's a hundred kids around here."

Alicia's face no longer bore a playful expression. Instead, it bore the look of a stone-cold killer. Mai's voice, always light, was barely audible: "I know all about blood and death but this won't stand."

As if by telepathy, they knew what they had to do. Drake picked his way swiftly through the uneasy throng, his training helping to make him aware of the area where the shooter stood. Mai and Alicia drifted rapidly toward his associates, mingling with and emerging from the crowd like deadly wraiths. In rapid movement, they struck and withdrew, leaving crumpled men in their wakes but never attracting immediate attention.

Drake faded behind a group of brightly dressed women, all wearing tight zebra-print leggings and yellow jackets, all part of some girls' night out or work party. He slipped around the group as it passed the man with the gun held by his side. Although he tried to conceal it, he couldn't hide from Drake.

The gunshot had been designed to bring them out, and it worked. But far better than their pursuers would ever know.

Drake brought an arm around the man's throat and shouted a big *"Hey!"* as if in greeting, while simultaneously breaking the wrist that held the gun, then bringing his free hand up in a pincer grip around his throat.

The man gargled, struggling furiously.

Leaning right in, Drake whispered, "Twenty of you bastards never stood a chance." He held the man fast until he began to slump, then used his immense strength to drag him carefully over to the steps that surrounded the fountain.

Sirens began to sound in the distance. It made no difference to the Londoners and the tourists as, convinced now that the gunshot had been a backfire, they carried on about their business.

Drake left his man slouched, made a quick decision to throw his firearm into a nearby trashcan, and met Alicia and Mai outside the local Cinnabon shop.

Alicia was licking the frosting off a bun. "Took your time, Drakester."

"Piss off."

The sirens were approaching. Mai turned toward Leicester Square. "This friend of Wells," she said, "has no idea what trouble he's into, does he?"

"We hope so." Drake cautioned her. "For all we know, he's as bent as Wells was."

"One thing's for sure," Alicia said around a mouthful of cinnamon frosting. "In about an hour, he'll be telling us *all* he knows."

SIX

Kinimaka jammed his foot to the floor as the three black sedans loomed large in the rearview. The cars were jam-packed with bad guys, sitting three abreast in front and jostling for position in the back. Kinimaka glimpsed at least two of them pressing ear mics and listening intently, nodding with faces as emotionless as granite. One of them took out a gun and slid down a window.

"Uh-oh," he murmured "I think they just got the kill order."

"Not a chance," Gates told him from the back seat. "We're heading toward central Hollywood."

Kinimaka wrenched the Chevy around a tight curve. Screeching tires came from behind as all three sedans fought hard to close the gap. Dahl twisted around in the back seat. "Well, we're in the right place for a car chase."

There was a *ping* and a quick explosion of noise. Dahl shook his head, unruffled. "So now they're shooting. Bloody Americans."

But Belmonte was far from calm. "Shooting! Get a move on, big guy. My God, you take one step out of London and you're in the Wild West!"

Kinimaka said nothing, just rolled his eyes toward Hayden in the passenger seat. As they took another bend, weaving around two SUV's, Hayden's window went opaque, turning into a spider-web of tiny cracks.

Gates shrank in the back seat. Kinimaka increased the speed again, but he was getting close to becoming dangerous and there were hundreds of civilians around, both mobile and pedestrian.

Hayden pointed to a sign. "Drop onto the I10, then head for the hills." She sighed at her own choice of words. "If they want a fight, we can give it to them there."

A black sedan roared up behind them, barely an inch off their rear bumper.

Kinimaka evaded the vehicle with a quick shift to the left. "If we can get there," he said and spun the car at the last moment, taking the off-ramp to the I10 Freeway. The car shot up, slewing dangerously before he got it under control, and barreled into the flow of traffic. The sudden maneuver put some space between them and their pursuers, and Kinimaka used the advantage to move into the emptiest lane and floored the Chevy.

But the sedans were powerful, and they were reckless. They began to close the gap almost immediately. Another shot boomed out, this one glancing off the side.

Hayden jammed down a speed-dial button on her cell phone. "Ben? Tell me you got something on the location of that third tomb?"

The reply made her forehead tighten. "Well, work faster. We're screwed out here. Time just became our enemy." Then she shook her head in exasperation. "I can't talk now, Ben. This is real fucking life!" She ended the call with an abrupt shake of the wrist.

Kinimaka jammed the brakes hard as a BMW drifted

arrogantly into their path. The driver's eyes nearly popped out of his skull when he saw all the guns waving in his direction and shunted swiftly away. The Hawaiian drove cleverly, always using other cars to block the sedans and employing varying speeds to keep them guessing and off-balance.

"Get off here!" Hayden shouted. Kinimaka saw a sign that read "Hollywood Freeway" and again took a late turn, hitting the ramps at speed and swerving onto the hard shoulder to evade a white Chrysler being carefully driven by a couple of tourists.

The sedans came hustling down the ramp. One of them clipped the Chrysler and sent it slamming into the concrete wall. A crunch of metal rent the air, loud even over the screaming engine. The sedan went into a spin. Hayden took the chance to smash her window, lean out and fire a whole clip into it, striking chassis, windows, wheels and engine. In another moment, it struck the curb and flipped, tons of metal in mid-air, and landed with a deathly sounding thud. Debris scattered all across the road.

The other two sedans left it behind, still in hot pursuit.

"Those other people—" Dahl said.

"It's a Chrysler," Hayden told him. "They'll be fine."

The 101 Freeway took them north past West Hollywood and toward the famous hills. Hayden used the time to call in the pursuit to her local CIA office and Gates finally found the nerve to sit up and make a few calls.

After ten minutes, they both sat back, uneasy expressions on their faces. "If I didn't know better, sir," Hayden said with a glance back at her boss. "I'd say our asses were being hung out in the wind."

"You underestimate," Gates almost whispered, having

turned whiter than Wite Out. "I'd say it's more like a hurricane."

"We on our own, boss?" Kinimaka asked, concentrating hard on the rolling lanes in front of them.

"Not in so many words," Hayden replied. "I can't believe they would truly abandon us."

"Do you not *know* government?" Dahl snorted. "It's what they do."

"Not to a US Secretary of Defense," Hayden shot back. She wished now that Gates was firing on all cylinders, running at his best, rather than floundering underneath weeks of hell and hardship and unspeakable loss. If he were on top form, they might be able to dig their way out of this.

What would her father do? What would Drake do?

"Fight," she said aloud. They would seek out the group behind all this and they would make them pay dearly. Drake had found the Blood King for God's sake, the myth made real, and pursued him through the gates of hell. Drake had shown her the way—now it was up to her to heed the lesson.

The off-ramp for Mulholland shot by on the right —her first route into the hills. "Take the next off-ramp," she told Kinimaka, annoyed.

The office had responded to her call with a subdued concern. They hadn't asked any questions. Hadn't given her any instructions. They hadn't passed her up the line.

Were Ben and Karin safe?

Kinimaka hit the off-ramp hard, sending Hayden's head bouncing against the window frame. Her gun fell to the floor and it took her a moment to pick it up and check the whereabouts of their pursuers. By the time she looked around, Kinimaka was weaving desperately between rows of crawling cars and gawking tourist vehicles through a wide entrance and suddenly they were inside an enclosed approach, heading uncontrollably toward a row of ticket boots and flimsy barriers.

"Dude," Hayden said in a confused voice, "why the hell are you heading into Universal Studios?"

SEVEN

"I didn't mean to!" Kinimaka cried. "It was the only way to get through traffic without stopping!"

"Well you're gonna have to stop soon," Hayden said sarcastically. "Personally, I prefer the *Jurassic Park* level. Kinda reminds me of work."

Belmonte shifted uncomfortably in the back. Emma's body was slouched in the well between his knees and the back seat. "Can we get out?"

"This might work," Hayden said, thinking hard. "We could lose them in the City Walk." She turned to Dahl "What do you think?"

The City Walk is an urbane entertainment complex, a lively mix of restaurants, bars and shops, normally crowded.

Dahl bounced around in his seat as they negotiated a series of ramps and almost scraped a high concrete wall. A multi-story car-lot opened out before them.

"I don't like any of it," the Swede said dubiously. "Get close. The authorities will be on our arses any minute."

"Yeah, but which authorities, bud?" Kinimaka muttered.

At that moment, there was a shotgun blast. Hayden's wing mirror disappeared in an explosion of lead and plastic. Then the rear window shattered, sending shards of glass bursting through the car. Kinimaka ducked and twisted the wheel, slamming them into a parked SUV. The Chevy shuddered as it came to an abrupt stop.

Dahl was the first to move, unbuckling his seat belt, opening the back door and shouting at them to get a bloody move on. The two chasing sedans squealed to a halt about twenty feet away. Hayden and Kinimaka rolled out of their doors, guns up.

Hayden ducked behind her door for cover, shouting at Gates. "Stay low!"

The sound of gunfire erupted across the parking lot.

Cayman's men were rushing forward, ten of them, staying low and firing constantly. Behind them, newly arrived vehicles were slamming brakes on or turning around and racing off. The sound of multiple fender-benders split the air.

Bullets impacted Hayden's door, pinging into the metal. She fired blindly around the frame. Kinimaka was having better luck, using the Chevy's roof to lean on and picking his targets. Three of Cayman's men had already collapsed, groaning. But the rest came on. There were too many to stop them all.

Dahl raced off around the back of the SUV they had hit. He went so fast that no one except Hayden saw him, and within seconds, he had re-emerged from the vehicle's far side, running hard, heading straight for the advancing men, but from their side, a flanking maneuver. He fired four bullets, four head-shots. The sudden onslaught made Cayman's remaining three men duck for cover. One of them rolled and fired at Dahl, but the shot hit the overhead concrete ceiling and glanced off into the hood of a parked car.

Dahl looked around, shaking his head. This was a family place, a kid's sanctuary. He would never have let them enter

The Tomb of the Gods

the City Walk; he would have surrendered or died first. Some operatives and even some governments accepted collateral damage. But he would never allow it.

Beyond the parking lot, he saw a long escalator packed with families. Past that he saw the flickering lights of the City Walk itself. Too close. This fight not only had to be contained here, it had to end here.

At that moment, there came the roar of an engine and one of the black sedans inched forward. *The drivers!* He had forgotten about the bloody drivers. No matter. Before the vehicle picked up any amount of speed, he sprinted toward it and leapt onto the hood, landing on his side facing the driver with his gun pointed at the man's face.

Sporting the big smile he usually reserved for killing megalomaniac fashion designers.

The driver's expression fell. Dahl pulled the trigger. The windshield exploded and blood sprayed the inside of the car as the vehicle veered sideways. Dahl let himself slide off, rolling when he hit the concrete.

Just in time to hear the second sedan roar.

Behind him, he heard Hayden and Kinimaka firing at Cayman's remaining three stooges. One of them screamed. All good. He fired at the sedan's tires, bursting one, but then the gun ran out of bullets. Still, Dahl was not perturbed. As the vehicle slewed out of control toward him, the Swede leapt feet-first onto the hood and then, with the grace of a dancer rather than the bulk of a six foot six inch Special Forces soldier, sprang lightly onto the roof itself.

A second before the vehicle crashed, Dahl jumped clear, rolling until the momentum dispersed. Out of his peripheral vision, he saw the driver smash against the windshield, not full-force but with enough of an impact to render him insensible.

Dahl came up, slightly disoriented, and saw Hayden struggling in hand-to-hand with one of their assailants. Hayden was still below par, having been stabbed again by Boudreau recently. Dahl bounded forward and waded in, giving Cayman's soldier no chance. A knee to the back, a huge, stiff arm across the throat, and a judo flip ensured the man's head impacted hard with the concrete floor and put an end to any evil aspirations he had ever had.

Hayden panted, holding her side. "Thanks."

"No problem. But, just to be clear, I'd advise against being stabbed more than once a week."

Hayden was already used to the leg-pullers. Drake and Dahl were from the same army mold, different educations or not.

Kinimaka looked over the top of the car. "Aloha. We seem to be out of bad guys."

"Get in." Dahl eased Hayden into the passenger seat before running around to the driver's side. "You okay, mate?"

"I'm good." Kinimaka took the wheel once more. "Where to?"

Dahl checked on Gates. "You okay, sir?" Then Belmonte. "Our thief friend seems alright. Your friend still dead, mate?"

The lack of response told Dahl what he needed to know, that Belmonte, the renowned British thief, did indeed have a heart. He turned to Kinimaka as he climbed into the back. "Start her up, my friend. In the words of most Hollywood couples—*let's split*."

The car engine rolled over with a purr. Kinimaka pointed the hood back the way they had come and drove down the exit road. Sirens were blaring over the high concrete barriers, dangerously close.

"We ought to have frisked them." Hayden looked back at the bodies strewn across the concrete.

"No time," Dahl said. "We're barely gonna get out of here without a good Tasing as it is. Kinimaka," he said with a smile, "try to look... touristy."

Hayden quickly dialed Ben as they drove. "How we doing?"

The words, spoken quietly across distant airwaves, felt like warm syrup to her brain. "We have a location for tomb number three."

Hayden abruptly forgot all her aches and pains. *"What?"*

She could tell Ben was smiling as he repeated his words. "We have a location for tomb number three."

Hayden thought quickly. "Listen, Ben. We're on the run. I don't know who we can trust. Get out of the building and meet us at LAX. Do it now. Plan B. You get me?"

It had been Drake's idea, of course. Ben was, by now, comfortable with the concept of a plan B—a "drop everything and get the hell out of there" scenario. This was it. Dahl was signaling her.

"Terminal?"

Hayden nodded and asked. "Which country, Ben?"

"Germany. You won't believe this, but we're looking for an extinct volcano beneath one of the world's oldest castles. Awesome, eh?"

"Ok. We'll find you. Be. . ." She faltered. "Be safe."

"I will."

Hayden heard him mutter something to Karin as he cut the line. She watched Kinimaka thread the needle between two slower cars and approach the exit. So far, so good. No one stepped out to stop them. Of course, there had been a mass desertion of cars in the last few minutes. Their misfortune was now also their security. Flashing blue lights were just entering the park as they left. Big, black unmarked vans were pulling up to the ticket booths.

Dahl shook his head in sorrow. "This'll ruin some poor kid's day," he said with meaning.

Belmonte looked askance at him, still holding Emma. "You thick-skulled Viking." He sputtered. "How can you?"

"I'm sorry," Dahl said, much to everyone's surprise. "But she's dead, my friend, and your love for her will not bring her back. You can only get even now."

"Love?" Belmonte said quickly. "She was my protégé. My friend's daughter. That is all."

"I think not, but have it as you will. In any case, I believe in the magic of places like this. The cynics call them dens for big business, places for fat cats to get even richer, but I pride myself in one thing—being able to see as a child sees. Disneyland can bring a tear to my eye. Universal and Sea World can fill me with wonder. I see no shame in that. And the person who can't feel at least some wonder in their hearts as they stroll around the Magic Kingdom I pity because they have no magic left in their lives."

Belmonte stared at him.

"My children," Dahl said, "will experience all the wonder of childhood. Because you're an adult for a very long time."

Belmonte nodded at him and then laid Emma's body down gently along the rear footwell. "I get what you're saying and you're right. I'm sorry too. I misjudged you. You're right about getting even. Did Cayman kill Emma?"

"He sure ordered it," Gates spoke up again now that the action was over. Hayden could see the darkness in his eyes and the black circles surrounding them. The secretary was on a collision course with twin-paths of exhaustion and depression. It was just a matter of time.

"But someone *ordered* him to order it," Gates finished. "And they're the people we need to find. They're the people who are looking for the third tomb and the doomsday weapon inside."

Dahl nodded in agreement. "I'll try my man in Iceland," he said, pulling out a phone. "See what luck he's had in deciphering the ancient language."

Hayden looked at her own phone. "If we're on our way to Germany, heading for the third tomb," she said, "I guess it's time to call in Matt Drake."

EIGHT

Drake jabbed the button on the central dash to answer his ringing mobile through the cars Bluetooth connectivity device. "Hayden?"

"Ben and Karin cracked the location of tomb three, Drake. It's in Germany."

He sensed Alicia and Mai suddenly rise from their respective positions of repose. Hayden recounted the incidents in LA as quickly as she could. Alicia whistled. "Sounds like we're missing out on all the action here."

Drake didn't look at her. "We've had some action of our own."

Alicia snorted. "We joined playtime at nursery."

Drake told Hayden about their day so far. "Which leaves us about twenty miles out in the middle of nowhere. Nearing Sevenoaks, and the home of Wells's friend."

"According to our online gurus, we'll be landing in Germany about three a.m., German time. Can you make it by then?"

Drake made a few quick calculations. "If we get lucky with the flight times, we won't be far behind you. So long as Wells's old friend is cooperative."

Mai said, "Excuse me. You say you're 'on the run' now. Are you not CIA? Are you running from your own agency?"

"No. It's a whole new ballgame now. We're *choosing* to run because we don't know who to trust at government level. Because every second counts if we're to beat Cayman to that tomb, and because we have the resources to seize it."

"You think?" Alicia sounded surprised. "Cayman seems to be bollock-deep in resources by what I'm hearing."

"The Secretary has some major pull, as you know," Hayden said. "The only problem is when you start to exert that kind of pull—most everyone hears about it."

"So. . ."

"So we're calling on people from smaller units that owe us. Units from Europe. Some of Dahl's buddies. Komodo's men. Whoever and whatever's available are hauling ass to meet us there."

"I know some people," Mai said quietly. Drake eased the rental car, a snazzy new Nissan Juke, off the country road and onto an even quieter B-road. He pointed at a property ahead, lit by a patch of soft garden lighting. "We're here."

Hayden pushed one last time. "The race is on, guys. We need to get to that tomb and find this doomsday weapon before Cayman does."

"Understood," Drake said. "I'll find some men. Wells wasn't my only friend in the SAS."

He killed the engine and the phone call. They quietly exited the car. Drake took a moment to look around. Moonlight threw a stark glow across the scene. A large two-story house stood in front of them, curtains drawn against the night, a soft glow emanating from a downstairs room. Sporadic shrubs dotted the garden as if planted on a whim. Drake noticed that the garage door was only halfway down, the telltale sign of a man unused to late night visitors and not worried about local thieves.

They formed a wary huddle outside the front door. "Eyes peeled," Drake said and knocked.

In a matter of moments, the porch light clicked on. Then a voice came from behind the door, a shadow outlined through the patterned glass. "Yes?"

"Andrew Black?" Alicia spoke up because a woman's voice coming from outside your door on pitch-black night was always going to be less threatening than a man's.

"Who is it?"

"We're friends of Wells."

"Who? I don't know any Wells. Now please—"

Mai shook her hair out, unbuttoned her coat and stepped into the light. "Just check, Mr Black. Just check whatever hidden camera you have. I'm Mai Kitano. Wells may have mentioned me."

Silent moments passed, measured only by the unruly blasts of a menacing wind and the ragged gusts of storm clouds across the silver-patched skies. At length, the shadow returned. "There should be a password," an inscrutable voice whispered. "I hope to God you know it."

"It's either *Maitime* or *sprite,*" Mai said with impatience. "Now open the damn door."

A fumbling preceded the appearance of an old man's head in the frame. Andrew Black was bald and probably rounding sixty, but when he stepped into sight, Drake saw he was still fit, shrewd and capable.

"The legend herself." Black stared at Mai with genuine delight. "Never thought I'd get the pleasure."

"You won't," Mai said. "But try Myles here. If you live in the UK, you're probably related to someone who has."

"Oooh." Alicia laughed, not taking any offence. "The sprite

cracked a funny. What next? Stories of her *undercover* years in Thailand?"

Andrew Black led the way into a warmly lit living room. Pristine leather sofas and easy chairs stood all around, as if trying to occupy the space. Old family photographs crammed the walls. Wells's old friend had all the trappings of a man who'd raised, loved and set free a family, and now lived only for the everlasting memories that remained imprinted on his heart.

"Wells did talk about you." Black motioned them toward the chairs. "Sometimes he talked about little else, truth be told. But he was very clear with his instructions. If you ever came by, *ever*, I was to give you everything. Every bit of his research."

"Research?" Drake frowned. "What on earth would Wells be researching?"

"The Shadow Elite, of course." Andrew Black looked at Drake as if he were a shop-floor dummy. "Wells was making careful investigations into the small group of people who run our world, Mr. Drake. And he was making some remarkable progress."

*****

"Shadow Elite?" Mai's voice was the essence of politeness, but forced Black to get to the point.

"I know very little." The old man's eyes flicked nervously toward the pictures that hung on his walls, perhaps fearing repercussions.

"No one will ever know you told us," Mai assured him quietly.

"I know only a few things I overheard and what Wells would spout off about in moments of anger or insobriety. It's all on here." Black reached under the big, puffed-out arms of his chair and removed a strip of tape. A small, black device fell into his hand, which he held out to Mai.

"A Dictaphone?"

"He recorded everything on there. Never wrote a thing down. My old friend had his failings, Miss Kitano, but he never forgot a thing and he was a gifted commander."

"Before we listen to that," Drake spoke up, "please tell us what you know, Mr. Black."

"This Shadow Elite—it's what they call themselves—are made up of individuals from a group of old families. A very old group that date back to when rough and rugged men were first making their fortunes. Their wealth is ancient. It goes beyond heritage, beyond royalty. It's the *original* wealth of our world. And thus, it can never be tainted."

"Go on." Mai prompted him gently.

"That's most of what I know. Wells opened up one night about the origin of the families. Their leader is called the *Norseman*. He's God, so to speak. The supreme ruler."

Drake shook his head. "With the third tomb, the eight pieces being *relocated,* and now this, I'm beginning to think we're nowhere near done with the bones of Odin yet."

Mai reached out and pressed the Dictaphone's *play* button. Drake frowned to hear his old commander's voice fill the empty room. It took him a few moments of readjustment.

"Above all I am a patriot. A servant of Britain. When Cayman first came to me, he convinced me that the Shadow Elite were, in fact, the ruling body of this world. Simply put – they gave every government its orders, including my own. So have I truly not

become a greater patriot by serving them?" There was a lengthy pause. *"A question for a more insightful mind than mine. But it later became clear to me that the Shadow Elite did not have the people's interests at heart. What government does, I hear you ask? I would like to think—my own. I believe that every British man who becomes a politician starts out wanting to help his fellow man, no matter where he ends up."* Another pause.

Alicia said, "How long has he been digging?"

Black shrugged. "Seven? Eight years? Wells became a changed man." He shook his head regretfully. "Terribly changed."

That was around the same time Alyson died. Drake did not miss Mai's meaningful look.

"I decided, after the conclusion of the Doubledown operation, to delve a bit deeper into the motivations of my employers, and perhaps learn their intentions. Were they just men playing chess with civilian lives? Or did they have hidden, honorable aspirations?"

Mai paused the recording and again glanced at Drake. "Have you ever heard of Doubledown?"

Drake felt the icy trickle of unhappy memory crawl the length of his spine. "It was an operation I headed. My last. At first, we made excellent progress. The whole thing fit together perfectly and it seemed we were going to finish in record time. Then. . ." He shrugged. "It got shut down. No explanations. We were ready to move on this big guy."

Drake thought back. "He owned some kind of mansion in Vienna. Then, Wells came in and told us we were done. *Pack your bags. First flight home.* Even—*take some time off.* Then, about a week later—" He sighed. "Alyson died."

"Doubledown seems to have been some kind of catalyst," Mai said. "For Wells and for you, though you didn't know it at the time."

She restarted the Dictaphone. Drake tried to block out the sound of the wind as it swept and scoured the dark garden paths and the scraping of trees at the windows. Wells's ghostly tones filled the room.

"The Norseman is the key figure of the Shadow Elite, though obviously all six of them are principal figures. Still, I have no names, but I do have a possible location, and other more personal revelations that will not put me in a good light. But I cannot tell it all here. Even this is too public. There are files. Many files."

The voice stopped. Drake and the others in the room all looked at each other.

"You old bastard," Mai said vehemently. "Not like this."

But then the voice spoke again. *"There's a stash of old and new stuff at the secret SAS facility in Luxembourg. It's in my archived file. I know because I put it there. I ask you not to judge me, Mai, no matter what you find. I remain, above all, a patriot, and I carried out what I judged to be the course of action that best served my government and my country."*

Drake let out a deep breath. "That doesn't sound good."

"Which bloody bit?" Alicia exploded, unable to keep her cool any longer. "Wells's admission of guilt? The fact that all his papers are inside a friggin' SAS base! Or his hint that there's worse to come? *Fuck!*"

"Exactly," Drake said. "My friends in the regiment would do anything for me, but I can't ask them to steal for me."

"Of course," Mai said without hesitation.

"So *we're* going to have to do the stealing," Drake went on. "If we want to know what Wells found."

"He might have found the Shadow Elite," Mai said, and Black nodded in agreement. "Six men who rule the world.

And they're connected to Wells, to Cayman, and to the tomb and the doomsday weapon. We can't ignore them, Drake."

"So you intend to infiltrate an SAS base, steal some documents, and then escape without being noticed?" Alicia hissed. "Are you serious? Those guys *invented* stealth." She grunted. "I mean—*us guys*."

Drake smiled. "But even the best of the best ain't seen anything like us," he said with conviction in his voice. "What was it Wells used to say? *Heroes never quit. They stay strong until the end.*"

*****

The drive to Heathrow didn't take long. Drake tried Hayden again, but didn't expect to reach her. She was in the air, en route to Germany where the last and deadliest tomb of the gods had been located by both the good and the bad guys. Tomb three held all the vilest gods. The worst of their kind.

The race to reach it first was well and truly on.

"No luck," Drake said and cut the call. He looked at Mai swiping away at her 3D smartphone. "A three a.m. flight, you say? That will get us in two hours after Hayden. Hopefully, she'll wait."

"She'll wait." Alicia echoed. "That girl has faith. And, naturally, she needs us." A bounce of energy sent her blond curls flying.

Drake typed in another number. He wasn't surprised when the man from Hereford answered on the first ring.

"Drake?"

"Hello, Sam. Thanks again for guarding the Blakes for me, mate. A debt like that—" He faltered.

"Never needs repaying between friends." Sam finished for him. "You saved my life a hundred times. Now, what's up?"

"How're you fixed for a German op?"

There was a brief pause. "Not too well, mate. Of our people, I can get three for about two days. Four including me."

"Then go now," Drake told him. "Meet me in Singen, Germany, as soon as you can."

Drake saw the bright lights of Heathrow swinging around to the left and ended the call. He raised an eyebrow at Mai. "I got four. How about you?"

"Two." She half-smiled and then threw a glare toward the back seat. "How about you, Alicia? How many friends can you count on?"

Alicia let out a loud snore, as if asleep.

Mai snorted. "Thought so."

NINE

Russell Cayman knew hardship. His junkie parents had abandoned him in a ditch when he was four. They were caught and tried, but that didn't save Cayman from being shuttled from one cruel, uncaring foster family to the next. Having never known love, he would never know how to give it or recognize it.

Children of the "system" were always on the radar of the more clandestine sections of governmental agencies, and in particular, the ones who ended up demonstrating a brilliant skill-set in one area or another. The CIA moved in when he was fourteen, and with no real guardian and no family, Cayman was happy to accept their friendship. It was many years later that he understood it was to be a friendship with fangs, and with no way out.

Now, Cayman threw his keys onto the tiny table by the door and headed into his apartment. The place would have made a Spartan happy. There were no furnishings, no home comforts, just a chair to sit in, a bed to sleep on, a table to eat off, and a TV to keep up to date with the world news. But it gave him some peace. Here he was happiest.

Cayman possessed no social skills beyond what the agency had taught him. So now, stressed to the point where he wanted, needed, to kill, he walked into the kitchen and quickly began choosing pots and pans. He rummaged through the fridge and picked out a chicken breast, some Italian chorizo sausage, peppers, celery and green beans. Furiously, he began mixing up some meat stock whilst he fried an onion and added fresh garlic.

Slowly, the tension seeped away.

The mix of concentration, aromatic smells and simple exercise worked to drain the pressure from his body. Cooking was his only release, and then only when he was home because nowhere else felt the same.

As he chopped the peppers, the knife slipped, cutting a tiny chunk of flesh from his finger. He left it nestled amidst the peppers as he swept them into the big pan and let the blood drain into the mix. Time ceased to exist. Jambalaya was his masterpiece, the pinnacle of his long-practiced culinary skills.

After a while, Cayman laid out a knife and fork on the empty table, the noise echoing around the empty apartment as if to mock him. He sat down, carefully thinking about nothing, still dressed in the standard suit and tie, and ate with robotic, measured strokes.

Hayden and Gates had escaped his trap in L.A. Where would they turn up next? Their cohorts, Ben and Karin Blake, had fled the CIA building a mere twenty minutes before Cayman's men arrived.

He stopped eating. The anxiety made him want to fling the meal to the floor. Made him want to stab the fork through the meat of his hand and suck at the blood and the torn flesh for solace, using the hand like a grotesque dummy. He'd done it before.

But the heady aroma invaded his senses again. He returned to the meal. He finished the bowl, stood up and walked over to the window. The neighborhood outside was busy, full of parents and children hurrying about their daily routines. Cayman had chosen to live amidst a bustling civilian population, though he didn't know why. Was it the need to feel he was a part of something? Something real, as opposed to the shadowy cutthroat world he thrived in?

He watched the young mothers, familiar figures by now. The children. He was a monster in their midst, the Halloween ghoul come to life. But the government indulged his whim and let him live amongst them.

No, not the government. The people *behind* the government. They didn't have a conscience. They didn't care where he lived, so long as they got what they wanted. The American government, the top brass, had actually balked at the idea of allowing him the use of this location. . .but they'd been overruled.

The Shadow Elite. They were the towering silhouette behind the monster. The blackness at the heart of the gloom. A body of six men, Cayman knew, who played the world's governments like puppets. Their interest, already piqued at the discovery of the spectacular tombs and preserved bones of so many legendary gods, had skyrocketed into the stratosphere when they learned of the doomsday device. The response had been immediate. First, it must not fall into the hands of anyone else, for that person might then be able to wield some influence over them, and second, *they* should be the ones to control it since they always had been, and always would be, the world's governing body. It was an irony to them, Cayman knew, that they should possess the power of old gods, since they were the new gods. And the Norseman, their leader, was an unstoppable force. On a whim, he could start a war. On the toss of a coin, he could wipe out a village—anywhere in the world. Cayman had witnessed his power first-hand. The memories still gave him night terrors.

Cayman turned back to the emptiness of his home, as his cellphone began to chirp a standard ringtone.

"Cayman here."

"This is Mackenzie, sir. I'm in charge of coordinating all the data we collect from tombs one and two that might relate to tomb three."

"I know exactly who you are. What do you want?"

"It's tomb three, sir. We have a location."

Cayman was careful not to let his excitement show. *This was it!* The Shadow Elite would be, literally, ecstatic.

"Gather everyone." He spoke the words slowly and succinctly. "Send them all to the location at once. Now—where is it?"

TEN

Drake's flight landed at Zurich airport a little before six a.m. Swiss time. He'd already received coordinates in-flight from Hayden so, as soon as they passed through security control without a hiccup, they found a taxi rank and gave the driver a local address. Within twenty minutes, they turned off *Zurichstrasse* onto *Wisentalstrasse* and dropped off outside a gray, nondescript building with the initials IMI painted onto a very old, very shabby sign, which hung precariously over the front door.

Drake, Alicia and Mai eyed the area suspiciously as the taxi pulled away.

"An awful lot of flat ground," Alicia said warily. "You sure about this, Drakey?"

"I didn't choose it," he said testily.

The door opened and Torsten Dahl stood there. The big Swede had a lopsided grin on his face.

"Aye up, it's the mad Swede," Drake said with warmth in his voice. "I remember that same stupid grin being on yer face when you stood on the edge of Odin's tomb, staring down at his bones."

"As did you, my friend." Dahl came forward. "When I finally let you have a look."

The pair shook hands. "The bloody A-team," Dahl said. "Back together."

"Well, by all accounts," Drake said seriously, "we're gonna be needed."

"Jesus!" Alicia said, brushing them aside. "Make sure his thong doesn't cut your lip, Drake, when you pull it down with your teeth."

Drake stared after her. "Bitch always had a way with words."

Mai followed Alicia. "Let's see who else came to the party, shall we?"

Drake let Dahl get his back and followed Mai through the ramshackle door. Once inside, the building abruptly changed, everything looking more modernized. A fortified, brick-lined passageway led to another door—this one a big, riveted hard steel affair—with a nearby keypad. Hayden was waiting for them, and after giving them all a brief, tense greeting, she entered a sixteen-digit pin to unlock the door.

She ushered them through. Drake tried to shake off his ideas and plans for the forthcoming trip to the SAS facility in Luxembourg and concentrate on the job at hand. Wells's material might hold the key to Alyson's killer, but it might also blow the lid off the Shadow Elite—an organization even now immorally involved in trying to acquire the doomsday weapon that might exist inside the third and final tomb of the gods.

He saw Ben immediately. The young man stood uncomfortably in one corner of the big room, next to his sister, a pint of coke in hand and looking like the geek hanging out at the school disco. The bar behind him glistened with liter bottles full of the sweet nectar of forgetfulness. Drake's eyes lingered a moment too long.

Dahl clapped him on the back. Hard. "Check that out, mate."

Alicia had sashayed into the middle of the room, like a

capable and confident model surveying an invited audience that, for some reason, never understood it was really the prey, until she came face to face with Daniel Belmonte, the British master thief, her ex-lover.

Drake could hear them speaking. Belmonte, to his credit, had recovered quickest. "Always good to. . .bump into you, Myles."

Drake saw Hayden watching them too. And Ben watching Hayden. Such an odd rectangle of ex and current lovers.

Alicia didn't miss a beat though. "The only thing you'll be *stealing* tonight, Belmonte, is glances." And she walked right by him, continuing toward the bar without looking back.

Mai had watched the exchange too. "She's good. Though I'd never tell her."

"Your secret is safe with me, Miss Kitano," Dahl told her, a big smile lighting his face.

Drake took a moment to study the room. Clearly, this was some kind of local police safe house. Someone, Gates or Hayden or even Dahl, had probably called in a favor, an occurrence that would probably be happening a lot during the next few days. As he thought about it, Drake decided it had been Dahl. The Swede was the least likely of them all to pop up on an enemy's radar and no doubt had a vast amount of friends and colleagues in mainland Europe. The room was furnished with a couple of big sofas, a solid oak table long enough to seat a horde of Vikings, and at least three makeshift beds in the corners. The bar, of course, was the main feature, especially for those having to deal with a terrible new knowledge.

Dahl took out his wallet and took a moment to study a picture of his two sons and his wife. Still holding it, he turned to Drake. "This is why we fight," he said. "This is why we try to make things better. So our children can grow up in a safer world."

Drake opened his mouth to reply. A sudden, unexpected lump of emotion lodged at the back of his throat. Dahl stared at him. The Swede didn't know Alyson had been pregnant. Even now, Drake was still dealing with the fact that he would never have children, and that the child he had made had been so viciously torn from him.

"I will kill them all," he whispered. "No one will get away with what they did."

Dahl looked momentarily confused, then returned the picture to his wallet. Maybe he thought that Drake, in his way, was just agreeing with him. "I have a man on the inside," he said with a grin. "In Iceland. He's translating the ancient language as we speak. I should be hearing from him any time."

"About what?"

"About *everything*. Bloody hell, why are Yorkshire men so dumb? The whole story is there, mate. About why the gods lay down to die. About the time-travel devices you found near the Bermuda Triangle and in Hawaii. About the doomsday machine. About how they *created fate.* They hopped through time, Matt, literally *hopped,* like we would visit different stores in a mall. Do you remember that poem, the one related to Odin?"

Drake collected himself. "Vaguely."

"The ending went '*Forever shall thou fear this, hear me sons of men, for to defile the Tomb of Gods is to start the Day of Reckoning.*'"

"Yes?"

"We believe that it has begun. The day of reckoning is fast approaching."

"The Day of Reckoning? Something to do with Armageddon. Or the Viking's *Ragnarok?*"

"Exactly. *Ragnarok.* Either heroes will rise to save the day or villains will end it."

Drake stared at his Swedish friend. That sentence struck a chord in him. *Either heroes will rise to save the day or villains will end it.* "So we'll stay strong until the end," he said. "And we'll win the day. For our children, and our friends."

"No matter what." Dahl gripped his hand and the two men shared a moment that would lock them together for the rest of their lives.

ELEVEN

Drake watched Hayden walk through the crowd as Alicia had done. But this time the crowd parted with respect and expectation.

He saw her command attention with a look, a sigh. He saw Ben staring at her and suddenly felt a wave of sadness for his young friend. There was no future there. Ben, though exceptional in his own right, was not the man for Hayden Jaye. And widening his field of vision, he noticed Komodo—the Delta team leader who had helped him win the day against the Blood King in Hawaii. Drake made a point of catching the man's eye and nodding in respect, though Komodo seemed more intent on chatting with Karin than noticing Drake.

There were men scattered around who Drake didn't know. Probably colleagues of Mai and loyal soldiers attached to Jonathan Gates, a US Secretary of Defense who could realistically trust no one except the few people in this very room.

"We're in desperate times," Hayden said. "You all know that the third tomb of the gods houses the nastiest of their kind. So we have no idea what to expect. And even worse—it may also contain some kind of doomsday device. We don't know with any certainty, so we can't rule anything out. What we *do* know is that Russell Cayman—under the command of some all-powerful group—will stop at nothing to reach the tomb. The race to reach it first has already begun. If you're willing to risk your life to become a hero, then stay in this room. Otherwise—just walk away."

Not a man or woman listening moved a muscle.

Hayden smiled. Everyone was scared, but they stayed anyway. She nodded toward her boss. "The US Secretary of Defense would like to say something."

Jonathan Gates didn't move, but his voice carried around the room. "I can only reinforce what Agent Jaye has already told you. The tomb is vital. The remaining eight Pieces of Odin, now in Stuttgart, are vital. Russell Cayman is vital, and if at all possible needs to be captured alive. We don't know"— he paused—"if the eyes of authority consider us the bad guys here. But we're monitoring the news services and nothing has come up so maybe someone, somewhere, has our backs. There's a group—calls itself the Shadow Elite—who think they own the world. Let's shake it up and show 'em who it really belongs to. The people."

A cheer went up. Drake could hardly imagine the variety of characters a man like Gates could enlist to find the Shadow Elite. Something would shake loose soon. When Gates stopped speaking and the room started to mobilize for their short journey to the tomb, Drake drifted over to Ben and Karin.

"You two nailed down the tomb's location, I hear. Not bad for a head banger and a dropout."

Ben's face fell. "Don't remind me, mate. Just don't remind me." He sounded suicidal.

Drake blinked rapidly at Karin. "His nappy rash flared up again?"

Karin smirked. "Worse than ever. But on top of that, he's just heard that, in his absence, the band released their CD when they came out of police protection and have been invited to guest at a festival near Leeds."

"Isn't that good news, mate?"

"Not when I'm *here*," Ben whined, "saving the world."

"Worse thing is—" Karin couldn't contain herself any longer. "The festival's being headlined by Ben's two favorite groups. Pretty Reckless and Evanescence."

Drake whistled. "Bummer. Don't worry. Maybe the world will have ended by then."

Ben glared at him. "I thought you, at least, would understand."

"Life's tough, Ben." Drake cast a sideways glance at Hayden. "And if you don't *realize* that pretty soon, you're gonna find out in a way that'll cut you off at the knees." Drake turned away, an old memory of Kennedy playing through his head. "Stick to working the internet, Blakey."

Karin put a hand on his shoulder as he made to walk away. "There's something else bothering him too. Well, both of us. This Shadow Elite—we found literally bugger all about them on the net. Not a trace nor a trail. Not even a sniff of digital footprints."

Drake nodded. "I understand." Ben and Karin working together could crack into the NSA without breaking a sweat. He walked them over to where Hayden, Mai and Alicia were talking. "Now, if you're up for it, there's the last tomb of the gods to raid."

Hayden heard his last comment as they approached. She looked up, eyes hard. "You'd better be up for it. You think you've gone through hell so far? You ain't seen nothin' yet."

PART TWO

The tomb, the thief and the train.

TWELVE

The industrial city of Singen in Southern Germany had no idea of the storm that was set to strike. Sitting pretty and picturesque under a clear, blue sky, surrounded by forests, lakes and mountains, and overlooked by the landmark it was made famous for—the volcanic stub on which was built a fortress, now ruined—it basked in dangerous ignorance.

Some of the world's most ruthless men and women approached. Some were already there.

They made the trip in less than an hour. During that time Drake, Alicia, Mai and Dahl swapped stories and jokes to help alleviate the tension. Drake kept half an ear on the conversation, but concentrated mainly on checking the gear he'd been issued back at the safe house. Of course, as always, Dahl had chosen that particular place for a major reason. Not only was it an SSG facility, it was also a military bunker and stored enough weaponry to outfit a small army. SIG and Glock pistols, American M16's, and M4 Carbines. Pump-action shotguns, rocket launchers, grenades and flares.

Alicia and even Mai had approached the stash eagerly, like kids at Christmas, but Drake had grabbed the bare minimum, while making sure both Ben and Karin were outfitted with easy-to-use "point and click" handguns. At first, he had tried persuading them to stay behind, or at least stay hidden.

Ben had shaken his head immediately. Karin, in the way of a close sister, had put his thoughts into words. "We've come this far. We might be scared, but we're doing it anyway."

Drake looked at them, looked at them all. "That's what makes a hero."

"My life," Karin said, "hadn't been worth living, until I chased a madman down a black hole in a tropical paradise. Until then. . .I purposely destroyed my life."

"Why would you do that?" Drake had asked.

Karin had shaken her head. "I lost my faith in people. Even now, I can't find it. I just...can't."

"We'll try to help." Drake said to her, painfully aware that two months ago his words would have been *trust me. I'll save you.* But not now. Not ever again.

"Like I said, we're coming with you."

Now Drake began to prepare himself mentally for what was to come. Their toughest battle yet. The streets of Singen streamed past, the stump of *Hohentwiel* now commanding the horizon. Lush fields, stands of green trees and a few houses encircled the volcanic stub and its old castle and, as they drew closer, something else.

Something completely out of place.

The chatter began to fire up the airwaves almost immediately. "I see three choppers, sir. All military." A voice from the lead car.

Dahl's voice. "Markings?"

"Sir, I think you should know this first. *They're just landing.* Men are e-vaccing as I speak. I think we should consider an immediate strike."

A stunned silence followed. Drake's adrenalin spiked and

he caught a look that flashed between Alicia and Mai. They were up for it too. They all nodded at Dahl.

"We hit them before they can set up," Drake said. "Before they can prepare, settle, or plan. That way, even though we came second, we still have the element of surprise."

"Strike through their lines." Mai joined in. "Break through, outflank them, and decimate. We'll come upon those already inside the tomb without warning."

Alicia scowled. "In an ideal world, little sprite."

Dahl was already speaking into the walkie. "Plan is a go. We do this now. No delay."

"Lock and load." Hayden's voice came over the walkie. "Nothing changes. We hit them harder, that's all. Remember, this is one of the most important military strikes in living memory. We're talking about a third tomb of the gods *and* a possible doomsday device being acquired by an unknown group. We simply cannot afford to fail. "

The military convoy picked up speed as it left the city and approached the old volcano. They made final weapons checks, clicked live ammo into place and tried to attain the mental focus it was going to take to win the day.

At the base of the steep hill, they abandoned the vehicles and took to the trees. Beneath the priceless cover, the special multinational force hotfooted its way to the volcano's summit.

"We aim for the choppers." Dahl breathed into the throatmics. "Cayman and his men either found the entrance or made one. It wouldn't be too risky with the proper GPRS systems."

Drake remembered that ground-penetrating radar was the Swede's specialty. He listened to the chatter but eyeballed every inch of the surrounding hostile territory as he ran. The competence of the people around him gave him confidence.

He was used to venturing into the unknown and striking a supposedly superior target. Though Kennedy's death had been avenged and even now the Blood King, Dmitry Kovalenko, was suffering in prison for all his terrible sins, Drake couldn't help but look forward to the dark violence that was to come. He had been forced to embrace it for Kennedy.

It would always be a part of him.

A deep rumble came from up above. The ground shook for a few seconds and in between small gaps in the trees, he strained to see a plume of spreading smoke. Cayman and his men had made their entrance, maybe even destroying part of the ancient castle. Nothing would get in the way of their arrogance and their progress.

Except us. Drake saw the four SAS men at point, Sam and his colleagues. All four had once worked with Drake and with Wells. He trusted their judgment with his life. Next came the two Japanese, Mai's friends, and Gates's four secret service agents. Komodo and his three Delta soldiers had volunteered to watch their backs and allowed Belmonte, Ben and Karin to join them.

Hayden, Kinimaka, Gates, and the rest of them formed a formidable central column. Up they went, eyes peeled for trouble, but it was their ears that easily pinpointed Cayman's position. Loud shouts and curses rang around the hillside. The mercs who worked for Cayman were in a hurry, making no effort to keep their presence under wraps. The DIA operative would know that Gates followed and had no doubt left orders to quickly enforce the perimeter.

They were soon among a set of old ruins, now closing in on the castle. The signal went up for absolute silence and readiness. A whisper rattled down the throat-mics, asking for half a dozen men to circle around the staging area. Drake crouched behind a rough free-standing concrete archway that might once have been a window. A cursory glance ahead and he saw the staging area. Cayman's men rushed around, setting up a communications array and a makeshift HQ. They lugged equipment from three stationary choppers as their rotors whirled gently. The old castle's tumbledown walls made a crazy backdrop to the proceedings, its gaping doorway emitting clouds of smoke that drifted up from somewhere deep inside.

Drake heard the Bluetooth squawk that signaled the flanking team's readiness. Mai, Alicia and Dahl knelt in readiness alongside him. In the stand of trees behind them lay Komodo and his team with Ben and Karin among them.

Hayden took them all in with an enigmatic expression. "The doomsday device and Cayman," she whispered, a ghost in their ears. "That's what we're here for."

They broke cover with devastating force, coming at Cayman's men from three sides, dozens of professional soldiers firing in short, accurate bursts. The screaming began immediately, bodies and equipment struck and sent smashing to the ground. Even then, Cayman had had the foresight to conceal a few sharpshooters in the castle itself. Shots rang out, and the grass around Drake's feet was peppered with gunfire, sods of earth kicking up as if they'd jumped out of the ground. Immediately, one of Mai's men fell and the rogue Japanese agent dropped to one knee, squeezing off shot after shot, each one at a different window to keep the shooters neutralized.

But the mercs were hardened fighters. Showing no sign of panic at the onrushing force, they located weapons and held their ground. Drake smashed his rifle into the face of the first he came to, aware that Cayman would already know the enemy had arrived and would be hatching a plan.

When the man went down, Drake shot him and moved onto the next. Hayden was struggling beside him. Nowhere near healed yet, she had no choice but to fight until they could find someone to help them, someone they could trust. Drake felled his man and looked around. A few dozen mercs were down. The chopper pilots were dead or tagged and gagged. Alicia was already tailing the SAS soldiers as they ran for the wide castle entrance. Mai fired without pause, and had now been joined by more men. It seemed a couple of sharpshooters still remained, but the SAS would soon take care of that.

Dahl kicked a man's knee out. When the man fell and let out a shriek, the Swede hesitated. But Daniel Belmonte didn't. Coming up with the rear guard, he stepped around Dahl and shot the man point-blank in the head.

When Dahl turned a confused expression on him, Belmonte's cultured tones were frayed with pain. "One of them killed Emma. That tars them all. None of them deserve to live, not here and certainly not among civilized people."

Drake caught hold of Dahl's shoulder. "No time to argue. Go."

They ran along the path and passed under the castle walls into a suffused dimness. Alicia was just descending a stairwell to the left, hissing with distaste.

"Bloody regimentals got to 'em first. That leaves me with a zero body count so far." The Englishwoman looked glum.

Mai caught up. "So take point and stop your whining."

"My pleasure."

"Alright." Drake spotted two exits. He was about to follow Hayden and Kinimaka as they stalked toward the farthest when a stream of enemy soldiers suddenly burst from both doors. Drake rolled as gunfire erupted. Everyone evaded as best they could, leaping sideways or even falling backward. A hail of bullets was not something to confront standing up. But when Drake hit the deck, he was already aiming and squeezing the trigger of his M16. His skull struck concrete, but his aim didn't waver. Bullets strafed the room, whizzing and zipping from wall to wall. Boots came toward his face. With his hands full of rifle, he had little chance of defending himself.

He braced for the impact and hoped not to lose too many teeth.

Then the boots skipped sideways and folded. A second later, a body landed beside him. He found himself staring into the newly dead eyes of a pock-marked mercenary.

A hand appeared. A voice. "You owe me. Saved your looks." Then a sigh. "Such as they are."

Alicia had gotten her first kill. Drake jumped up, saw a man wearing leather leaping at him, pounding hard, gun drifting up. Drake moved faster than his opponent's eye could follow. Hand strikes to the body and the head, all purposely aimed and weighted to rupture organs and snap bones. Another enemy body came at him, but his focus was solely on the parts of the body where he could cause maximum damage in minimum time. He didn't even see the face of the man he killed.

He finally earned some breathing space. Hayden and Kinimaka fought at the front of a pack, which included the four SAS soldiers. Dahl battled over on the other side of the room, helping Komodo and his Delta team while also protecting the non-fighters. Alicia fought on her own. The joint prowess of his team members impressed him, and they swiftly overtook their opponents.

But it was Mai Kitano who cut them down. Wherever she went, men lay convulsing in her wake. Fear spread among their enemies as the Japanese woman inched toward them. When a man tried to spray the room with automatic fire, Mai grabbed his arm and shoved it down so the first burst fired into the floor. With superhuman speed, she twisted his wrist, snapping it, but keeping the barrel steady so that the second burst ravaged his nearby colleagues. When he fell to his knees, Mai made sure the third burst ended up in his skull.

Between them, Mai and Alicia mopped up the remainder of their assailants. When they had finished, the two women stared at each other.

Alicia said, "Maybe we should start keeping a head count. The winner gets to—" Her eyes swiveled toward Drake as Hayden's shout drowned everything out.

"Let's go!"

Mai ran to the hole in the wall, peering through and then signaling the all clear. They jogged after her, leaving their dead and dying enemies behind. The castle was a warren of rooms, some partly furnished and some left barren and bare. Modern displays and cabinets clashed with ancient austerity. The empty rooms felt haunted and lonely, things that could not quite be seen shifted among the dirt and the dust, befitting for a structure built atop a tomb of the most wicked gods ever known. The wind whistled through gaps in the windows and through hidden loopholes among the battlements. More than one empty shadow made the group turn their heads as they ran past.

Mai led the way, following footsteps and wisps of smoke

and damage left by the modern-day invaders. Bluetooth chatting kept them organized and highly alert. Drake swapped his mag for a fresh one. A head count confirmed what they all already knew—three of their number had fallen. Both of Mai's agents and one of Gates's. Sam was still human and frosty enough to give Drake a look as Mai led the SAS team forward. The regiment leader seemed in awe. *Oh no,* Drake thought. *Not another.*

Through another room where tapestries and paintings had been torn off the walls and flung to the floor. Cayman must have been looking for something. Maybe something explained by the whorls—the ancient language they had found in the other tombs. Drake wondered if Dahl's language expert had been trying to contact them.

At last, they tore through the open doorway of a grand state room, throwing flash-bangs before them. Mai had heard the voices of whispering guards from two rooms away. Once the guards were taken out, they finally arrived at the blasted hole in the wall—a wide, ragged void through which a frigid, keening breath of wind blasted in intermittent gusts.

Drake paused for a moment and looked at Dahl. "One more time, mate?"

"Let's hope so." The Swede's serious face spoke pessimistic volumes.

Ben's small voice spoke up from the back of the group. "Can you tell why they chose this place to break through? Any clues are good right about now."

Drake lifted his eyes to the demolished wall for the first time. The far edges and some of the top blocks were intact. A picture of some kind had been carved into the wall. Hard to decipher at first, but then Torsten Dahl's eagle eyes figured it out. "Look at both edges of the wall, and the base, where part of the wall remains. You have the base and far side of a triangle. This—" he said.

"Was a carving of Odin's symbol, the *Valknott*." Ben finished. "A symbol of death."

"And there." Karin moved closer to the wall. "The whorls again. The language of the gods. Odin, it seems, really was the father of the gods."

"He sacrificed his eyes for wisdom." Ben recalled their search for the first tomb. "For future knowledge. He knew what was going to happen."

"In that case," Hayden said, "his eight pieces—the ones that seemed redundant after we found the first tomb—might be more important than we thought."

Mai and Alicia were itching to move forward. "We'll learn nothing stood around up here," Mai said softly and Alicia grunted.

Drake and the other soldiers agreed. The enemy shouldn't be allowed any more time to prepare.

Mano Kinimaka eyed the hole and the narrowing passageway beyond. "I'm not even sure I can fit down there."

"But the gods are waiting," Hayden said carefully. "And so is Cayman. Sir—" She half turned toward Gates.

"Screw it, Jaye. I'm coming."

The darkness beckoned them, a darkness that crawled with the presence of evil gods, evil contraptions and evil men.

THIRTEEN

The four-man SAS squad took point with Mai Kitano, closely followed by Hayden and Kinimaka. Drake shadowed the big Hawaiian closely, impressed by the big man's agile moves as the passage started to descend quite steeply. The walls turned from smooth clad stone to ragged earth and then to roughhewn rock as they moved down. The breeze died for a while and then began to sweep past them again, carrying with it the stench of ages, the reek of old things gone bad.

They heard whisperings on the wind. Faint voices tugged at their ears, that caught their attention like the suggestions of a malicious temptress. Down and down the passage ran. Their feet crunched through ancient debris, their heads brushing against bruising rock and stone. The way was already lit, but the SAS team left nothing to chance, stopping the team regularly whilst they scouted ahead.

Everyone knew they were heading into a trap. There could be no other outcome. It was simply a matter of when and if they could identify and counteract it.

Time slipped by. The real world fell away. There were no traps they could see. The malevolent air would be enough to warn most people away. They passed a high gothic archway with supreme care. A foul miasma drifted up and began to swirl around their bodies as if sniffing, testing, and touching, and even the Special Forces soldiers shivered.

"I. Don't. Like. This." Alicia was the one who spoke up, enunciating her words like bullet shots, probably trying to chase away her own feelings of dread with her form of ammunition.

Farther down and underneath another gothic arch, they still couldn't hear their enemies. Drake began to wonder if this passage was a false lead, and that Cayman was somewhere else. The backs of his calves burned. Several times something dropped on his head, something that skittered or squirmed quickly away, making him swallow hard to conceal the revulsion.

Then, from a distance, they heard faint voices—many men shouting. The team halted for an agonizing five minutes and then began to proceed even more cautiously. Drake knew even the shouting could be a ruse. Where Russell Cayman was concerned, nothing could be taken at face value. Behind him, he heard Komodo whispering at Ben and Karin that they should now prepare for absolutely anything, even running back the way they had just come.

At length, and after interminable minutes of sneaking slowly through the awful creeping dark, an enormous archway could be seen ahead. Still some way to go, but Drake, craning his head around Kinimaka and Hayden, could make out the floor of a well-lit cavern. He could hear men shouting back and forth. He could hear heavy gear being dragged.

But he saw no one.

He whispered to Hayden. "They can't risk a firefight in the tunnel. It might cause a cave-in and trap them. They'll wait until we emerge."

"Agreed."

Kinimaka grunted. "So get ready. I got a Christmas luau to get to soon. Time off and everything. Nothing like Christmas in Hawaii, man."

Drake got a glimpse of how lonely his Christmas might be, when only a few weeks ago it had held such promise. Whoever said "life can turn in a dime" sure knew what they were talking about. He thought about the dynamics going on in their little group and couldn't think of anyone who might look forward to cast-iron Christmas happiness. Except Kinimaka.

"We'll do our best, Mano." No guarantees.

A whisper came back up the line as they approached the light. "We're going to punch it. Fast and hard. Keep moving."

There was one more moment of pause and then the SAS team broke cover with extreme prejudice. But they didn't just run and shoot, they threw flash bangs and smoke grenades all while staying in perfect fighting formation, covering each other as they ran. Mai fitted in perfectly with them as she would any specialized team. Hayden and Kinimaka burst out next, staying calm, then Drake, Alicia and Dahl, ready for the fight of their lives.

Mayhem and violence confronted them. Heavy lifting gear and abseiling equipment was piled in the center of the huge cavern. Cayman's men were arrayed around it and around the far walls, weapons spouting fire as they discharged their weapons. Drake and Alicia veered sharply to the right, firing into the central mass of the enemy. The SAS team advanced at pace. Komodo and his men burst out a second later, adding to the firepower. For several moments, the cavern floor was a warzone, a lethal free-for-all where skill was outmatched ten to one by pure luck.

Drake skidded to one knee, rifle to shoulder, squeezing off a shot every second after a minor adjustment. His bullets struck bone and flesh, his aim only thrown off when sizzling lumps of hot lead zinged too close for comfort. He was immensely aware of the stunning tomb architecture all around him but didn't have even a millisecond to appreciate it. His team had no cover, but they more than made up for that in sheer ferocity and perfect aim. Within a few minutes, the men Cayman had situated in the center of the room were falling back, intimidated, decimated and abandoning their only cover. The mercs around the walls had sustained fewer injuries, but even they were trying to inch away.

Then the SAS team took a hit, a young soldier falling backward with a shot to the head and one of Komodo's Delta team collapsed clutching his throat. Gates's secret service detail was thinned to just one when the third member of his guard took a stunning round to the vest and then, as he gasped for breath, another to the face.

Drake looked up for the first time. Of course this tomb was a multi-level affair. Still unable to take it in, but fully aware it was one of the wonders of the world, Drake ignored the tomb and pinpointed the places where Cayman's men were sniping down at them. He nodded at Alicia and Dahl and the three of them fired continuously at the hidden men as the mysterious gale blew and raged around them again.

"Whatever you do," Alicia cried, "don't hit one of those fucking coffins!"

*****

Hayden had fanned out to the left, spying a spectacular staircase. Wide at the bottom, it narrowed drastically all the way to the top of the vast cavern, ending in a point where it touched the very heights. The staircase offered a way up to the several ledges and tiers that ran around this circular tomb, and the many niches beyond. Kinimaka followed her, picking off mercs stationed near the stairs.

As she neared the first step, a merc pounded toward her. Hayden shot him point-blank, desperate not to get into hand-to-hand. Her knife wound hurt like a bitch. It would only take one hard, precise punch to incapacitate her.

But she fought anyway. She fought to win the day for her country, for her father, but most of all, for her friends. As the bullets flew, she prayed for them all. As she stepped foot on the high staircase and saw a dozen mercs suddenly jump from the first level up and come screaming toward her, she began to pray for herself.

*****

Ben Blake stood directly behind the Delta soldier who collapsed. He fell with the soldier, aware that Karin and Gates were at his side, and tried to see the wound. But the man's hands were holding onto his own throat with a death grip. His eyes were wide, full of pain, focused on nothing. Ben touched the man's wrist gently, feeling the blood running slickly like dark oil. Within seconds, the man had died, his hands falling apart to reveal a fatal wound.

Ben stared, choking back tears and bile. This was about as up close and bloody as war got. There were more terrible aspects of it, Ben was sure, but this soldier, lying still and dead where seconds ago a virile, young man had stood, shook him to his core. It showed him how his daily worries and struggles were irrelevant. How every second of life should be savored. How horrifying death could be.

He rose to his feet, temporarily alone. The remaining Delta

man inched forward, covering their international teammates with precision-placed shots. Karin stood next to him, saying nothing. They knew how each other felt. Gates was still on his knees, holding the dead soldier's hand and whispering something about sorrow.

Ben's eyes were drawn to the cavern itself. The enormous structure rose hundreds of feet and was as wide as it was tall. It was a huge bowl, comprising of three different levels, not including the floor. Around each level ran a wide ledge. Beyond the ledge, hewn into the rock of the ancient volcano, were hundreds and hundreds of niches. Tombs.

Tombs of the Gods.

The floor level was also ringed with tombs. Ben squinted at several opposite, but unlike the niches in the first two tombs, these were sparsely appointed, containing little except the oversize coffin itself and a few austere carvings. Of course this place had been where the gods had imprisoned the worst of their kind. No tribute necessary.

Komodo glanced back at them. "Stay close!" He gestured for them to join him before turning back to the battle. Ben saw Hayden stuck on one of the two staircases with Kinimaka at her side, beset by the enemy, holding her side in agony.

Komodo veered his team toward her.

*****

Drake kept the snipers pinned down as best he could. When it became clear even their sharpshooting wasn't going to pin down the enemy for long, Dahl took off toward the cavern's second staircase with a crazy, weaving run. Drake shouted a warning, but the mad Swede was already up to full speed. He hit the staircase at a dead run, leaping up two steps at a time. Drake saw no option but to follow. The Swede was reckless, but their team really needed to get up higher.

A bullet zinged by, whistling as it parted the air in front of his nose and then Alicia's. One handed, Drake fired blindly into the enemy as he ran. He hit the staircase six steps behind Dahl and one behind Alicia. Even among the mayhem, his pride took a hit. Then, a man flew over from the side and collided with him, knocking him off his feet. The rough stairs scraped his face. Drake struck toward his opponent's eyes and throat and brought his knees up to protect his stomach. A knife flashed. Drake palmed it aside. It came again, but Drake shifted inside it, caught the man's wrist and snapped it. Even then, the assault didn't stop, but Drake hadn't expected it to. The knife clattered away. The mercenary brought his bulk to bear, trying to pin Drake to the staircase and smashed his large forehead downward.

Drake slipped aside again. The merc's forehead connected solidly with the stone edge of the staircase, temporarily stunning him. Drake flipped him over, finished him with a stiff-fingered jab and looked up.

Dahl and Alicia were already partway along the first level. Fierce opposition had forced them to take cover in one of the niches, next to a bullet-pocked coffin.

Drake grimaced. Alicia wouldn't be happy.

*****

Hayden staggered as the pain ripped through her side. Oddly, it hadn't been an enemy blow that had hurt her, but a misstep on the stairs, sending both her and her weapons crashing to the ground. Instantly, the mercenaries were among them. Hayden forced herself up, gritting her teeth to hold in the pain, and swiped the first one off the step with a swing of her rifle. The second she clubbed right on the nose. A bullet fired from a handgun pinged off the concrete between her legs and zipped on through. Kinimaka was a giant at her side. Men actually collided with him and rebounded right off the staircase, landing heavily in the dust below. But Kinimaka's real strength was his surprising speed. Three assailants fell before they even knew the man had grabbed hold of them.

Then, Komodo and his men were with them. They advanced up the stairs. Hayden stayed in place for a while and used her elevated position to fire down upon the disorderly mercenaries.

Then Ben was at her side. "Are you ok?"

"No. Are you?" The lad's face was deathly white.

"Death is everywhere." His eyes darted from the fallen soldiers to the tombs of the gods.

"This place was built for death." Hayden squeezed off another shot, sending another mercenary folding in a wheezing heap.

"Look at the floor," Ben said quietly. "Just look."

Hayden paused for a moment and removed her eye from the gun's sights. What she saw made the hairs on her arms rise. The floor of the tomb, dusty and strewn with debris was slowly being covered in blood. Thick, red pools were spreading from the many dead and dying men across the wide expanse, making it slick and slippery for men's boots. Even the SAS down there were losing their balance, drenching their fatigues and turning red themselves.

"And look."

Ben pointed out something that, amidst the chaos, Hayden had so far failed to see. Arranged around the outside of the cavern, in a circle, were a number of small altars, each one with a different shape carved into its surface.

Hayden looked down on them, momentarily at a loss for words.

"There are eight of them," Ben said as if in explanation. "And the whorls." He gestured toward all the ground floor walls. "Are everywhere."

Hayden's eyes traveled from the ground floor up, past three levels of niches, and it was then that her eyes fell on a figure she partly recognized.

She patted Ben's hand. "That's Russell Cayman," she said. "He's up there, watching how this whole thing goes down."

*****

Drake scurried up the stairs double-time, pausing at the ledge as his two teammates laid down covering fire and then leapt into the niche. Instantly, it seemed a clammy hand took hold of his skull and gripped it with ice-cold fingers. He shivered.

"Not exactly Starbucks."

"Shut it," Alicia whispered. "This place gives me the creeps."

The niche was long and narrow, cut back into the rock about forty feet. The overall impression was that it had been constructed quickly and with little thought. The walls and ceiling were irregular and jagged, as if cleaved by a mighty weapon or hand.

Alicia shook her head at something down below. "Your baby boy's causing us trouble, Drakey."

Drake glanced over and saw Ben distracting Hayden as she tried to pick off bad guys. "I'll talk to the little fool."

Dahl appeared at that moment, coming from the rear of the cave. Drake eyed him "Bit of a risky place to take a piss, mate."

"For you, maybe." Dahl flashed a brief smile, then turned serious again. "I discovered several relatively crude carvings back there. And a statue. I think this is the tomb of Amatsu, literally the god of evil. This is a very bad place, my friends."

"Well, for now," Drake said, "let's deal with the evil we can see."

He refrained from lobbing a grenade toward the enemy, but leaned out and let loose a burst of automatic fire. The mag ran dry. He dropped it and clicked another into place. "One-two combination?"

"Do it." Dahl fell in behind him. Alicia took rearguard. Firing together they hopped out of the niche and rushed to the next one along, felling startled enemy soldiers and then taking cover behind the next big coffin.

As they ran briefly along the ledge, the entire cavern opened up for them. Drake saw the SAS team and Mai directly below, crawling among the heavy equipment as they took cover whilst peppering bullets at the few remaining mercs. He saw the great staircase to his right. A contingent of Cayman's men were being beaten back by Komodo's Delta team and Mano Kinimaka. Hayden was sniping the snipers, her eagle eyes seeking out every niche.

Back near the arched entrance, Gates and Belmonte had taken cover, armed but holding their fire for fear of harming a member of their own team.

And two levels up, standing rigidly still, he saw a figure watching them. A figure he guessed could be only one man.

The figure observed until the last of its men on the ground floor was killed and the group on the stairs beaten back. Only then did it raise a hand.

"Stop this," it cried. "Your efforts, though noteworthy, are trivial. You cannot win this battle."

Then, hundreds of men suddenly appeared around the third tier, silent, weapons carefully aimed. Cayman began to laugh.

FOURTEEN

Drake took a deep breath. Cayman had them hopelessly outnumbered. It was do or die, or run like hell. Behind him another coffin sat in ancient stillness.

"We stand a virgin's chance in hell," Alicia commented. "That means fu—"

"We know what it means." Dahl and the Englishwoman still hadn't had chance to become properly acquainted yet. Of course, for each of them, the idea had totally different meanings. Dahl pointed out the stairs, and a wicked grin twisted the corner of his mouth. "There's our play."

Drake stared and understood. "No way. You're fucking crazy, Dahl."

"Yeah, but *good* crazy." The Swede scanned the cavern, and tapped his Bluetooth mic. "Let the bastard talk whilst you figure out a move. Then go on my signal."

Squawks of static conveyed understanding. Cayman, the DIA ghost, the wetwork specialist, the business end of the Shadow Elite, shouted in a voice that dripped with disdain.

"I was a child of the system," he said. "A child in time, nothing more. Now I rank above presidents. You should feel honored, being allowed to die by my word." He spread his arms. "I am the voice of the Shadow Elite. No common man could achieve more."

Drake stared hard at this individual. There was a chance he might soon hold the fate of the world in his hands. Cayman looked like an ordinary man, slightly built, average height, not outstanding in any way. But an aura of menace surrounded him. A sense that this man had never known compassion, love, nor forgiveness. That all his days were filled with ice-cold fantasies.

Cayman laughed once more, the sound strained and foreign. Drake knew then that Russell Cayman had never had a good hour in his life.

"You would be too late anyway. I have sent for the eight pieces of Odin. They are already on their way here, and once they arrive—the doomsday device will be ours."

"The eight pieces *are* important?" Alicia grumbled. "What a twat. Dahl, you should really have hung on to those bad boys."

"The advice is duly noted. I'll file it where I think it belongs."

"Don't get testy, Torsten. They're in Stuttgart, right?"

"They were."

"Well, he can't have gotten 'em that far. Maybe we can intercept them."

Drake shushed them. "We have bigger problems." He pointed out the eight altars arrayed about the floor below. "Ben just Bluetoothed me. His guess is the pieces fit in there."

"And that activates the device?" Dahl shook his head in disbelief. "So the nastiest tomb holds the nastiest weapon. And it all seems to revolve somehow around Odin and Norse mythology. We really need to learn more, you know, and talk to my language guy back in Iceland's tomb."

"We will," Drake said. "As soon as we get out of here."

And then he stepped forward. "Hey! Cayman!" He stared up at the emotionless man. "Do you know me?"

Silenced stretched as taut as a tripwire, then Cayman shrugged. "I know all of your names. But the names of dead men mean nothing to me."

"Ah, but I'm not dead yet," Drake said. "You'll find that I'm pretty hard to kill. Maybe one of the hardest you've ever known. Do you know why?"

Cayman said nothing.

"Because I'm looking for the man who ordered my wife's murder. And for the man who murdered her. And I think you know something about that, Cayman. You and Wells. What is it that you know?"

Cayman licked his lips. "You're about to die, Drake. Do it with honor and stop whining."

"Did it involve the Shadow Elite?" Drake asked. "Are they connected to her death? Who is the Norseman?"

With that one word, Drake got a reaction he'd never imagined. Cayman's body literally *lurched* in shock. His face and his clenched fists turned bone white and he opened his mouth to scream an order.

Dahl was quicker. "Move!"

All hell broke loose. Dahl burst from cover and sprinted for the stairs, Drake and Alicia right behind him. Drake and even the daredevil Alicia were gritting their teeth in anticipation of Dahl's next move. . .

. . .at the same time Mai and the SAS force leapt *toward* the tomb walls and the weapons of the soldiers who stood above them, reaching for the abseil ropes that Cayman's men had been attaching earlier to help move heavy equipment. They were *attacking* the enemy. . .

The Tomb of the Gods

...as Hayden and her team stood their ground and focused all their firepower on the superior force!

Dahl rushed to the top of the stone staircase and then jumped into space. Anyone watching would have stopped in shock, wondering what on earth the Swede was up to. Was he committing suicide? But then he landed, gun aimed and firing, on the stone railing that ran down the side of the stairs and slid, gathering speed, loosing bullets, screaming and with hair flying all around him, at high speed toward the ground floor.

Drake came next and then Alicia, also screaming to help dull their anxiety. The trio slid down the stone railing, their weapons firing on full auto.

Mai and a single SAS soldier grabbed ropes and scurried up the walls as fast they could whilst Sam and the remaining men unleashed a devastating salvo of covering fire. Up they flew, just twenty feet, and then threw timed grenades into the air. It seemed a random, hopeful move, but in fact was carefully calculated to disorganize and disorient the enemy.

Then they let go, jumping to the ground...

...and Hayden's team made a break for the exit, using the mayhem as cover. A Delta soldier took a round that killed him instantly, but for a second his legs kept going under their own momentum and he took another round meant for Komodo, the man saving his commander's life even after he was dead. Hayden bounded to the floor and then Gates and his last remaining agent and Belmonte slipped from cover and added their own firepower to the lead-filled fray.

Mai and the SAS soldier landed together, rolled, and came up just as the grenades they'd thrown detonated in the air at the center of the cavern. Fragments exploded outward in every direction, striking enemy bodies on all sides of the tomb.

Dahl, Drake and Alicia descended speedily down the stone rail, but even at that speed, their aims proved accurate. Enemy soldiers twisted and fell from the third level, plummeting over the edge and down to the ground. More danced like puppets as shots riddled them, falling back amongst their brethren and pulling them down. Dahl flew off the end of the railing and, with nothing to stop him, crashed into the ground at speed, his graceful flight turning into a wipeout landing. Drake and Alicia couldn't help but follow suit.

"Fuck me." Alicia mumbled into the ground. "That's one way of showing a girl a good time."

Drake pulled his aching body up. Most of their enemy, in shock at being assailed by a weaker force from three angles, stood in temporary disarray. Those that weren't readied their weapons. Drake spied the exit.

It was now or never. No choice

"Hurry."

He led the way toward the exit. A few bullets slammed into the stone around their feet, but not nearly as many as it might have been. Even the superior soldiers among their enemy were thrown off by their screaming accomplices. Drake knew that no soldier, no matter who he worked for or what agenda he followed, could stay fully focused whilst his comrades screamed and died around him. Then Drake saw that Hayden and her team were already there and laying down some first-rate covering fire. As he passed one of the eight altars, he slowed to take a better look.

A rectangle of stone sat, fused into the rock floor of the cavern, with the oval altar set on top. Within the body of the altar, a precise shape had been carved. Cayman, it appeared, was right. The eight pieces of Odin were meant to be fixed into the eight altars to, presumably, activate the doomsday device.

And the eight pieces were already en route.

Game and set to Cayman, it seemed. But not yet *match*. Not by a long way. And if Cayman's reaction was anything to go by, then the Shadow Elite and its leader, the Norseman, were not only fully invested in the terrible events unfolding around the tombs of the gods, but also responsible for the horrors of Drake's past.

As was Cayman himself.

Drake needed to get to that SAS facility and find Wells's research. The way this thing was panning out—everything was connected.

Hayden met him with a pained grin. "Survived again, huh?"

"At least until she's avenged," he said with a grimace. "How many didn't?"

"Too many," Hayden said, and Drake saw Ben standing behind her. The young lad's face was drip white, his hands bloody. Just then, bullets began to pepper the sides of the archway behind Drake.

He pointed the way back up the long passage they had followed down here. "We should get moving."

*****

The team retraced its steps. At first, they proceeded quickly, but without haste. Then Hayden voiced her concerns about the eight pieces of Odin.

"They can't be that far away. It all depends how Cayman transports them. My guess is he'll have to do it covertly and quietly, since that's how his masters work. So it will take a bit longer. But even then—" She left the obvious unspoken.

"They must be intercepted," Dahl said. "It's imperative that we get to them before Cayman takes delivery. And, as soon as we get out of here. . ." He glanced ahead through the deep gloom. "I need to talk to my man in Iceland. He's had time to decipher at least *something* by now."

"What *is* the doomsday device?" Belmonte spoke up now. "And how does it work? Does anyone know?"

"Not yet." Dahl breathed as he started to pick up the pace. "That's part of what my language expert in Iceland is looking into."

"I bet it relates to Odin in some way," Karin said. "The Norse gods are all over this. It all seems preordained, as if we're following a path set down in ancient history. . ." She paused. "But to what end?"

"If, like you say, it has anything to do with Norse mythology—Odin and Ragnarok—it'll be pretty earth-shattering," Dahl told her. "Ragnarok was the last stand of the gods. If they all laid down to die before it happened, then—"

"It hasn't happened yet." Belmonte finished for him.

Karin nodded. "I bet it was Odin who first saw the future and realized that the gods died in a different manner. At first, he would've laughed and ridiculed it, but maybe. . .*seeing that it had happened made it happen.*"

"Whoa." Ben was struggling to keep up. Drake half-grinned as Komodo half-dragged the lad along. "That's some very deep shit, sis."

"Very, very deep," Karin replied. "But probably true."

"And the shield started it all?" Hayden wondered. "Your brother and Parnevik were always rambling on about it being the principal piece."

"The finding of the shield started a chain of events—"

Karin told her. "That led to the finding of tomb three. That, I'm sure of."

"And as for the Shadow Elite." Jonathan Gates was being helped along by his last agent and Komodo's last remaining Delta soldier. "We still don't know who to trust."

"Speaking of the pieces," Hayden said, grimacing as she held her wounded side. "Let's move."

They began to really pick up the pace, lights bobbing as they ran. The going was strenuous and, at times, painful, but they all knew now what was at stake.

Every minute counted.

FIFTEEN

Daylight greeted their eyes as they emerged from the eerie tunnel. The dead and the dying still lay all around. One enemy soldier had managed to crawl all the way to the edge of the tunnel shaft, gun in hand. He looked startled when the entire team emerged in front of him.

Hayden pointed. "Grab that guy. His reward for perseverance will be telling us all he knows about Cayman's plan for the eight pieces." She nodded toward the other rooms. "Gather any other survivors too. Check outside."

Kinimaka, Komodo and the other Delta soldier took off. Sam and his SAS colleagues followed after a brief consultation. Drake took a moment to bask in the sunlight, enjoying its soft, mellow beams flickering through the many windows and the disturbed dust motes drifting through the still air. Beyond these old castle walls lay a busy city, jam-packed with men and women who had no idea of the immense conflict going on around them.

Torsten Dahl walked toward one of the windows, taking out his mobile phone and jabbing at several buttons. Drake, Ben and Karin joined him and they were soon joined by Belmonte. Alicia and Mai stayed to cover the tunnel.

Dahl looked dubious as the phone rang and rang. After a minute, he glanced at his own screen and switched it to speakerphone. "Bloody hell. Does he not have voicemail?"

"He might not know how to use it." Ben smiled. "These crustys don't have much of a grasp on modern technology, do they, Matt?"

Dahl heard a click. "Hello?"

"*Ja?*"

"It's me—Dahl. Are you alright, Olle?"

"*Ja.* I am good. Where are you? I thought you were dead."

"It will take more than a few gorillas with guns to kill me, Olle."

"I have something for you. Actually, more than something. I have many things."

Dahl pulled a face at the others. "He's an odd sort of guy."

Drake nodded. "You don't say."

"Akerman." Dahl added some weight to his voice. "If you can talk freely, now would be the time."

"Talk freely? Bah. I'm lucky I can talk at all. No, *you're* lucky. Because if they killed me, Torsten, *you* would be the one I came for." He paused. "To haunt. As a ghost."

Dahl frowned in concern. "Do they know you're working for me?"

"They might do. They never trusted me since they caught me with all the pictures."

"What pictures?"

"The ones of your wife. Ha, ha. Ha, ha, ha."

"Akerman. . ."

"*Ja, ja.* Okay, I get the hint. The tomb language is very tricky. You know that. I had to take pictures and work on it back in my room. It was the only way."

Dahl shook his head. "Go on."

"It's a mix of old Akkadian and Sumerian. Maybe some old Babylonian, just for fun. My findings are very preliminary right now, but I can say that much at least. It's possible that ancient languages actually first began when some enterprising soul discovered this so-called god language. As you know old Akkadian was written on clay tablets using a *Cuneiform* script—adopted from early Sumerian. Once I translated the frequent *logograms*, I was away."

"Logogram?" Drake wondered.

Karin whispered. "Pictures that represent words."

"Fill in the gaps?" Dahl said with a fond smile.

"It's a little bit more complex than that, Torsten. I know most of what you soldiers do is point and click, but translating an unknown language—well, that takes a little skill."

Dahl waited.

"Anyway. Once I discounted the logograms as a somewhat secondary script and realized the rest of the language was, in fact, a complete syllabary, I began to make some headway."

Drake glanced at Karin. The blond-haired Blake girl said, "A syllabary is a set of symbols that represent all the syllables of a language. A complete writing system."

"Admittedly, there's a bit of ancient Greek, some *Nu Shu* of ancient China and even some Mayan, but it seems to blend in quite well."

"That makes sense," Dahl said. "The tombs are full of gods from every land."

"After trawling through some dross, I started to piece it together. To make it easier for you, Torsten, I'll stick to the simple stuff."

"Kind of you, Akerman."

"I know. It was pre-ordained that the unearthing of Odin's shield would start in motion a series of events that would lead to the discovery of all three tombs. That includes the portal devices found in Blackbeard's ship and the gate you found in Hawaii. You see? They were not discovered at this time by accident."

"It had occurred to us," Drake murmured.

"But—" Akerman shouted the word. "It goes on to say that the sequence of events will reveal all of the god's secrets and 'mankind's decision to save or destroy itself'"

Belmonte whistled. "I don't like the sound of that."

"*Mankind's* decision?" Dahl said wonderingly.

Karin gave a weary sigh. "To use or not to use the doomsday device," she said. "It's all in our hands."

"Of course. Odin's poem—*forever shall thou fear this, hear me sons of men, for to defile the Tomb of Gods is to start the Day of Reckoning*. Akerman, go on."

"As for the gods themselves? Odin was the one who saw the future—then literally traveled through time. It so happened one day that he traveled to a time when no gods existed. They were dead. When he took his findings back to his Council and his sons, they laughed at him. They would not believe him. It was then that he crafted the teleportation devices and allowed several of the more trusted ones to see the future. What had come to pass *would* come to pass. You see? Before that moment, the gods saw themselves as perpetual, an undying breed. But a hard truth can reveal one's true mortality, and so it was with the gods."

Karin smiled at her brother. She had been right.

"It is said that no god is truly evil," Akerman went on. "But some are definitely nastier than others. It was these few, of course, who wished to use the teleportation devices for their own ends—imagine the chaos they could cause—and so progressed Odin's plans apace. The great gods and he built tomb three first to negate the threat. Then the one in Iceland. And then the one in Hawaii. Apparently, there is some kind of throne there?"

Drake nodded to Dahl's questioning look. "Yes. A huge, dark throne overlooking the biggest cavern you ever saw."

"It's where Odin sat," Akerman told them. "Before he died. The last of the gods contemplating his momentous decisions. And then he returned to his own country to die."

It's where Odin sat. Drake's heart pounded in disbelief. *I climbed over the throne where Odin sat.* For a moment, his vision blurred.

"Odin created fate," Akerman continued. "He created the fate of the gods and of mankind, and I have no doubt, planted many turning points in the course of our history. Not just this one."

"Do the texts explain anything about the device itself or how it may relate to Norse mythology?" Karin asked impatiently.

"Who said that?" Akerman blustered. "Never mind. The female is aggressive, but I suppose I may have been getting a bit carried away. And yes—it does. My main focus was, of course, on this part of the text." Akerman coughed uncomfortably.

"Go on, old friend," Dahl said gently.

"The doomsday device is a weapon designed to cause an overload of the elements. The earth will quake. The air will be split apart by megastorms of unbelievable ferocity. Chains of volcanoes will erupt. And the oceans shall rise."

"The worst scenario we can imagine." Ben nodded. "Naturally."

"Thor was the god of thunder and lightning. Poseidon—of

the seas. Loki—of fire. And both Loki and Poseidon are also known as the gods of earthquakes. You have found them all, have you not?"

"Among thousands of others." Dahl's eyes were bleak.

Drake wanted to reassure him, but the words dried to ash in his throat. Assurance was beyond him now.

"That's the point. The device will use the natural elements to rip the planet apart. But it's based around the Norse version of the apocalypse—Ragnarok. Ever heard of it?"

*****

Hayden had no wish to hurt the man, but her obligations ran far deeper than his pitiful wish to cling to life. A right he'd given up the moment he chose to become a mercenary.

If he chose it, Hayden thought, remembering the plight of many of the Blood King's men.

She searched his eyes. "What do you know of the eight pieces, huh? Where are they?"

His expression didn't change. Hayden tapped his skull with the barrel of her handgun. "Tell me. Now."

"Cayman sent for them." The man spit out at last. "He. . . They were at Stuttgart. Not far."

"Sure thing, I know all that. But how is he transporting them to Singen?"

As she said it, the answer popped into her brain. There was only one way to do it quickly, safely and quietly. But she needed confirmation.

The man shook his head. "I don't know."

Hayden scowled. She looked around. Kinimaka labored over another man a few feet away. He came up with a similar expression.

Then Sam, the SAS Commander, appeared a nearby decrepit doorway. "We found their communications array and worked one of the operators until he came up with the answer. Cayman went for secrecy and stealth, probably at the insistence of his masters. The pieces are being transported overland, by civilian train."

Hayden jumped to her feet. "Get ready for another battle, guys. We need to stop that train—at all costs."

*****

At Dahl's urging, Akerman explained as quickly as he could. "Ragnarok is the great battle of battles. The one that ends it all. It is, basically, the last stand of the gods. The last stand of all the heroes. Heimdall blows his great horn. The midguard serpent thrashes, causing immense tidal waves. Cliff faces are sundered. People walk the road to hell and the heavens split apart. The great World Tree, *Yggdrasil,* shudders. The gods do battle with the invaders. Odin dies at the jaws of *Fenrir.* Freyr fights *Surtr* and loses. Odin's other son, Vioarr, avenges his father and spears the enormous wolf. Thor, the Protector of the Earth, desperately fights the great serpent and defeats it, but is only able to take nine steps afterward before falling to his death, poisoned. People flee their homes. The sun turns black, great storms batter the earth and it sinks into the sea. Stars vanish. Fire and steam rises and flames touch the heavens."

"But it never happened," Dahl said.

"Maybe not. Maybe not *yet.* Odin was always considered the wisest of all beings. He may have found a way—this way—to postpone the inevitable. In any case, your battle, our battle, is real. As real as can be. This is *our* Ragnarok, my friend."

"Interpreted how?"

"Heroes must rise to save the day or villains will end it. Whatever you believe in doesn't matter. A last stand is coming. A battle of battles. You must make this stand together and you must win."

Drake suddenly felt the presence of Mai and Alicia. They had heard and were looking suitably shocked. "The Shadow Elite are behind all this," he said aloud. "They want the eight pieces to hold the world to ransom. We'll stop them."

"So why bring the pieces here?" Dahl momentarily turned away from his call.

"To prove the worth of what they have," Karin said in a sickened voice. "They mean to give the world a little taster."

Drake thought it a little ironic—that the eight pieces they had thought at one time irrelevant were now turning about to be crucial. He watched, lost in thought, as Karin broke away from the conversation to talk to the approaching Komodo.

Hayden joined them. "It's time to move."

Dahl thanked Akerman, told the Swedish language expert to leave Iceland immediately, and ended the call. "So," he said. "Who wants to catch a train?"

*****

Karin intercepted Komodo as he walked to join the group and took the big soldier to one side. They passed through a narrow, crumbling doorway and into a quiet alcove with more windows and collapsed masonry than walls.

"I missed you, Trevor."

The big man blanched a little at the use of his real name. It was Karin's way of teasing him. They hadn't known each other for long, but they had known each other long enough.

"And I you, Kazmat." His nickname for her was based around the abbreviation for Hazardous Materials—the family, he said, to which she belonged.

Karin kissed him hard on the lips. The soldier had to bend down to reach her. By the time they broke away, they were both breathless.

"You're the first thing I've believed in since Rebecca died." Karin said the words again as she'd said them to him many times. "Don't make me regret it."

"Not a chance."

"I threw my life away all those years." She buried her head into his shoulders, not caring about the dust and grime.

"When this is over," Komodo said quietly, "we'll work something out."

"I *tried* to help. I tried. But I was so young. . ." Karin blocked out the memories, brought to the surface now, she thought, in reaction to the danger they had just escaped and her feelings for Komodo.

"It wasn't your fault. It was the others. The grown-ups who ignored you."

"I do know that." Karin breathed. "But—"

"It was their fault." Komodo reiterated, trying to make her believe.

"We need time to make this work."

The soldier pulled away a little. "We will have time. I promise you."

"Your work—"

"All that bullshit will not get in the way. There are other jobs."

Karin looked dubious. "For a six foot six, tattooed, beefy Delta commando who looks like a biker and has the name Trevor? Unlikely."

"I'll guard your body." He moved closer.

Karin choked back a laugh. "And sometimes talks like a nine-year-old. Ugh."

"You wanna fight me?" Komodo pulled away with a laugh. "You really wanna tussle with this shit?" He puffed out his chest.

Karin glanced toward the foliage outside the window. "Just grab my ass and drag me over to those trees. Then, we'll see who wants to fight."

But at that moment they heard the unmistakable sounds of their team breaking up and moving out. Ben's voice shouted over the hubbub. "Sis?"

Komodo shrugged. "So? First, we'll go save the world."

SIXTEEN

The team negotiated their way out of the castle and headed back down the hill toward the waiting cars. Hayden believed that Cayman, since he had remained below with his men and showed no signs of pursuit, had called in reinforcements. But that wasn't the main reason they were moving out double-time.

As they ran, she dry swallowed painkillers. Every movement sent a bolt of fire through her wounded side. So far today, she'd taken enough painkillers to poleaxe a horse, but the adrenalin spurred her on. Twisted brush underfoot and thorny shrubbery to the side attempted to send her into a headlong tumble. As she emerged from cover, the entire city of Singen opened up before her, sprawling to the horizons.

Kinimaka steadied her with a huge arm. "If you'd let me carry you, boss, I'd do it."

"I know, Mano, but not today."

Jonathan Gates thoughtfully tapped his phone against the side of his leg. "So I stand here, a US Secretary of Defense, trying to decide who to call upon for help." He gave them all a cheerless smile. "But I can't think of a single person – with the right connections – who I trust."

Hayden took a moment to steady herself. Over the last few weeks and months, she felt like she'd lived an entire lifetime. Her hopes, her dreams, her future – everything had changed.

She kept imagining that one day she'd wake up to find it had all been a crazy dream. That Matt Drake and Ben Blake and Alicia Myles didn't really exist – they were nothing more than the warped and fevered ghosts of her imagination.

But here she stood on the tree-dotted hillside of an ancient castle, above what had once been a volcano, long ago. Her boss and her colleagues were with her. The world was at stake.

A train ran between Stuttgart and Singen, bringing with it a cargo of civilians, mercenaries and death. One way or another, she had to get aboard that train.

She turned to Ben and Karin. "Get me the train's details. I need exact times. I need all changes. The works."

"On it," Karin said immediately. Ben gave her a dull look before fishing out his iPhone. She didn't smile at him. It was as if he knew her thoughts. Knew that they were as good as over.

Time to grow up, Ben.

Drake had been conversing quietly with his SAS buddies. Now he caught her eye and drifted over. "You grab those pieces," he said in his Yorkshire accent. "Or destroy 'em. Or hide them somewhere. Just fuck those bastards up. Whatever it takes."

"You're not coming?"

"Alicia, Mai and I will be hitting Luxembourg. Wells was spying on Cayman and this Shadow Elite crowd for a decade. He worked for them. Knew their moves. I see a point coming in the very near future where that knowledge might be helpful."

"And you'll find your wife's killer too?"

"I hope to get his identity. I won't go after him until this thing with the tomb of the gods is over."

"Make sure you keep in touch."

"Every hour."

Drake gave her a look, something full of respect and admiration and more than a little love. She knew right then, in a post-Ben world, that Matt Drake would remain her friend. She watched him walk away.

She turned toward Kinimaka, hoping to get a little heart-warming camaraderie, but Daniel Belmonte planted himself between them.

"You haven't had need of my services so far," he said with an impish smile. "But there goes a man who just might." He nodded after Drake. "Do you mind?"

"Sure. Why would I mind?" Hayden sighed. "You're here because you got caught up in the flow. You're useless to me."

"I'm the best at what I do."

"Stop with the double-entendre's, Belmonte. We had sex. Just the once. It was..." She met his eye. "Not bad, to be fair. But first and foremost, you're a thief." She looked at Drake. "So go be one."

"My pleasure."

"But, Belmonte," she warned, "I know you think you're god's gift and all that, but take a piece of advice?"

"Try me."

"Stay clear of Alicia Myles. She's. . .blue-eyed disaster."

As Belmonte walked away, deep speculation on his face, both Ben and Karin came walking over to her. Kinimaka shot her a "chin up" look. Gates put a gentle arm around her shoulder.

Ben said, "Stuttgart to Singen is over a four-hour journey. We have the time to drive to Zurich train station, where it stops for forty-five minutes, and board there. The trip from Zurich to Singen takes one hour. . ."

"Giving us sixty minutes to search the train, find the pieces and neutralize them." Karin finished in classic sisterly fashion. "One way or another."

Dahl had finished up on the phone to his *Statsminister* and caught the last part. He too stared after Drake. "Do not repeat this, but I'd give my career to have that man with us."

"This is a team," Hayden said firmly and felt Gates grip her shoulder hard. "Not a one-man effort. Between us, we'll board the train, find the pieces *and* unmask the assholes behind all this. Now"—she started walking toward the cars, the throbbing wound in her side temporarily forgotten—"mount up."

SEVENTEEN

Drake hurried over to bid farewell to Sam and his SAS pals. The man they'd left behind, Rob Ingles, was being quietly mourned in the way of soldiers. Mai had also lost loyal friends and was standing silently to one side. Drake waited for the somber moment to pass.

"We're heading out," he said at length. "How's your standby situation, Sam?"

"As of now, mate, we're good. We're able to remain in Europe for at least a few more days. But within the week…" Sam made a face. "Some shiny arse is gonna catch on and this thing's gonna have to be explained."

"It will be," Drake said, thinking of Jonathan Gates's influence and Wells's hidden research. An uneasy memory of his time in the SRT resurfaced then, like a bone-white hand rises from beneath the bed in the dead of night, to clasp its cold, clammy fingers around a man's ankle. It was the time when his unit had been ordered not to interfere in the interrogation of the village. Orders from on high. Orders from who though? Maybe he'd find more than one answer among Wells's papers.

"We'll wait as long as we can," Sam told him. "There's three more teams currently operating in Europe. Just so you know." He winked.

The Tomb of the Gods

Drake thanked his friend and jumped into one of the cars, along with Mai, Alicia and Belmonte. Within seconds, they were leaving *Hohentwiel* and their friends in the rear-view and driving quickly to a private airstrip on the outskirts of Singen. Dahl's people had secured Drake and his friends a special charter for their trip to Luxembourg – the general feeling being that the quicker he got there, the quicker he'd get back.

Silence reigned in the car. Belmonte tried a few quips to engage some kind of conversation but, for the other three, this was their down time. The drive afforded them the chance to unwind and recoup a small part of their tattered reserves.

As he drove, Drake found his brain dipping into waters so murky, he'd rather leave them undisturbed. Old fears had been raised, and with them, the non-resolution of newer fears. Mai Kitano, by his side, had given the teleportation device to the Blood King in return for her sister's safety. An understandable act sure, but one she still needed to answer for. She had also kept the secret of his wife's death from him for years.

And then there was Alicia Myles, lounging in the back seat, head back, blue eyes aimed toward the window, staring sightlessly at the fields and trees rolling by. She had not only kept the same secret, but she had been a part of Abel Frey's murdering gang, and he was sure she was still highly motivated by hard cash. What she'd done for it in the past, he didn't want to know.

But what might she do for it in the future?

His thoughts switched toward Ben Blake. They'd started this adventure together, only a couple of months ago. Now they were poles apart, separated by love, loss and necessity. Drake hadn't even asked Ben to accompany them to

Luxembourg. He'd known what the answer would be and, quite frankly, he judged they'd be better off without him.

A soldier's judgment, not the decision of the civilian he thought he'd become. Life had turned again. As it often did.

But now was not the time to process any of it. If Dahl's man in Iceland was right, then some kind of battle was coming, a battle to end all battles, and its outcome would decide who ran the world. The factors were already fighting in a narrowing theater of war. It was only a matter of time before they would all meet. The Shadow Elite had already shown their hand for the first time in an age, and were maneuvering toward a terrible end game. Drake and his friends were being isolated, cut down and impeded. Their window of opportunity was shrinking.

Hence Hayden's crazy plan to board a passenger train.

"You give any thought as to how we're going to do this?" Alicia spoke up without moving her position.

"It's a suck-it-and-see scenario," Drake told her.

"My favorite."

"All I know is that the facility is near the airport. It's nothing special, just a way-station of sorts. Only problem – it'll be guarded by the best soldiers in the world."

"Time for Mr. Belmonte to show his mettle." Alicia watched the scenery flash by.

Drake pulled up outside the airfield. "You ready?"

*****

The flight lasted only thirty minutes. All Drake could think about was Hayden, Dahl, Ben and the others who were currently speeding toward a crazy encounter. He wanted to be with them. But the fact that Wells had researched the Shadow Elite and taken the time to hide his findings in such an obscure place told Drake he would be better prepared by having it. And Alyson's ghost had more than a chance of being laid to rest.

The plane dipped and then landed smoothly. Even though the airport was the expected eyesore of concrete and steel, the countryside that surrounded it looked picturesque and agreeable. Within minutes of leaving the plane, they were shown to a waiting vehicle. Then they were on their own.

Drake programmed the sat-nav with figures he'd taken from Wells's recording and drove out of the airport. The secret facility was only a twenty-minute drive. About ten minutes before they got there, they passed a dingy-looking pub. Battered cars and gleaming bikes littered the car park. Even as they drove by, Drake saw a man crash through one of the windows to land headfirst in the dirt. A big bruiser filled the new gap, grinning and pouring half of the man's pint on top of him. The other half he drank with gusto.

"My kinda place." Alicia gave a grin.

"Aye up, Belmonte," Drake said. "Do you wanna drive by now and have a little reccy, or stop and come up with a rough plan?"

"The reccy," Belmonte said immediately. "Better to see what we're dealing with."

"Well, don't get your hopes up," Mai said. "This secret facility won't come with its own guidebook."

Drake slowed as the sat-nav announced they had reached their destination. The car skirted the back of the airport, where an industrial area had sprouted up. Warehouses and fast food shops, car showrooms and walled-in businesses. The one to their immediate right was a long, low warehouse surrounded by an iron gate with spikes and a high wall topped with razor wire. Nondescript signs had been fixed to the wall and the top of the warehouse itself. *Horne Manufacturing.*

"Good area for me." Belmonte started a commentary. "Plenty of places to hide around here. Plenty of places to use as a staging area and a fallback point. Three ingress points are available, the fourth hard up against another unit. See there? A flat roof. Another plus. The warehouse isn't too high, either. Razor wire everywhere, but that won't be a problem. I spotted a discreet guardhouse inside the main gate, behind the posts. The extra security there rules it out for our use."

Drake nodded. "Discount anything that will take time."

"The best don't need much time. In any case, we're left with the walls, the air, or the other unit. Do you have any idea what that other unit might be?"

Drake shook his head. "My guess? Part of the same facility. From what Wells said, there are some storage rooms against the back wall of the big warehouse. Nothing fancy. We are talking army here, after all. He stashed his research there."

"Why here?" Mai asked.

"Opportunity," Drake said. "His status brought him here often. It's chiefly a way-station, meaning it can be used for literally *anything*. Wells would've been called out here a lot."

"But it's still just a warehouse," Belmonte said. "The men guarding it are good, yes, but chiefly it's a brick, block and metal structure with the same basic design as any other. They wouldn't have beefed the construction up."

"No. But they wouldn't have been complacent about the internal security, either."

"One problem at a time," Belmonte said. "Trust me. I'm the world's greatest thief, after all." A grin. "The weak point is where the walls of the first and second unit meet. There's a return on the wall there – see – that runs back to the building and could give a good man access to the grounds and the roof." Belmonte traced an imaginary tick in the air. "First problem – overcome."

Alicia groaned. "And I let this clown into my pants. In my defense I was pissed at the time."

Belmonte didn't even look at her. "There are no windows. The door we can see is off-limits. This leaves us with only one play. The roof. But I'll need a special tool. And it'll be noisy."

"Then come up with another plan." Drake let his impatience show in his voice.

"There is no other plan. It's a warehouse, not Buckingham Palace. There are only a finite few places of ingress. Besides, the roof plan will work. We just need a distraction."

His eyes roved over Mai and Alicia. "And what better distractions could we possibly hope for?"

"You're not seriously thinking of sending us in to. . .woo the guards?" Mai asked with a touch of incredulity.

"Oh, no. Nothing like that. What I have in mind is far more dangerous."

EIGHTEEN

If chasing the Blood King through the Gates of Hell had been the most dangerous moment of Matt Drake's life, then walking into a bar full of truckers, junkies, cutthroats and thieves didn't lag too far behind. Belmonte, the prissy Brit, went first. Then came Drake, and last of all came Mai and Alicia. Drake drifted through the smoky bar like a wisp trailed by a forest fire. Hard men with big arms and tattoos craned their shaggy heads around to check out the girls, their pints still poised at their lips. Scantily clad cage-dancers stopped their jaded gyrations, gripping the bars and poking their heads through to get a better look. Burly bouncers wearing tank tops and imitation Levis, patted their exposed Tasers and stood to attention, sensing the mood swing. Men propping up the bar halted their conversation and swung around as if they, too, sensed something different. Behind the bar itself, both barmen reached slowly underneath the wide length of chipped, scarred wood.

A hush fell over the place. After the men had checked out the girls, their cruel eyes sought out any opposition they might find – Belmonte and Drake.

Drake didn't even have to scout the place. Knives were on tables. Lines of coke and heroin laid out in plain sight. A man with long hair and a Metallica T-shirt sat in the corner, kissing one of the girls deeply whilst twirling a pistol around a finger.

A gang bar. A serious one. He was surprised. On the whole, Luxembourg was a safe country, a prudent place to live, except for a few areas around the train station and the airport. Like this.

Smoke and harsh intentions thickened the air. The click of safety switches being slackened off made a sound like a startled rattlesnake. Drake imagined that any outsider who even tried to order a drink here would be lucky to leave the place alive.

Then Drake took out a wad of one-hundred euro notes almost too thick to hold in his hand. Slowly he flapped them in the direction of the hardest table in the room.

A bullet slipped through the stunned fingers of one of the bikers and the man's mouth fell open faster than a spring-loaded trapdoor.

"So," Drake said, "We're looking to make you an offer you can't refuse. Who do we need to speak to?"

*****

They were going for a three-pronged operation. It had been deemed too dangerous for Drake to take part. The repercussions for getting caught would be bad for any of them, but for Drake, it would be infinitely worse. Belmonte had used his connections and skills to find the nearest location that could source them a laser cutter and a few choice tools with which to splice an operations board into an electronic panel. At first, Drake had doubted such tools could be so easily found, but when he saw their everyday nature and the ways Belmonte could adapt them for his own use, he soon found his confidence in the thief beginning to grow. Even the laser cutter itself was not a special tool. Most merchant tool outlets sold them.

So, Alicia had joined force with the bar gang—an experience she seemed to relish. Drake, hanging at the back of the crowd, had already winced several times in anticipation after some of her finer insults, but unsurprisingly they served only to make the bikers grow fonder of her. Already he'd noticed an exchange of numbers and a Bluetooth sharing of mobile data – photos or videos. He shook his head.

Alicia thrived on danger, got drunk with it. Tonight, she was in her element as the crowd of bikers and thieves approached the secret SAS facility.

*****

At first, Belmonte and Mai stuck together. Staying to the shadows, they skirted the warehouse until they reached the point where its two buildings came together. Here they crouched for a while, impatiently waiting for the signal.

Now Belmonte, in addition to thievery, had one other delectation. The appreciation of beautiful women. Getting close to Mai had been the other reason he opted to join this operation and now seemed as good a time as any to get the ball rolling.

"You did the right thing," he said. "You got your sister out. Then you got Kovalenko."

"Drake got him, actually," Mai said lightly. "I got Boudreau. And Chika will always be my first choice."

"And what does your agency say to that?"

"My agency," Mai repeated, "affords me some slack. Because they know what I can do."

Belmonte wondered briefly if that was a veiled threat. But he was a confident man, and the more he talked, planned, and used his wits, then the less he would dwell on Emma and what had happened to her. "I hear you're one of the best. I imagine you've heard the same about me. . ." He paused.

When Mai didn't answer, he went on. "People like us, we should make the most of our time. Who knows how long we have left?"

Mai didn't even look at him. "Which movie did that come from?"

"I'm good at what I do. *Everything* I do."

"That's so original. Save it for the next time you get drunk with someone like Myles."

Belmonte peered around at the dark shapes of hedges swaying and ugly brick walls blocking out the faint stars. "I do believe you're right. This isn't quite the best setting."

"You sound desperate, Belmonte," Mai said evenly. "And I think we both know why. Get it straight in your head and then have another go." She flashed him an unexpected grin. "Now a girl can't be fairer than that, can she?"

Belmonte was about to answer, his own face creasing into a smile, when a loud explosion shattered the air.

Alicia's signal.

Mai nodded up at the wall. "Mask on and move."

*****

Drake watched from the shadows, an act that now struck him as purely alien after the last few months of being called constantly into action. He couldn't even listen to proceedings on an earpiece for fear of interfering with the facility's or

Belmonte's delicate communications frequencies. The facility was an unknown quantity, thus they had had to base their plan on several informed assumptions. It had never been broken into or even challenged before, therefore it was assumed that, when a mob targeted it, most of the personnel inside would be sent to investigate and resolve the issue.

Most, but not all.

The warehouse would not have dedicated guards. The trained men inside would be considered enough, especially since no sensitive material was housed there. Drake watched as Alicia ran with the pack, flirting with drug dealers and gunrunners, and reminded himself not to get too comfortable with her presence. Or with her loyalty.

She was a woman apart. One who lived, worked and played only for herself.

His mind flickered backward in time, to Kennedy Moore, and the brief months they had shared. Her loss was a scorched and ragged hole in his heart, one he'd tried to fill with forgetting, but now was trying to overcome. God, it was hard. Even in the midst of all this, with barely a second to think, the grief and the loneliness threatened to overwhelm him. And now, Alyson's memories had also swirled up from the bottom of the deep abyss he'd buried them in, clutching for purchase in his already scarred and battered brain.

And Ben Blake. Poor old Ben had been on his own since the moment his hands were literally stained with Kennedy's blood. Drake couldn't help that. It was a harsh way to grow up. But at least it was growing up. At least it was *life*.

Ben still has a chance with Hayden, Drake thought, *and he needs her*. He needed every good, stable and combative thing about her. Hayden was a woman who knew how to fight for the good things in her life. A true warrior. But Ben's chance with her was quickly diminishing.

At that moment, one of the lead bikers launched his petrol bomb against the wall of the compound. There was a smash of glass and a brief flame, then belching smoke and an aggressive cheer. Even Alicia joined in. Drake shook his head and secreted himself in the shadows.

Men of the British elite forces were rushing to the gate.

*****

Belmonte climbed first, Mai a foot behind. When he reached the horizontal wall, he flattened his frame and scurried across like a rat through a narrow drain. His balance and technique were perfect. He paused on the edge of the warehouse roof, hugging the curve, just one more shadow against the black. Mai slithered next to him.

Belmonte unhooked the device he'd fashioned and lowered his body precariously until he was level with a junction box, legs and feet hooked around the eaves of the building and the brick wall. Mai scampered over him and quickly found the position they had pinpointed from the ground earlier. If she gained entry here, she'd be able to lower herself into the warehouse, into the section containing the box files. Now she took out a laser cutter and, without waiting for Belmonte, started to quickly cut through the sheet steel roof decking. Belmonte had said it would be made up of 1mm metal lying atop Rockwool sandwich panels with a polyurethane backing. The laser cutter made short work of the metal, slicing through in seconds, and then allowed her to take away the Rockwool in one thick chunk, granting her the option of replacing the roof elements if they made good their escape without drawing attention.

"Wait," Mai whispered, seeing more men heading toward the burning fires at the gates. "Give them all a chance to get out there."

Then she signaled him, and it was suddenly do or die. Belmonte had told them early on that, as this short notice and without specialized equipment, he couldn't possibly circumvent the alarm system, but he *could* rig something that would be able to splice into the electronics. Not a major problem.

He flicked a switch and the facilities main door came crashing down. Now most of the soldiers were locked out.

Mai had already rigged her descender, the hardest and most expensive of the items they had had to source. Now she threw herself through the hole and toward the warehouse floor. As she fell, she hurled half a dozen of the gang's improvised smoke bombs in all directions, her sharp eyes clocking the positions of six men. There would be others.

She landed softly, bouncing on the soles of her feet. Despite the restrictions of the mask, she could clearly see the ordered rows of box files that stretched to her left and right. The box immediately before her was lettered C.

Then she heard the sound of choking men and thumping boots. Of course someone had seen her. Even amidst the smoke, they would know how to search and track and corner her. She had to move fast.

Dashing to her right she followed the letters to F and a box junction. She could either move down it and search for W or keep moving. At that moment, a figure emerged out of the billowing gloom. With the advantage of surprise, Mai made

The Tomb of the Gods

sure her first blow was effective, staggering the man to his knees. Even then, he somehow blocked the second, but Mai was no lightweight and her third rendered him unconscious.

Down the junction she rushed. Another aisle opened up. She glimpsed the letter S. She ran that way and soon came to W. She was lost among the box aisles. She thumbed her way until she found the small box marked "Wells," an unassuming cardboard drawer that might hold the secrets to unlocking a shadowy organization and a killer. Mai emptied out the contents, replaced the box carefully, and stuffed Wells's research into her backpack.

Then she crouched and waited, letting her senses stream in every direction. It was always best to hold your nerve and wait, to scout out your aggressors rather than rush in headlong, hoping for the best.

They were advancing up the main aisle. They couldn't stop the smoke from getting into their throats, even with their training. It was just too thick, too acrid. Mai backed away in a crouch, hugging the floor, staying low as she exited her aisle and began to swing back around in a wide arc toward her original position.

She wasn't a woman who usually relied on hope. But this was a fast, fluid and high- risk operation. Her hope was that the descender wire hadn't been found. An image of the building's floor plan was firmly fixed in her mind, seen as she descended only minutes ago. Now she deftly negotiated her way around a long wooden table littered with cups, plates and utensils and surrounded by dozens of abandoned chairs. One of the guards, a man with red cheeks and streaming eyes, passed within a few feet of her, but her crouching, rigidly immobile figure never registered on his radar. To help her cause, there suddenly came the banging of many fists on the main warehouse door and then some shouting to get back.

The SAS would be through in seconds. No doubt they had weapons, but even if they hadn't, they would quickly jury-rig some kind of device that would open the door. And then the smoke would quickly dissipate.

But Mai was fleet of foot and reached the stationary black line of the descender in seconds. With a quick movement, she hooked it to her harness and pressed the button. The machine took her up toward the rafters, now above the heads of the searchers below.

And out into the cold night. Smoke filtered through the gap behind her. Mai spent twenty seconds replacing the roof components and wedging them tight, then slid back onto the brick wall.

Belmonte was crouched at the far end, waiting. "Poetry in motion."

They quickly dropped to the pavement, draping themselves in the deep shadows. Drake and Alicia were already waiting up ahead.

Mai nodded in answer to Drake's questioning glance. "I took everything. If Wells had anything on this Shadow Elite group or your wife's killer, it's right here. All that's left is to read it."

The Englishman almost smiled.

NINETEEN

In the dark and haunted places below our chaotic world, there are evil men who contemplate diabolical deeds. It's not that there is no light in their lives; it's that they feel great joy in bringing darkness to others. The more limitless their power, the more it consumes them, eating through their heart and soul until only an icy, uncaring shell remains.

Russell Cayman had been a child once, a blank slate. But not even being left to die in a ditch by his junkie parents had turned him into the man he had become today. Nature or nurture might have molded him differently, but he had had neither. Instead, the system swallowed him whole and churned him out, a child forgotten, a child alone. A vulnerable adult who the government could manipulate with deceit and trickery.

Now he was a machine, but ironically, a machine working for the people who owned the very government that had beguiled him. Down here, in the dark pits of the earth, he felt at home. The lone reminder of his life were the men tramping around the tombs. If they were to depart, he might very well lay down in one of the coffins, in the arms of Kali or Callisto, finding a comfort and a solace amongst the long-dead, evil gods that he had never experienced in life.

He directed his men. He supervised the clearing of the floor areas around the eight altars so they could receive the eight pieces without obstruction. He reviewed the points that might come up in his forthcoming call to the Norseman—the boss of bosses.

But his eyes lingered on the tombs. On their Spartan, uncluttered perfection. He needed that lack of disorder to calm his mind. He had been told that the tomb of Amatsu lay at his back, a deity literally called the God of Evil. In a quiet moment, Cayman ventured inside and used all of his strength to crowbar open the lid. It didn't move far, but an ancient dust blew out straight up Cayman's nostrils.

The protector of the Shadow Elite breathed deeply. A soft susurration rustled around the roughhewn room. Cayman could quite happily die here. He bent over the edge and reached blindly inside. Something clunked over in a dark corner. His sharp eyes saw nothing. A tiny whirlwind skipped across the floor, stirring dust and debris, originating from nothing and imploding a moment later as if it had never existed.

Cayman's fingers closed over hard bone. It was cold and rough. The edges were sharp and might have cut him had he been given time to press his wrist to them.

But an alien beeping noise tore him back to the present. The sound of his watch alarm.

It was time to return to the surface and call the Norseman.

Cayman withdrew his arm with a depressed sigh. The feel of the old bones still stayed with him as he headed back out of the darkness and into the sunlight. The perfect tomb clutched at his heart, but the Shadow Elite's clutches were far tighter and went much deeper. Once he had followed an old protocol and checked his perimeter, then locked himself inside one of the military choppers and switched on its frequency blocking system, he finally used an untraceable sat-phone to contact the Norseman.

"Where are we?" No greeting, no compromise, just the deep melancholic tones demanding a status report.

"The pieces are on their way here," Cayman said, equally blunt. "There have been no problems to date. The tomb is prepared."

"What of the escapees?"

"Dispersed. Undoubtedly trying to thwart us again. Their kind will never leave well enough alone. But our discipline will win the day."

"*Your* discipline," the Norseman said after a pause. "That is why you are our disciple and our word. It is your discipline that will hold your unruly men together and win this day."

"Thank you."

"It's not a compliment, Cayman." The Norseman sighed. "It's a threat. Do you see?"

"Yes." Cayman kicked himself for not remaining focused. With half a brain still consorting with Amatsu in his tomb, the ex-DIA man was no match for someone as formidable as the Norseman. Claiming to be a descendant of the great exploring Viking Eric the Red—and who was there to refute him?—the Norseman was a larger-than-life figure who had inherited untold wealth and the senior position in the Shadow Elite council upon his father's death. Since that time, decades ago, the Shadow Elite had not stagnated or regressed. They had taken great strides forward in securing their already redoubtable position.

"They may know about the train." The Norseman was always pragmatic. "They may even try to stop us. It is always their way, to flounder and thwart. The Elite are gathering in Vienna right now. You know where."

"Where they have always gathered." Cayman was used to the Norseman's chatter. He believed the great leader liked to hear his own thoughts spoken aloud and used Cayman as a sounding board.

"The old place. Grey. Aldridge. Thomas. Leng. And young Holgate—always the upstart. But his deportment has changed of late. It is something I will be addressing once I reach Vienna."

"You're not there?" Cayman immediately kicked himself for the stupidity of the question. If one of his own men had asked that kind of question, Cayman would be tempted to shoot him on the spot.

But the Norseman was seemingly lost in expressing his thoughts. "I'm at home. The Prague fortress is impregnable. Not even an army could get in here. Once I know the pieces have been activated, I will depart for Vienna. Now tell me, Cayman, has the Wells thing been cleaned up?"

"Yes, sir. All checked and clean. No leaks there."

"Good. And Drake?"

Cayman hesitated. "Drake?"

"We know him of old. You know that. If he were ever to find us—"

Cayman was truly stunned. He had never heard even the slightest expression of fear in the Norseman's voice before. The ex-DIA man thought back to Drake's prowess in the tomb and quickly revised his opinions.

"If he shows his face again, sir, I will obliterate it."

"We cannot fail then." The Norseman's voice came as close to happiness as was possible for one such as him. "Short of a miracle, the pieces can't be stopped. The entire world will cower before us. Our rule, already absolute, will be preserved forever."

TWENTY

Hayden and her team made Zurich train station by the skin of their teeth. Once inside, even as she ran and scanned the big blue boards for their platform number, Hayden was struck by the polished cleanliness of the station. The vast floor seemed to shine, the arched alcoves that led to retail outlets looked cozy, warm and inviting, quite the opposite of most train stations she'd ever visited. Bizarre and colorful balloons hung from the ceiling. Tourists dressed in all manner of clothing drifted and bumped past each other, focused on their own schedules. The noise level swelled and decreased as groups marched past them.

Karin was first to spot it. "Singen!" She raced off in the direction of the platforms and Hayden and the rest rushed after her, painfully aware they had only minutes to make the train. When they found the big engine burbling loudly, the CIA agent heaved a sigh of relief.

Karin sent a questioning glance.

"Just get on," Hayden shouted. "We'll worry about the 'where' later."

A red and white stripe ran for a few carriages at the point she jumped on to the train. She noticed a huge green Starbucks logo as she leapt through the door. The craving for a double-strong Caramel Macchiato hit her like a bullet, but at that moment, there was the sound of the doors locking and the engine's note strengthening. They were on their way.

Dahl spoke up immediately. "We have one hour," he said, "to find the pieces and stop them reaching Singen. Let's move."

Hayden stepped up. She led the way through the first carriage and then, as if in odd answer to her prayers, the Starbucks logo appeared once again and she was suddenly walking through a coffee shop right there on the train. A fully functioning outlet.

Ben's voice could be heard from the back. "I never heard of a Starbucks on a train before."

The Barista popped up from behind the counter with startling efficiency, making both Dahl and Kinimaka flinch and reach for weapons they had decided not to risk carrying through the busy station.

"It's a trial train," she said, blond hair tied fiercely back. "Built here in Zurich." The lilt in her voice betrayed her pride. "If it works— it could go global."

"Smart idea," Ben said. "Do trial trains offer free drinks?"

The Barista's eyes twinkled. "We stop at waitress service, I'm afraid. And that's only at trial."

Hayden paused as she reached the next carriage, studying the passengers. Every seat was taken. But all she could see were women and children, students and tourists. Big backpacks stacked everywhere. A thumping musical beat heard through tiny earphones. A youth talking loudly into his mobile phone.

She walked on, clearing the carriage in seconds. The next proved to be a mirror image of the first. When they reached the third and it too was jam-packed with a mixed bunch of happy-go-lucky tourists and blithe locals, Dahl called for a halt in the corridor between cars. Quickly he tugged down the window and stuck his head out.

"Three more standard carriages," he said after securing the window. "Then two extra cars at the back of the train. . ." He paused. "With blacked out windows."

Kinimaka grunted. "Could they be any more obvious?"

"They're the type of people who can pull the right strings to get two extra cars put on a civilian passenger train at short notice," Hayden said grimly. "They don't *care*, Mano. They believe they're all-powerful."

Dahl nodded. "Hayden's right. These people expect—they don't ask. Let's go."

"So we're gonna simply walk up to their carriage and charge inside?" Karin asked, her quick brain trying to come up with alternatives. "It's a big risk to take."

"We're soldiers, miss," Dahl told her. "That's what we do."

"And into the valley of death. . ." Karin recited, then to the blank looks she said, "It's a poem. 'The Charge of the Light Brigade.' *Into the valley of death rode the six hundred.* Remember?"

Dahl nodded. "It's a poem about great heroism."

Karin nodded. *"Charge for the guns. . .*don't forget these guys were on horses and wielding only sabers. *Cannon to the left of them, cannon to the right of them, cannon in front of them. While horse and hero fell."*

There was a moment of silence. Then Hayden turned an eye toward the next carriage and what lay beyond. "Let's go."

In silence they threaded through the next three cars. The tension rose among them. They had no weapons and no plan. All they had was the courage in their hearts and the knowledge that the eight pieces could either hold millions of innocents to ransom, or destroy them. Nothing else mattered right now. As they entered the last carriage, Hayden felt Dahl shoulder past her and, for a moment, felt a little begrudged, but then she realized—the Swede had taken point, not because he doubted her, but because he was, simply, the man who would always step up. He knew no other way.

Toward the rear of the last civilian carriage, Dahl slowed. Hayden peered around his big shoulders. The next car was accessible through a sliding door, but all the glass was tinted. Not even the vaguest of shapes could be seen in the compartment beyond.

Hayden put a hand on the Swede's shoulder. "Just wait a moment." She cast around, desperately seeking inspiration. Anything that meant they would not have to walk blindly into the dragon's den.

At that moment she heard a voice behind them.

"Excuse me. Can I get through? I have coffee for the rear carriage."

She turned. The voice belonged to the Barista they had passed a few minutes ago. Hayden smiled. "I sure hope that coffee's good and hot."

*****

A few seconds later, Hayden had donned the green tunic and balanced a tray full of paper cups in one hand. The Barista was sitting in a window seat, staring at them with pleading eyes and intimating that her district manager was going to be super pissed, this being the maiden voyage and all.

Kinimaka held her wrist. "Uh, boss. You sure 'bout this? They have male Baristas too, ya know."

"Mano, I'm fine. What the hell's wrong with you? You didn't care this much before I got stabbed. Twice."

Kinimaka turned away. Hayden stared after him for a second, then met the eyes of Ben Blake over the huge Hawaiian's shoulder.

He nodded at her, no expression on his face, but a shimmer of love in his eyes. Hayden didn't have time for it. She breathed deeply, faced down her fear, and stepped forward.

Straight into the dragon's den.

TWENTY-ONE

Matt Drake could barely contain his feelings of anxiety and dread as he walked into a restaurant near Luxembourg airport and headed straight for the bar. It was all he could do not to rip the rucksack off Mai's back and start leafing through its contents.

Alicia pulled him back. "Wrong way, Drakey. You're s'posed to be trying to give up the good stuff, remember?"

He let her lead him to a dimly lit booth, eyes locked onto the amber nectar the whole way. It took a huge inner effort, and some as yet unresolved arguments about the depths both Mai and Alicia had already stopped to over the last few years, to steady his resolve.

Mai had exchanged a time travel device for her sister. Not only that, she had given it to a madman, a crazy billionaire. She had also killed Wells, Drake's ex-commander and a man Drake even now believed would be exonerated by his research.

Alicia had been part of Abel Frey's plot to steal the bones of Odin. She had kept too many secrets for far, far too long. Drake had yet to fathom her true motives, and still couldn't decide whether she would stay loyal or sell him out to the highest bidder.

But all that was light entertainment compared to the secrets they were about to unearth.

Mai unstrapped the bag and sat down in the corner. Drake

took the seat opposite. Alicia squeezed in next to her. Belmonte took a look and then drifted off to the bar to order some food.

"He took Emma's death really hard," Mai said. "It's the only reason he's helping us."

"He's good," Drake admitted. "The way he located those parts out of nothing. The hack. And, not forgetting the money he gave us to pay off the bikers."

"That's partly what worries me," Mai said as she unfastened the rucksack. "Belmonte's a thief. He takes what he wants and gives nothing away."

"Perhaps Emma's death brought him some perspective." Drake restrained himself from reaching for the sheaf of papers that fell on to the table. Mai took a moment to divide them into thirds.

Belmonte returned with four glasses of water and a round of black coffees. "Ordered a load of tapas," he said with a shrug. "Seemed like a plan."

Drake barely heard him. Wells's writing was small and spidery and difficult to decipher. After a while he realized he was reading about Wells's secret investigation into the Shadow Elite's headquarters. Reading it like this, all at once, diminished the danger and skill that Wells had employed. Almost every paragraph was written in a different pen. Drake remembered that Wells had been digging for a decade.

One paragraph spoke of a journey to Vienna. Another of a man called Russell Cayman being admitted to the "inner circle"—an achievement only afforded to one outsider every lifetime. That outsider would fight all his days to further the organization's aims and to keep their identities concealed. After the initiation it would be all he lived for.

"If there was ever any doubt," Drake said aloud, "this confirms that Cayman's our way in to the Shadow Elite. Maybe we should have grabbed him back at Singen."

"Not even sure *we* could have handled that." Alicia snorted.

"No. But Dahl's a machine." Drake smiled. "Just point and command."

Mai spoke up. "I don't like what I'm reading here." She looked up at Drake. "It's about Operation Doubledown."

"What?"

The tapas arrived. Belmonte cleared a space, allowing the waitress to carefully place the small bowls around the table. As she walked away, Mai started to read aloud.

"The op was running smoothly, but then took an unfortunate turn. Unexpectedly, the roads started to lead toward home and Drake wasn't letting go."

"Doubledown was my last op," Drake said to the table. "Everything was perfect and then we received orders to walk away." He paused. "We were about to investigate someone who we thought might be a covert terrorist. A man who lived in Vienna."

Mai had been reading to herself. "Oh, Matt. This gets worse. The operation would have led, ultimately, straight to the Shadow Elite. Wells was under deadly pressure to terminate it. One way or another. The interrogation you witnessed..."

Drake flashed back to that dreadful day as part of the SRT team when he had witnessed a bunch of soldiers interrogating some villagers. Worse, when he had immediately called up Wells, his field commander, he'd been told to leave it alone. Leave it well alone. It had been the beginning of his disillusion with the army and had turned his priorities severely around.

"I remember." He was aware of Alicia's nod. She'd been there too.

"That day also had something to do with the Shadow Elite. They were looking for someone, seeking information. *'Their arrogance,'* Wells has written. *'Their righteous, self-serving, disgusting arrogance.'* These people"—Mai looked up—"they do whatever they want to whoever they want."

"I get that," Drake said. "What else?"

Mai read on and then suddenly stopped. Her eyes widened. The color drained from her cheeks and she looked up at Drake, open-mouthed. "I'm sorry," she whispered. "I'm so sorry."

Drake closed his eyes and took a deep breath. "Go on."

"I. . .I will read it word for word. *'Drake was just too headstrong. Doubledown was his baby and he was loving it. It needed to stop, and stop quickly. The council gave me the ultimatum. I compromised by offering up a new idea. I proposed the 'accidental' death of his wife. In the middle of the op, I ordered a brief break, sent everyone home and gave the order. I procured Coyote and gave him the go. It happened on the night of an argument, which was perfect. . .'* " Mai stopped talking. "There's more. But—"

Drake opened his eyes to stare at her in horror. "Wells ordered Alyson's murder? *Wells?*"

"To divert you—us—away from the Shadow Elite," Alicia said in an undertone, even her hard resolve fractured by the revelation.

Drake's throat was rasping as he said, "So Wells knew about Doubledown and where it was going. Which was Vienna. He knew about the murdered villagers. He ordered Alyson's death. Wells was a fucking snake."

"Who gave his life to the Shadow Elite," Belmonte said. "But what did they give him in return?"

"Wells was a patriot," Drake said. "A true English patriot. It would have taken a lot of convincing for him to betray his country."

"I don't believe he thought he was betraying his country," Mai said now as she read on. "There's something else."

TWENTY-TWO

Hayden pushed through into the blacked-out carriage, smiling as a dozen suspicious glances nailed her. But then she saw the true power of the Starbucks logo as every one of those stern-faced bad guys sat back and relaxed upon seeing her, like toddlers all lined up in a row awaiting their party drinks.

"Venti misto, two extra shots, with whipped cream and a drizzle of caramel sauce." She stepped forward into their midst, taking advantage of their uncertainty as the train thrummed and swayed along the tracks.

Most of Cayman's men turned to stare at each other, confusion written clearly on their faces. Hayden saw skepticism in only two pairs of eyes and it was toward these that she quickly stepped.

And hurled two paper cups of boiling hot coffee. She had already loosened the lids and the steaming liquid flew out in a scalding stream. The men screamed, hands flying toward their faces. Hayden leapt on one man's lap, wrestled his handgun out of its holster and spun, firing across the carriage.

At the same time, making lots of noise, Dahl, Kinimaka and Komodo burst through the door, a fearsome sight on any day, and threw themselves at the mercenaries. Cayman's men were experienced and recovered quickly. Dahl destroyed the first's face with a haymaker, but when he turned to a second opponent, he was already jabbing with an elbow. Dahl took it in the eye, growled, and grabbed the man's neck. With no time to pause and throttle the life out of him, he simply threw him across the car to fall among his compatriots.

Green trees and fields flashed by the two-way windows. A gun thumped to the floor, right at Kinimaka's feet. The Hawaiian had been clubbed on the head and was falling, but scooped the gun up and fired in a single movement before crashing to the carpeted floor. A mercenary fell, one knee shattered. Kinimaka lay prone, eyes switching to the front and toward his boss.

Hayden had taken out two of the mercenaries before they even had a chance to move, but two more had used those precious seconds to drag weapons free from concealed holsters. Now, as Hayden stared down those cold barrels, she saw the men who held them wrenched to the side as bullets passed through their skulls. Kinimaka had saved her life, firing from the floor.

Hayden rolled onto the floor a split second before another man fired, coming up level with his knee, so close she could have taken a bite. Then, she felt a huge presence above her and watched in awe as Komodo, having launched himself at full speed, took out the remaining row of mercenaries like bowling balls. He landed at the rear of the carriage in a heap, groaning. Injured mercenaries smashed their heads against the windows or tumbled to the floor in his wake. Hayden wasted no time in picking them off, shooting each one through the head in cold-blooded detachment. They all knew what they were doing when they signed up for this shindig.

The first private car cleared, they ran directly for the second one. Hayden heard a hubbub behind her. Passengers had

The Tomb of the Gods

obviously heard the shooting and were beginning to raise the alarm. One saving grace of this op was that no civilians were in the firing line. She saw Ben and Karin enter the first car and start collecting weapons.

Then she was inside the second car. But the reception this time was not as befuddled. She found herself facing half a dozen men with weapons raised. Another half dozen sat on seats at the rear of the carriage with the eight pieces of Odin arranged around them.

One of them men frowned. "You're on your own?"

*****

Dahl had paused in the corridor that separated the carriages and again lifted one of the windows. In the space of three seconds, he slithered out, gripped a tiny ledge that ran along the top of the speeding train, and hauled himself outside. Instantly, a heavy wind began to buffet his body, making him sway precariously. A tree flashed past close to the track, one of its branches whipping his back, tearing through his clothes and drawing a line of blood. With a quick lunge, he threw himself atop the train, staying low for balance.

A short gap separated him from the rear car. Ignoring the wind that slammed at him like Thor's hammer, he leapt over the gap and, even as he jumped, scouted out his options through the nearest skylight in the car below.

Komodo landed behind him. The two big men crab-walked forward, guns in hand.

The train suddenly emerged from a mountain pass into a long sweeping bend. A motorway ran alongside. Dahl saw cars and a coach traveling alongside them, their occupants going bug-eyed when they saw the men on top of the clattering train.

Dahl trod as lightly as he could, eyes locked firmly on his forthcoming victims. He moved to the second skylight, sighting on the group of mercs at the rear of the car, leaving the first group for Komodo to take care of.

A moment of extreme tension stretched on a hair-trigger.

*****

Hayden took a second to gain their attention. "It's just me now."

She saw them visibly relax. Even a few smiles appeared. None of them looked up. She deliberately let her gaze wander over to the window where the motorway had just appeared, knowing that most of them would follow her lead. She stared.

Silence fell over the carriage like a lead curtain. Hayden allowed her gun to dangle between two fingers.

The sound of gunfire and shattering Perspex tore the silence apart. Men were hit high in the chest and around the head. Blood and bone leapt into the air, painting patterns like random hieroglyphs. A cloud of red almost obliterated the front group of men. Hayden recovered her gun grip in a millisecond but found she had nowhere to aim. She couldn't even see the rear group of men.

A second's delay as first Dahl and then Komodo jumped down through the shattered skylights, landing like cats—on their feet but with guns ready. Dahl, in his distinctive way, calmly reloaded his weapon in free-fall, thinking nothing of it.

Another silence reigned. This one filled with the relief of being alive. Hayden flicked her gaze over all the slumped men. Kinimaka filed in behind her, closely followed by Ben and Karin.

The smell of blood and death laid a cloying stench like a shroud over the carriage. Hayden moved forward, glancing at the eight pieces of Odin. All seemed in order, though the Valkyries had taken a couple of stray rounds. Men were sprawled all around them.

And then Hayden saw one of the men snake his arm out to grab hold of a mobile phone. Within a split second he held it in his hand and his black eyes, crawling with malice, met hers. . .

*****

Mai looked up from what she was reading and locked eyes with Drake. The look she sent him was one of disbelief, of outrage, of incomprehension, that said even the best and most experienced Japanese agent alive could barely believe.

"These people." She breathed. "They will stop. . .at nothing."

*****

"No!" Hayden screamed.

But the man's finger hit the call button, sending the signal flying away into the atmosphere. The bomb exploded almost instantaneously. It erupted in a great, scything cloud of metal and fire, totally destroying the underside of the first private carriage where it had been positioned. The blast tore through the bottom of the carriages, making the rear end of the last civilian car lift entirely clear of the tracks. People were sent sprawling across the aisle and crashing into the seat in front of them. Bags and laptops, bottles of water and mobiles, Kindles and magazines all went skimming through the air. Screams of panic and yells of pain grew in volume like a hellish chorus.

Hayden and the rest of her team were thrown to the floor, landing in a tangle amidst the dead and dying mercenaries. Their weapons tumbled away. The force of the blast left them momentarily senseless.

Then, the worst happened. The last civilian car smashed back down onto the tracks but missed the rails. Instead, it hit the wooden sleepers, ballast, fasteners and subgrade with an almighty grinding sound and caused the entire train to slew to the side. Seen from afar, all the carriages tilted to one side and started a nightmarishly slow fall onto their sides. When it hit the ground, the train was still traveling fast, but the sudden impact with mercifully soft earth caused it to slow down fast. A bow wave of dirt caromed over the engine and the driver's compartment and the first carriage. The last few carriages sprayed out, away from the body of the train, and even as Hayden raised her head, still stunned and reeling, her heart almost stopped at what she saw.

The last two cars skidded away from the train tracks and struck a bank of dirt, causing the last car to veer upwards and swing so that its rear end swayed out across the motorway that ran parallel. Vehicles swerved and skidded to a halt. Terrified motorists aimed their cars in any direction except forward.

A small smart car slammed into the rear of the train. A Land Rover swung sharply sideways, but still hit the smart car with its rear end. Another vehicle pranged the Land Rover.

Hayden willed her body to respond, but sensed a heavy

blackness about to take over. The blast seemed not only to have disoriented her, but knocked out her sense of balance and reasoning. Even Dahl lay unmoving to her right.

And then, unbelievably, close to her ear she heard a voice crackle across one of the dead mercenaries mobile phones.

"This is Cayman. Train is compromised. We are on to plan B. Repeat plan B. Are you there?"

A response from a third party came immediately over the open line. "We have been tracking the train by road as instructed sir. The rear carriage is. . .well, it's actually in front of us."

"Get in there," Cayman ordered. "Recover the pieces and. . ." He paused. "New orders from the Norseman. Bring the bastards who tried to stop us. Bring them to Prague."

As the blackness claimed her, Hayden was left with only a single thought. *Call Matt Drake.* Bringing every ounce of her training, every contested second of her battle to match her father's name to bear, she endeavored to make the call.

Cayman's last words stayed with her. *"Prague is a fortress. Not even an army could reach us there."*

PART 3

The Shadow Elite

TWENTY-THREE

Mai was in full flow and no one dared interrupt her. "This *group*." She spat the word. "Targeted Wells so they could get an informer into the British army. They convinced him they were the ruling body of the world, that they controlled the British government. Not only that—it was *Cayman* who recruited him and convinced him that all governments did the Shadow Elite's bidding. I think Wells took patriotism just a bit too far."

"Weak men always have big secrets," Alicia said with a knowing smile. "Cayman will have had dirt on Wells, be sure of that."

Drake tried to stick to the facts they knew. "So Cayman is DIA, yes? Working undercover for the Shadow Elite. If that's the case, then we have to assume the CIA and the White House have similar moles, as well as every other agency in the world."

"Which is why Gates can't take the risk and the time to vet everyone above and around him," Mai said. "Which then leaves us out here, exposed and alone."

"But it also puts us right in the middle of the game," Drake said with a little smile, filling a little plate with chorizo sausage, *patatas bravas,* olive oil and bread. "We know where Cayman is. We know what the Shadow Elite want. Now all we have to do is find them."

"Vienna," Belmonte pointed out. "You were rather close to these bastards before. Do you recall anything pertaining to operation Doubledown?"

Drake took a few moments to think. Time tended to turn hazy around Alyson's death. He shook his head. "Sam might remember something. I can't."

"We could travel there," Mai suggested. "Call your pals and get them to meet us. We're still well within the window they gave you."

"It's a plan. But it's a bloody stretch, Mai. Especially with Hayden and the guys straining their bollocks off to acquire those eight pieces."

Drake checked his mobile, despite knowing that every method of contact was cranked to the highest level. "Thought we'd have heard something by now."

"Risky mission," Belmonte said, a faraway look in his eye. "People die."

"People die crossing the road or in car accidents," Drake said savagely. "I wonder who this *Coyote* is."

"That's another mission," Alicia said. "For another day."

"Whatever happens," Mai said, "the Shadow Elite cannot be allowed to continue. I work for one of the best intelligence teams in the world, and I've never heard of them. Yet they're the puppet masters. If they held our best interests..." She shrugged. "Maybe watch them from afar. But men who covet such weapons of mass destruction should never be allowed to rule."

"Fuckin' right," Alicia said. "At least me and the sprite agree on one thing."

"The sprite and I." Drake instantly corrected her.

"Don't encourage the bitch," Mai said pointedly. "She's

hard enough to tolerate. At the moment I only want to kill her once a day"

Belmonte looked between the three. "So I'm sensing some friendly history here?"

"Fuck off, Belmonte." Alicia picked at the food. "A thief like you wouldn't know the first thing about friendship, only liaisons."

Belmonte banged the table with his glass. "Don't presume to know me."

Alicia turned her gaze on him. "But I do know you, Daniel, as you often point out. I know you so well."

"I care for people. Cared." The thief sighed and shook his head. "I think the only bad thing that's ever happened in my life is going to be the worst thing that ever happens in my life. I don't even know why I'm with you people any more. What good will revenge do me?"

Drake tried not to stare at the bar. "I'll let you know. Soon."

"I'm not like you, Drake. I'm a man of stealth and finesse, not of action and brawn. I'm no hero. Never will be."

"A hero should be defined by their actions in a given moment." Mai sounded as if she was reciting an old Japanese proverb. "Not by what they do normally, or don't do."

It was at that moment when Drake's mobile started to ring. He reached out quickly and grabbed it, looking surprised.

"Karin?"

The young woman's whisper conveyed tension, fear and urgency. "We're captured. They've got us. All of us. I. . ." A pause. "I'm going to try to leave my phone on. . ."

Then silence. Drake looked up. "We need to move now. Hayden's team has been captured. Let's go."

Without looking back, they raced into the unknown to help their friends.

TWENTY-FOUR

Hayden battled to focus her thoughts, as her exhausted body protested in every way. The concussion of the blast had knocked her momentarily unconscious, but it had done worse to her equilibrium. It had made her sick, made her have to grope through a sludgy mist to remember where she was. It had done the same to Dahl and Komodo, leaving Kinimaka, Ben and Karin slightly better off, but still with stability issues.

Now she lay bouncing around the hard metal floor of a van. The movement of the vehicle, being driven fast around bends and over bumps in the road, did nothing to hasten her slowly returning sense of balance. Her eyes were a few inches off the floor.

Her arms were tied behind her back, her ankles too. Dahl and Komodo rolled listlessly beside her as the journey went on. She was vaguely aware of Karin wrestling a hand free, then a brief conversation before the blond girl locked her phone and thrust it deep into a pocket.

Some time later, as she drifted, the van slowed and began a stop-start motion. She heard curses from up front. They were stuck in traffic, maybe traveling through a city or around one. Her head was starting to regain some of its sharpness. She still had no idea how long it had been since the train crash that followed the shocking explosion. She could never have guessed that the Shadow Elite would plant explosives in one of its own train carriages, but it was a lesson she had now learned and would always remember. She hoped to God no civilians had been hurt.

Ben's voice drifted through the thinning fog. "Hayden. Hayden, are you alright?" A dull monotone she'd been aware of for some time, but unable to process.

Her nose cracked against the rust-spotted metal floor, bringing tears to her eyes yet again. "Not. . .not really." She managed to mumble.

She felt huge relief when the voice of Torsten Dahl spoke up. "Do we know where we are or where we're going?"

Negative replies came back. Karin spoke softly. "I managed to call Drake and leave my phone on so he can track us. The battery should last a while. But the back window's blacked out. They'd know if I scratched at it."

"Untie us." Hayden knew the fuzziness in her head explained why Karin hadn't already tried.

"With what? We're secured with plastic strip ties and the van's empty. And—" she murmured, "they've been checking on us."

The van lurched around a bend. Hayden rolled, crashing into Kinimaka. She was vaguely aware of the Hawaiian piling into Komodo and pinning the poor Delta man against the side of the van. Not a great position to be caught in.

"Sorry, bud." Kinimaka said.

A panel in the front bulkhead suddenly slid back and a man appeared. He was bald, clean-shaven and mean-looking. A scar extended across his forehead. "I hear wagging tongues," he said. "And I don't want to. The Norseman wants to see you, but he didn't say anything about your tongues. Keep it quiet. We're almost there."

The head vanished along with the East-European accent. Hayden felt a shockwave travel the length of her body. She turned to lock eyes with Dahl.

"The Norseman?" She breathed.

"End of the line," Dahl said. "The leader of the Shadow Elite wants to punish us for ruining his plans. No prizes for guessing what happens after that."

"Sure thing, but it's what happens *during* it that bothers me more." Hayden struggled to rip her hands free of the bonds, but got nowhere. She thought about the civilians, Ben, Karin and Gates behind her. She thought about what these terrible men might do to them.

Please, Drake, she thought. *Come for us.*

*****

At that moment, Matthew Holgate, the sixth and youngest member of the Shadow Elite, was being served a light lunch at an upscale restaurant inside Vienna's Museum of Natural History. The menu was short and never varied, but that didn't matter. They knew what he wanted. He spent a brief few minutes chatting with the amiable waitress and then turned to his waiting coffee.

Staring into its black depths, he saw a reflection of himself floating there, confined. A symbolic image. Not long ago, Holgate had been one of the world's richest playboys, a man with a house, five cars and a dozen women in every major city around the globe, a setter of trends and even a philanthropist. Behind all that lurked the Shadow Elite, a group he had

The Tomb of the Gods

figuratively belonged to since the day he was born, his father's son. Actively, he had belonged for decades, loving its limitless power, basking in its unaccountability, relishing the times when its leader—the melancholy Norseman—allowed them to play games with random people's lives. Even in a jaded rich man's world, there was nothing quite like picking a person or a family and subjecting them to endless indiscriminate torment.

It helped reinforce the group's belief in their own power, the Norseman said. The end always justified the means. So if there was just another peasant family on the scrapheap who would notice?

But recently, a chance event of its own had transformed Holgate's life. The world at large knew it as the recession. But Holgate knew what it really was—the big decision-makers had decided that the world was advancing too fast and needed to slow down, that progress was moving too quickly, that common men were simply becoming too affluent, their lives too painless. A decision had been made at the top, a level below the Shadow Elite, who had discussed its meager worth to the group but decided to allow the period of austerity to happen. It wouldn't affect them. It would actually help to reinforce their positions and extend the scope of their powers and their games.

But then, in his blind arrogance, Holgate had been caught in one of the big bank crashes. After that he'd lost much more in property value slumps. He'd invested heavily in hedge funds and start-up businesses that simply vanished.

All so quick. All that virtual wealth wiped away. When he realized the extent of his actual paper wealth, he almost threw himself off the top of his exterior Italian-carpeted marble staircase and onto the roof of his gleaming black Maserati

MC12 supercar. But deliberation saved him. He'd thought about his fellow Elite members and believed they'd help him. It was only later, when broaching a few carefully crafted questions, he realized they would certainly crucify him, their lifelong colleague, if they ever found out.

And then the whole Odin thing happened. The Shadow Elite had convened more times in the last two months than in the previous two years. Holgate sat and listened, and gave his input without really getting too involved, constantly aware that his five brothers might, at any time, find out about his bankruptcies.

But, like the predator that lies in wait ready to strike, the answer had come to Holgate in the form of the eight pieces of Odin. So crucial. The heart of everything.

Holgate smiled as the waitress placed his warm food on the table. Then he picked up an untraceable mobile phone he'd recently been given by one of the most dangerous men in the world.

When the call was answered with a curt, "Ya?" Matthew Holgate took the first steps down the diabolical road that was his master plan.

"I can get them. It's all in readiness. Now, how many of the world's richest, craziest terrorists can you actually gather together in one place?"

He paused for a beat.

"That many? Good. Now sit back and listen."

*****

Hayden braced herself as the van skidded to a sudden stop. Laughter, deep and coarse, came from the front and then two doors banged. Shouts echoed outside the van. Then the back door was pulled open and a man started laughing.

"Trussed up like turkeys. And here it is, not yet even Christmas."

She heard yells and guessed her colleagues were being pulled out of the van by their feet and allowed to crash to the ground. Again, she wrenched at her bonds and helplessness washed over her as she felt her own ankles grabbed and her body slid roughly over the van floor. There was a moment of weightlessness and then the hard earth rushed up to meet her, face-first. More laughter rang out. The laughter of many men.

Quickly, she rolled over. The harsh sunshine beat down at her face, making her eyes water. After a moment a shadow blocked out the light. "Up."

Strong arms looped underneath her armpits and dragged her to her feet. She stood there for a moment, swaying, unused to the new position and trying to let the queasiness subside. Dahl stood next to her, casting around furtively, Kinimaka and Komodo beside him. Beyond them she picked out Gates, Ben and Karin before dropping her eyes again, feigning shakiness.

A boot kicked her in the spine, making her stagger and cry out in surprise. Dahl turned in anger, but found himself facing the business end of a shiny Heckler and Koch. Hayden pushed past him, nudging him as she went. Time for that later.

They had been brought through a gate into an inner courtyard. The Norseman's mansion surrounded them on all four sides, built of old brick and stone, studded with bespoke windows and doors. The gate itself was a sturdy structure flanked on either side by massive stone pillars and a guardhouse. The surface beneath their feet was bits of tiny white gravel; the sky above their heads was cloudless and bright blue. Men stood around in easy poses, every one toting some kind of automatic weapon.

No way out, she thought, then berated herself. There was always a plan. And a plan B. The only obstacle was her fear.

A boot again connected with her spine. This time she stood her ground, turned, and stared hard at the wizened mercenary doing the kicking. "Untie me," she said evenly, "then try it again."

All the while hoping he didn't know about her knife wound...

...but the older hard-case just grinned, showing a mouth full of black teeth and gaps and a tongue missing an inch-square chunk. He motioned her onward, bringing his rifle to bear.

Hayden used the interlude to analyze their surroundings some more. The Norseman's mansion not only surrounded them on four sides, but rose three stories high. Wherever this place was, no doubt it resided among similar dwellings in an affluent area. From her vantage point, Hayden could ascertain no clues to their location.

She turned back again, walking toward a long brick wall. Her comrades had already been lined up against it, facing the courtyard. She too took her position at the end of the line.

Twelve men stepped forward and raised their weapons.

No! Her mind screamed. It was too soon. They hadn't even met the Norseman yet. Why bring them all this way just to shoot them on arrival?

The sound of a dozen rifles being cocked rang out across the sunlit courtyard. Hayden stared instant death in the eye with one last incredulous thought.

I didn't even get time to talk to Ben.

*****

Drake thought fast on his feet, faster than at any other time in his life. The immediate goal was to find a GPS tracker, something they could sync with Karin's recurrent signal and home in on. With Belmonte's expertise, it was a simple job, but required them to return to the "hot zone" around the airport's warehouse district they had just vacated. Drake didn't think twice. He led the way, purchasing the tracking device and returning to the airport in less than half an hour, just in time to catch the next plane to Prague, a journey that would take them less than seventy minutes.

Drake didn't waste a single one. "I have two plans," he told them. "A and B. . ."

*****

Hayden didn't close her eyes. Instead, she stared down the unwavering gun barrel, defiant to the last. Her thoughts became internally focused, her perceptions dulled. Time stretched before her like a piece of elastic, taut with expectation.

A balloon drifted through the skies above the courtyard, blood-red, with its long string dangling and twisted as if pulled directly from a child's hand.

The movement caught everyone's attention. When Hayden flicked her eyes back again, she was startled to see that a man had threaded his way through the gun barrels.

The Norseman. He stood before his soldiers, long blond hair rustled by the breeze, craggy face drawn in what some might have thought was sympathy, but Hayden knew amounted to nothing more than circumspect disinterest. It was the attention a young psychotic might give to a fly caught in the web of an approaching spider.

"Odin," he said. "He was the Father of the Gods. As I am the father of our council. We are alike, Odin and I."

Hayden shifted uncomfortably. Beside her Dahl managed a guffaw.

The Norseman's face tilted. "My wealth goes back to the days of the Vikings. My wealth's origins are the oldest known. I am descended of Beowulf, though the doubters would have you believe he never existed. The great poem—written in 800 CE, but only rediscovered in the seventeenth century tells of a real king and a real land. But Beowulf, they say, did not exist. Well here—" He tapped at the soil with his foot, the foundations of his home. "I have proof that he existed."

"And that he fought a monster?" Dahl said with sarcasm.

"We all fight our monsters. I only said Beowulf was real, not Grendel."

"You are the Norseman," Hayden said, still shocked despite herself.

"The man behind it all." His face gave no expression. "The shadow that rises above the Shadow Elite. Yes."

"And you would use the doomsday weapon?" Hayden asked.

"Use?" The Norseman sucked at the word as if it was a mint toffee. "Use? Such an ambiguous word. Yes, I would use it, my dear, but in what way do you mean?"

"To destroy the fucking world."

The Norseman's eyes barely blinked. "Don't be so fucking stupid. Why would I do that? Why would I destroy that which I own?"

Dahl laughed. "Because you're crazier than batshit, mate."

Hayden winced. She heard Ben's sharp intake of breath and even Komodo swallowed hard.

The Norseman didn't waver. "The doomsday device will be *used* as our security net. Once in place, it will never need to be called upon." Then his eyes went far away. "But imagine. Imagine if one day it was let loose. Fire and water, storms and lightning and thunder, earthquakes and mega tornadoes engulfing the world. What beauty. What an end!"

Hayden knew he wasn't kidding around. This man didn't have it in him to joke.

"Odin faced Ragnarok," the Norseman told them. "With his sons by his side, he marched into battle. He faced monsters. *Real* monsters—"

"No." Dahl interrupted the most powerful man on the planet. "He didn't."

The Norseman fixed a hooded gaze onto the Swede.

"I saw Odin's bones," Dahl said. "I touched them. I saw where he lay down and died. He certainly didn't die fighting on any battlefield. Ragnarok," he said softly, "is the real myth."

"He's right," Gates spoke up for the first time. "Ragnarok is *now*, not back then. Odin averted it once by making the gods die. But the finding of his shield started a chain reaction that had to end with the discovery of the third tomb and the doomsday weapon. It's now our choice. We decide. It is *mankind's decision to save or destroy itself.* The words are written in the Icelandic tomb."

"You refer to the day of reckoning." The Norseman studied the US Secretary of Defense impassively. "But it is all moot. Do you remember the Cold War? The days when the Russians and Americans pointed a thousand nukes at each other and waited for fate to take its course? A bad time, even for us. We can't possibly control every single itchy finger and one slip, one moment of rage, could've plunged the world into nuclear war. But now. . .we will be the only superpower, and we will hold *all* the weapons."

"What if we call your bluff?" Gates ventured.

"We are the Shadow Elite," the Norseman said simply. "If one voice rises against us, it shall be quieted. If many voices rise against us. . . then we'll wipe the fuckers off the map."

The Norseman stepped back then and took a long look at them. Hayden held her head high. The Norseman turned away and passed through the line of rifleman.

As one the weapons steadied, aimed, and held still.

A voice said, *"Fire!"*

The sound of gunshots, screams and bullets impacting against brickwork ruined the peace of an idyllic winter's day.

*****

No sooner had the plane landed than Drake and his friends were fighting past other passengers and racing to get through customs. If anyone thought them rude, they certainly didn't speak up. But then their hard faces would have put off all but the hardiest or oldest of complainers.

Outside the airport, into the bracing cold, the four could relax a little. Drake waved at a taxi and pulled out the tracking device that Belmonte had expertly cobbled together.

"Still strong," he said.

Mai, next to him, studied a map of Prague. *"Dejvice."* She reeled off a suburb of the old city and the taxi took off at pace.

As they rode, they reviewed the plan. It was rough, it was risky, but it was the best improvisation they could come up with under this kind of time limit and pressure. Drake was certain their friends would be killed today. It was just a matter of when.

"And the eight pieces of Odin?" Mai said.

"Are secondary," Drake said again. "Our friends come first."

"We should at least try—"

"Mai," Drake said forcefully, "I'm sorry. But you lost your say when you acted alone. You risked it all to save Chika. Now it's my turn."

Alicia turned bright eyes on the Japanese woman. "Hey. Look at it this way—a bitch who fucked up like you did— normally they'd just put you down. This way, you get a second chance."

"Put me down?" Mai echoed. "And who's going to do that? You?"

"I'll put you both down if you don't quit." In reality, Drake knew they were only mentally preparing themselves for the fight and the violence to come. He threw a glance at Belmonte.

"You'd probably be better off staying in the car. The *other* car, if you know what I mean."

The thief nodded. Drake's plan was verging on suicide, but it was all they had. At that moment, Drake's mobile rang, an old Dinorock tune, something about smoke on the water.

Drake listened for a moment, and then his face fell. "Oh no," he said. Then, "And there's no chance that—?"

The Englishman listened some more. The news did not look good. At the end he nodded and turned the mobile off. "That was Sam. His team can't meet us here in time. Balls."

"Doesn't change the plan one bit," Alicia said with some relish.

Drake nodded. "They're heading straight for Vienna. They will meet us all there later. Assuming. . ."

"We survive," Belmonte finished with a shake of his head. "Oh dear."

"Whatever happens, mate"—Drake turned to him—"You have to meet them there and tell them everything. If we die, the pieces of Odin will be in the wind."

Drake closed his eyes. "I just wish we knew if they were all alright."

*****

Hayden's hands, still held together with plastic ties behind her back, were roped loosely together and passed through a metal ring that had been built into the uneven brick wall at her back. The rope was tied. Her team, all shaken but alive, were lined up beside her.

So it was to be psychological torture to start with, at least. The firing squad had been accurate enough. Their bullets had smashed into the wall above their heads, showering masonry and hot jacket fragments over them. The Norseman's face hadn't even twitched. Then they had been dragged roughly inside the mansion and pushed into an unfurnished ground-floor room. Concrete floor. Brick walls. A large drain in the middle of the floor.

A killing room, easy to clean afterward.

Now, men with grins on their faces dragged big industrial hoses into the room. Normally used for sluicing, they were now aimed at the captives. Hayden braced herself for the impact. Then more men crowded in behind them, some holding machine guns, others equipped with an odd-shaped weapon. Large barreled and stubby, it somehow looked more menacing than the Heckler and Kochs.

"Rubber ball gun," Dahl said without emotion. "Hits harder than most men. Probably best to duck."

Hayden eyed the Swede tied beside her. "Options?"

Before he could answer, the Norseman's soldiers got started on their version of fun. The hose was switched on, slithering straight as the water surged through. Two men held the nozzle, unable to contain their mirth as a deluge of water jetted out and struck the helpless captives full-on. Hayden was blasted in the face and her head smashed back into the wall, making her see stars. The force of the water stopped her breathing. She felt like she was drowning, standing up.

Gasping for breath, she swallowed water, whipping her head from side to side and trying to turn away. But the stream of water was inescapable and terribly powerful. The last breath of air was forced out of her lungs. She had faced waterboarding before, but it had nothing on this. At the edge on consciousness, she heard the boom as the rubber-ball guns began firing.

The unmistakable sound of Ben's voice, screaming, reached her ears.

She swallowed more water, coughing, unable to get rid of it all in the face of the unyielding current. Then, when she had just passed the moment of surrender, the stream passed on to the next person—Kinimaka.

Hayden hung her head, almost spent. Her knife wound was throbbing again, the pain cutting through the cloud of helplessness that surrounded her. She gave thanks that one of the rubber balls hadn't struck her yet, for if one was to impact with the wound. . .even CIA discipline and all the training in the world might not stop her from begging for mercy.

So she hung from her bonds, showing defeat, feigning vulnerability whilst fighting hard to get her breath back and willing strength to return to her body. Again, she tested the plastic ties, hopeful the water might have loosened them. But if anything, it appeared to have tightened them, making the edges cut into her already-bruised skin.

Despair invaded and sought to occupy her heart. Her head fought against it, seeking an escape route, but deep down the terrible truth could no longer be denied.

There was no way out of this one.

She allowed her head to swing sideways and saw the water cannon had just reached Karin. Would the deluge damage and destroy her mobile phone? If it did, they were in for a long, painful and hard-fought death.

*****

Drake studied the mansion where his friends were being held until he had pinpointed Karin's exact position. The place blended right in with every other property around here. They were built right on the street, as if coveting every ounce of space they were allowed with minimal gardens, but imposing outer walls, high and almost unscaleable. Narrow, curtained windows looked out at street level, with the larger double-panes on the second and third floors. Drake couldn't even see a door. Maybe there was one around another side, but it didn't matter. He wasn't about to knock. He knew his plan was risky and fraught with assumptions, but the situation required an immediate and extreme response.

"There." He pointed out the exterior wall to Mai and Alicia, then left them to it. With Belmonte alongside, he prowled the nearby streets for two of the likeliest vehicles. Within five minutes, he had spotted a grey Land Rover and a powerful Toyota saloon. He pointed them out to Belmonte.

"Ready?"

"No, but I'm game."

*****

Hayden raised her head at last. A rubber ball caromed off the wall next to her right eye, the man who fired it laughing like a maniac and quickly reloading so he could try again. To left and right her companions tried to make themselves less of a target by scrunching their bodies up, but they were all drenched, and most of them had been hit in the most painful parts of their bodies.

"We're here all fuckin' day!" One of the mercs laughed and then brayed laughter like a strung-out donkey. He aimed and fired, his shot true. The rubber ball slammed into Komodo's ribcage, but the big Delta soldier never flinched.

Hayden sighed at his stupidity and saw Karin do the same. *Damn soldier boys and their macho displays.* The mercenary's laughter continued. "Now *there's* a challenge I accept. Believe this, bud, every hero I ever knew is long dead."

Dahl tried to flick his drenched hair to the side. "Good, lad. I'd have done the same."

"Then we'll all die as fools," Hayden whispered fiercely. "We have to be smarter than these animals, not stoop to their level."

"Suggestion?"

Hayden despaired. "Don't you have a plan? The great Torsten Dahl. The mad Swede. Whaddya say?"

"I say—" Dahl held up his ripped, bloody and *free* hands. "Let's go shove their fucking heads up their arses."

The mad Swede ran like the Devil rode his heels. Mouth wide, shrieking, with blood flying from his waving hands and water all around him, he charged down over a dozen armed men. In seconds he was among them, destroying the side of one man's face with a savage elbow and kicking a second so hard he didn't stop tumbling until he hit the back wall with enough force to knock him senseless. Hayden used the chaos to twist her own wrists again, but the pain of the ties ripping through her flesh made her cry out. How the hell could Dahl stand it? The man had to be superhuman. She saw Kinimaka and Komodo trying the same, faces contorted but full of desperate determination, and then Komodo wrenched a wrist free.

At that point, the whole place went crazy.

The Norseman strode in through the far door, shaking his head when he saw the melee and calling for more guards to come from the seemingly endless warren of rooms that made up his mansion. To his credit, he stood his ground, watching events unfold. Then, as if by great magic, Mai and Alicia suddenly appeared behind him, having gained entry through a ground-floor window. The Norseman immediately flung himself behind a unit of guards.

Suddenly, the tables were turned. With Dahl, Mai and Alicia free and able to battle, there wasn't a mercenary group in the world that would stay confident. The women bounded into the room, dealing wounds and injuries out as if they were distributing presents. Hayden gave up her struggle with the bonds, worn out with stress and pain of her wound, and waited for Komodo to find a weapon that would free her.

The Delta soldier broke free and fell to his knees. Groaning, he scrambled quickly to one of the men Dahl had left in his deadly wake, frisked the body and came up with a standard-issue knife.

The Norseman advanced farther into the room, unarmed, unfazed, his craggy face betraying not even the slightest hint of emotion. *What did he know?*

Hayden leaned forward as Komodo reached over and sawed through her bonds. She was in no condition to fight, but stumbled forward anyway, hoping to at least take one enemy out of the fray. Mai and Alicia had made their way over to Dahl, targeting the mercenaries with the deadliest weapons first and killing them.

The sound of gunfire ricocheted around the large space. One of the hoses was still running, sending water gushing up against a wall and rebounding back in a mini wave. Dahl slammed a man's head into it, rendering him unconscious, and left him to drown.

Behind Hayden, Komodo freed Kinimaka. The large Hawaiian grunted his thanks, hurdled a fallen mercenary to reach her side and held out a steadying hand. "You should fall back."

"You givin' me an order, Mano?"

"Yes, boss, I am. Now get behind me."

Kinimaka stood strong as a mercenary lined him up in his sights. The shot exploded from the big gun, the rubber ball impacting with bruising force against Kinimaka's thigh, but eliciting nothing more than a disdainful grunt. Kinimaka reached out and grabbed the mercenary by the neck, lifting him off the ground. The mercenary jammed the barrel of the gun under Kinimaka's neck.

The two men stared at each other, inches apart.

Hayden scooped up a small handgun and shot the merc between the eyes. Kinimaka sent her a grateful wink. "Mahalo."

"Any time. You do me, I'll do you. So to speak."

Kinimaka blinked in surprise, but then turned abruptly as a sudden hubbub filled the room, loud even over the noise of fighting and shooting and screaming.

Hayden stared too. Her hopes fell. A second substantial group of mercs swarmed into the room, all armed and looking hungry for blood. The Norseman crossed his arms and leaned against a wall. Game over.

A dozen guns fired at once, aimed high in an expression of strength and intent. Dahl paused in mid-flow, a mercenary in each hand. A deadly hush fell slowly over the room, the sudden silence ringing in their ears.

The Norseman stared at Mai and Alicia. "I commend your efforts. Breaking in here alone would make you worthy of being part of my team. But this—" He indicated the dead and dying mercenaries by their feet. "Proves your worth tenfold. But alas, your heroism is pointless. You see, there are no heroes any more. Not in this world. Your desperate plan B has failed."

Alicia stayed poised, ready to move. "Actually, we're plan A. *He's* plan B."

And then there came an almighty crash like the destruction of a mountain, and Matt Drake smashed through the far wall behind the wheel of a speeding Land Rover, utter determination carved into his face like foundations in bedrock.

Falling masonry, plaster and crushed timbers rained all around the speeding vehicle, along with the smoke of a dozen mini-explosives Belmonte had placed to weaken the wall.

Everyone scattered. The Norseman hurled himself out of the way, pretty spry for an older guy. One of his men got clipped by exploding rock, the big block crushing his skull before he could even blink. Mai and Alicia hit the deck; the rest of Hayden's team followed suit a split-second later. The revving of the mighty engine was the sound of a deadly behemoth in the room, and it was out for vengeance.

As soon as the big vehicle lost its momentum, Drake dived out the door, scooped up a couple of discarded machine guns and started firing, a weapon in each hand. Spurts of fire burst from the barrels. Mercenaries folded and pirouetted where they stood, blood painting the floor and the walls around them.

The Norseman crawled amidst the bodies, brick dust and blood clinging to him. His flight, his anonymity, was all that mattered to him now. He didn't even try to find a firearm. Dahl continued where he'd left off, grabbing the two stunned mercenaries again and slamming their heads together. Then, with a grunt, he discarded their bodies. No more would they take pleasure in the pain of others.

It was Hayden, soaked, bloody and limping, who reached down to grab the Norseman by the scruff of the neck. Roughly, she jerked his head upward until their eyes met.

"You see? There *are* still heroes in this world."

TWENTY-FIVE

Hayden hauled the Norseman to his feet by his hair. The old man struggled and cried out, but not a single sympathetic eye turned his way.

"We should kill him," Belmonte said, slipping from the back seat of the ruined Land Rover. "He instigated everything that's happened. It all started with this evil bastard."

"He's valuable," Hayden said, reverting to her CIA perspective. "Imagine the secrets he knows." She looked at Jonathan Gates. "Right? We might discover who we can really trust."

The Secretary of Defense nodded wearily and sat down heavily amidst the rubble. "We will. Just give me a minute."

Hayden threw the Norseman at Dahl and strode over to her boss, still limping. "Are you okay, sir?"

"Just tired," Gates said. "All this globetrotting seemed like a good idea at first. I fear I may have lost track of my mission objective. To form a chain of clean, reliable and trustworthy individuals all the way to the White House."

"Doesn't matter." Hayden settled beside him with a smile. "Now we have the Norseman, that task will be much simpler."

"If we handle it right."

"Yes," Hayden agreed. "If we handle it right." As the

The Tomb of the Gods

adrenalin subsided, the pain in her side increased. She still had some painkillers in her pocket and popped a few.

Ben dropped to her side. "You alright, Hayden?"

His girlfriend looked over his shoulder toward the men in the room. "I will be when the drugs kick in."

Dahl pinned the Norseman against a wall and held him there. Alicia appeared at his shoulder, studying the leader of the Shadow Elite as if he were a bizarre relic.

"Anything to say, you crispy old fuck?"

"I demand to speak to my lawyer?"

Alicia looked surprised, an unusual expression for her. "If you weren't such an evil wanker, I'd actually respect you for that."

But then, Drake pushed his way past and leaned in, lightly head-butting the man. "Tell me." He growled. "Was it you? Were you the bastard who saw me coming and ordered her death?"

The Norseman stared at him for a minute and then said, "Wells, your unit Commander, suggested her death would. . .divert your attentions. So yes, as leader of the group, I take all responsibility for allowing that to happen."

"And Coyote? The man who killed her. Who is that?"

"You think it was a man. . ."

"I'm sorry," Mai interrupted. "I really am, Matt, but we have a more pressing need. The world is still at risk. Where are the eight pieces of Odin? Tell us now, and your future might have less of a sharp edge to it."

"I have survived this long," the Norseman said, "by carefully weighing all my options and trusting my instinct. I will survive longer by telling you this—the Shadow Elite have their HQ in Vienna"—he gave a respectful nod to Drake—"as you almost discovered many years ago. I can give you the address. The eight pieces and the heads of all the other families will be there."

Now Dahl spoke up. "Why would the eight pieces be in Vienna? You need them to kick start the doomsday device, don't you? And why did that twat Cayman originally take them from Iceland to Stuttgart?"

"Do not think you are the only people who have a plan B. We too have contingencies. As the governing body of this planet, we have a new plan now, as anyone with an IQ over one hundred would anticipate."

"Which is?"

"We will try the threat first, as we always have. It's worked for thousands of years. It will work again. But. . ." He gazed without expression. "If we are forced, we will provide a demonstration. Vienna is close enough to Singen to be perfect for our ways and means. And…" He shrugged. "The base at Stuttgart was a similar way station. Just a more convenient resting place along the way."

"Your new plan sounds like a backward step to me," Drake said.

"It is the step that *I* originally advocated," the Norseman told them. "But I was overruled by the council. Now, using the fiasco *you* set in motion, I have exerted my authority."

"Fiasco?" Hayden said numbly. "We stopped you from using that fucking device. Did you even stop to think that once you got your rocks off by triggering it, you might not be able to stop it?"

The Norseman blinked, showing emotion for the first time.

"Your arrogance," Hayden said, "your superior, disgusting egotism astounds me. You think that because you are all-powerful, that you can second guess Odin?"

"The gods were once *real*," Dahl snapped at him. "Even now, you are too self-important to see that. Even now."

"Our families have governed this world for far longer than you can imagine," the Norseman told them. "When the world was new and unexplored, we were already wealthy. The global, navigated map only strengthened our hold. Our ancient families belong to the six foremost families in history."

"You think you are gods?" Drake snapped. "Is that it?"

"Gods of men." The Norseman almost smiled. "Of that I am sure."

"We are wasting time that we don't have," Mai said urgently. "You'll give us this address in Vienna and you will give us something more."

"And what is that?"

"At least three different ingress points."

"Well, my map drawing days are long gone—"

Drake gripped his neck. "Don't worry, old man. You start making up right now for all your past sins. You're coming with us."

TWENTY-SIX

Russell Cayman crouched like a big black spider in the corner of a shadowy tomb. He sang softly to himself, a spine-tingling litany that catalogued his life and all his woes. If any mercenary thought it a disturbing sight, none dared comment. But they did leave him there, eerie and troubled.

The pitted and scarred tomb beside him belonged to Amatsu, the God of Evil. Where Cayman did not believe in magic or fantasy or lingering spirits, he *did* believe that an old and terrible trauma might leave some kind of residue in the present. Stamped in time.

As if it were sunlight, he basked in its warmth. He had recently received orders that he and his men were to remain at the tomb for the foreseeable future, guarding it from the inquisitive and the downright nosey. The Shadow Elite's ghost network would take care of any curious authorities.

Deadly force must be used at all times.

Cayman and his men had no problem with that. It was what they were paid for. Now all they had to do was wait.

Cayman was convinced. The eight pieces of Odin had always been destined to be returned to the third tomb of the gods. Was there even a weapon or a person powerful enough to stop it happening? Sooner or later, by pure hand or foul, through good deed or ill, they would return to their rightful resting place and fulfill their bright and terrible destiny.

*****

Matthew Holgate strolled the sculpted gardens of Schonbrunn Palace, eyes blind to the great fountains, statues and seventeenth-century architecture that stood all around him. He meandered his way slowly toward the *gloriette*, each step a chore and a burden on his heart as he thought about what was to come.

His ancestors had been flourishing in Vienna even when this spectacular palace was being built. No doubt they had known its owners, its designers, and all of its occupants since. Now Holgate was about to destroy the family heritage. The legacy of centuries turned to ashes and dust.

He thought about the people his family had known. The kings. The princes. The presidents and prime ministers. And then, he thought about the utter scum he was being forced to contend with now. Men of no conscience, of no moral scruples whatsoever. Men who had been raised so hard and so ruthlessly that their hearts were made of black ice.

Not to say the Shadow Elite might boast about their grand humanitarian principles, but at least every leader of the six families bore some fragment of humanity.

Holgate was terrified in so many ways. He was terrified of walking this path alone—the first time he had ever had to do so—of not being able to go through with the deal, of the consequences of failure or disloyalty to his new benefactors. He didn't have a buffer—a Russell Cayman—he was a one man bring-and-buy sale.

And, most of all, he despaired of what would happen once the wrong man bought the right weapon.

But time marched on, and the rest of the Shadow Elite were running out of it, though they did not know it yet. Holgate turned to stare at the enormous fountain and, beyond it, the spectacular *gloriette*, his normally pale face aglow in response to the biting cold, his haunted gaze caught and held by the blood-red haze in the sky, a telling and silent accusation.

And then his phone rang. Unbuttoning his long black coat and reaching for an inside pocket, he took out the chirping mobile. "Yes?"

"We have made the arrangements," a heavily accented and clearly educated voice said. "The bazaar will be ready on time. Many, many. . .*attendees*, my friend. You had better get this right."

"It will be right," Holgate said quickly. "Just send me the men you promised."

"They are already there." The man reeled off a contact number. "Waiting for you. My part is done. Again, my friend, even *one* of these attendees would not hesitate to destroy a city to reach just one man, and you have invited more than two dozen to your bazaar—along with their bodyguards. For all our sakes, *do not fuck up."*

The connection was severed. Holgate started at the blank screen for a while and then at the bright-eyed faces of passing tourists.

Do not fuck up.

It wasn't one man destroying a city that caused Holgate's blood to run cold. It was that man having the capability to destroy the world.

Then don't do it, he thought. *Walk away. Tell the Norseman. Christ, even alert the authorities.*

But the proud leader of one of the six families just couldn't subject himself to such exposure. He was, after all, privileged. A god among men. He was allowed such quirks of character.

Everything would soon start to go his way. It always did.

TWENTY-SEVEN

Drake stared unseeing at the wintry, sun-struck streets of Vienna as Karin followed the detached directions of the inbuilt sat-nav to the place where the Norseman promised the Shadow Elite had kept their headquarters for thousands of years.

All those years ago, Wells had issued the order to kill Alyson. Time had enabled Drake to get past her death, but with the commencement of the Odin cycle it had cruelly thrust the details back into his face. That—and more.

Drake hadn't just lost Alyson in that crash. He had also lost his unborn child. Beyond strife, hunger, injustice and torture, there was one nightmarish absolute—a parent should never have to bury their own child, unborn or not. Now, Drake dwelled on what might have been and how his life might have been different, and had to physically shut down the pain that rose inside. A soldier's hard wall of indifference and denial struggled to intervene and compartmentalize the suffering.

Around him the streets of Vienna started to darken. Bright, colorful lights shone out warm and inviting against the night. Drake saw young children dressed in bobble hats and mittens, wrapped up with scarves, running between the shops, their parents struggling to keep up and keep an eye out for them. He saw the impressive architecture of a sprawling museum, its ancient facade artfully lit by a modern light show. He saw businessmen and secretaries, tourists and salespeople boiling up from the underground, many then darting across the wide roads whilst trying to avoid the metal bullets that flashed everywhere without thought—a cyclist rarely stops in Vienna.

Somewhere nondescript and unknown, they pulled over to the side of the road and accepted three men into the car. The men were hard-looking and rugged and carried big black holdalls. Sam, their leader, gave Drake a nod.

"Sam," the ex-SAS man greeted his old friend and his team, "thanks for joining us."

"Nowhere else to be, matey."

Beyond that, the throng thinned, but the old buildings with their eye-catching construction continued. A meandering park opened out to the right where, Belmonte told them, a superb restaurant sat right in the middle. A place frequented by and saved for the locals, cheap and delicious, not touted to the rich tourists. Still more streets and more sets of traffic lights and apartment complexes, and then they were in a tree-lined neighborhood. Even farther and the gateways became less frequent until. . .

The Norseman said, "Slow down. That is the place."

Drake observed a narrow gateway, lined on all sides with the requisite high trees. A razor-wire topped fence would no doubt stand behind the tee-line. He pressed a button to lower the electric window.

"Aye up. Well, you'd better not be lying to us, big man. The penalty for lies around here is slow and painful, and not something you usually come back from."

Mai raised an eyebrow at that one. "A date with Alicia?"

Even the Englishwoman grinned. "You're closer to the truth than you think."

Drake expected Belmonte to chirp up next, but the English thief was not himself these days. He said nothing, just stared out the front window, tapping the wheel. Drake turned in his seat. The second car had pulled up behind them. The rest of the Shadow Elite and the eight Pieces of Odin awaited them.

*****

With care, stealth and help from the Norseman, the team walked right through the front gates and melted quickly into the darkened grounds. No one challenged them at the gate, but then the Norseman had input the combination with his face just a few inches from the camera. The possibility existed that he had, in fact, entered an "intruder" alarm code, a set of numbers used to allow entry, but at the same time triggering a silent alert. Mai, Alicia and half the team slipped to the left, Drake and the others to the right.

And then they moved quickly, always alert, eyes peeled for guards and traps or any signs of movement ahead. They crept carefully for some time through the trees and ornamental gardens. The Shadow Elite's mansion was cloaked in a shroud of deep privacy. Then, after Drake began to wonder if there actually was any building ahead and that maybe the Norseman had sacrificed himself for his brethren, he saw the main road make a sweeping right curve up ahead.

And right on the cusp of that bend, standing as tall and wide and impressive as any house in Vienna, the secret headquarters of the group who ruled the world sat in silence.

Lights blazed from almost every window.

Dahl muttered, "Not exactly *green* warriors, are they?"

Drake dropped to one knee and dragged the Norseman up alongside him. Wetness soaked up from the grass through his trousers. His weapon clunked as it rapped the old man on the head. "Is that normal?" He hissed.

"No." The Norseman looked shocked. "It certainly isn't."

"And the front door?" Mai asked. "Does it normally hang off its hinges like that?"

Drake looked closer, marveling at the Japanese agent's eagle eye. The front door was small, overhung by a big arch and hidden partially behind a pillar, but the angles of the framework looked all wrong.

"Good spot."

"Something. . ." the Norseman began.

A gunshot echoed from inside the house. The Norseman drew in a sharp breath. "No. Oh no. . ."

Drake signaled and the group exploded from the trees like a well-primed and organized unit. Mai and Alicia flanked him with Dahl covering the rear and dragging the Norseman along. On the other side, Hayden and Kinimaka took point, with Komodo and the SAS team following and fanning out. Immediately behind them and staying impressively low came Karin and Ben, Gates and Belmonte.

Drake reached the house and took a quick gander through the nearest window before flattening himself against the wall. He shook his head. *Nothing.* Mai checked the next, and Alicia the next. Both women shook their heads.

"Front door."

Drake skipped past the windows until he reached the open door. He saw the thick wood had been hacked at and chewed through by bullets. The frame and concrete surrounds were pitted. Even the ornamental window above the door and the lintel had been pockmarked by flying lead.

"Not professionals then," Alicia said.

"Which makes it worse." Drake looked inside the house and quickly stepped back. "Spray and prey mercenaries are easy to come by, but hell to keep under control. Let's move."

The Norseman grunted something, sounding genuinely concerned for his five cohorts, but Dahl cuffed him and told him to shut his mouth if he valued his teeth. Inside the place, old paintings hung from the walls and rich furnishings sat upon Persian and old Egyptian rugs. The sculpted ceilings sported hanging chandeliers. First-rate sculptures of mythical and ancient beasts lined both sides of the corridor. Drake guessed they would not be reproductions. When he looked more closely, one painting depicted ancient Babylon with all its depraved delights, another Sodom and Gomorrah in immoral glory. Still another showed the devils of hell, corrupting young people whilst business-suited men stood and sipped whisky from crystal tumblers and watched, naked from the waist down.

"This?" Dahl growled into the Norseman's face. "This is how you live whilst so many struggle and die?"

Drake checked the first room. Hayden cleared the one on the opposite side of the immense hallway. Their ears were tuned for the slightest sounds. From somewhere up ahead, they heard low groans, a scream, and an order shouted in a guttural, foreign voice. It seemed to float from the back of the house.

Another room cleared, and then a fourth. Hayden and Kinimaka stepped into a fifth, this one with a wider entranceway and two enormous doors—the kind that were generally opened by waiting doormen. After a tense moment, when neither of them instantly emerged, Drake glided over to the entrance.

Hayden's back was to him, rigid. Kinimaka hung his head.

Drake, already fearing the worst, stepped past the big Hawaiian to appraise the room.

Horror froze his feet.

They had been nailed to the walls. Four members of the Shadow Elite, arms outstretched and legs bent in the crucifix position, their palms and feet shot through with heavy duty bolts right into the walls themselves. Rivers of blood ran down the priceless tapestries, furs and drapes that hung around them, pooling on the floor. The men's eyes bulged, their groans weak, full of pain.

The rest of the team filed into the room. Not even Ben and Karin made noises of surprise or regret on seeing the men. Live by the sword. . . taste the blood of innocents. . .die screaming, asshole.

No one moved to help the men. They hadn't been up there long. Drake's main concern now was over the individuals who had done this and the whereabouts of the eight pieces of Odin. He turned, weapon ready and eyed Sam and the SAS team, who had stayed to cover the hallway.

Sam nodded. *All good.*

He edged out. The voice of the Norseman stopped him. "What? You have to—"

Dahl smashed a fist into his mouth. "We have to do nothing. You should be thinking up ways of staying useful because as soon as you become obsolete. . .you're going the same way as your ancestor Beowulf and the Vikings."

"And what does that—?"

"Into the fucking ground. Now shut up."

The Norseman didn't even flinch from the blow, just stared at his colleagues with, at last, some emotion in his face. He seemed almost on the verge of tears.

The Tomb of the Gods

The team fanned out into the hallway and advanced. Four more rooms were cleared and now they heard only silence. Drake cursed inwardly that they had arrived too late, but moving forward now without care would only get one of them killed.

He turned to the Norseman. "We heard a gunshot. Someone still has to be here. What's back there?"

"A large room that leads to the rear gardens. The French windows are extensive, designed to give a full view of the—"

"Dahl," Drake said. The Swede silenced the Norseman with another punch.

Drake moved as fast as he dared. He noticed a bloody trail that extended along the wall at shoulder height. *Could one of the intruders be injured?* If they were, it was most likely due to being shot by one of their own men.

He stopped at the closed door and signaled for readiness. Kinimaka kicked it in and Drake leapt through first, closely followed by Hayden. Before him stretched an entire wall of glass doors and, beyond that, a spectacular view.

But it was the immediate sight of a crawling, bloodied man with a knife in his back and a gun in his hand that grabbed their attention.

"Holgate!" The Norseman tried to leap forward, but Dahl clamped a huge arm around his throat.

"Wait."

"Is he one of you?" Drake hissed without taking his eyes off the room, the man, and the spectacle beyond the windows.

"Yes. Matthew Holgate. The youngest member of our group."

Mai, Alicia and the SAS team flowed around Drake, taking point and responsibility for observing their perimeters. Drake dropped to the floor next to the man just as a coughing fit wracked his body.

"What happened?" Drake asked.

Holgate jumped and turned his head, trying to bring the gun around. Drake disarmed him with no regard to his wounds and repeated his question.

"They. . .they jumped me." Holgate coughed. "They made me watch—" He coughed again, screwing his face up in pain. "Whilst they. . .*crucified*. . .my friends. The only friends I have known."

The Norseman fell to his knees beside Holgate. "What happened here? Look, it is I. You have to tell me what went wrong tonight."

"Wrong?" Holgate spat the word as if it contained poison. "Everything has been wrong for years. But you? You never noticed. Your plans. . .your precious, flawless plans had to be executed. Day after day. Week after week." Holgate groaned and tried to reach around his body for the knife.

Drake grabbed his hand. "Probably best to leave that alone, dickhead."

The Norseman reached out too, but Dahl clamped his hand like a vice. Holgate took a moment and then continued, *"You never knew."* He suddenly hissed, and his eyes burned like fire as they turned on the Norseman. "You never even knew when I lost it all. You were unapproachable, a statue of ice in a suit and a tie. You failed *me.*"

The Norseman fell back, staring in horror. "I? What? You lost your fortune? The family's fortune? Impossible."

Mai reported from her position near a set of French doors. "We have movement out here. I see men among the trees behind the rink."

Drake tore his attention away from the exchange between the two Shadow Elite men. The question was—did they need to give chase?

"Wait," he interrupted Holgate. "The eight pieces of Odin. Do they have them?"

Holgate's face went whiter than snow. His lips moved, but no words spilled from his mouth.

"Do they have the pieces?" Drake wanted to throttle the man.

"Yes." The admission was like a death rattle.

"And where are they taking them?"

Absolute fear blanketed Holgate's eyes. "They double-crossed me." He rasped in disbelief. "They leave me with nothing."

"Where are they taking them?" Drake almost reached for the knife.

"To an arms bazaar!" Holgate cried out. "A vast terrorist market. The pieces are set to be auctioned off to the highest bidder."

Drake was on his feet in an instant. "Go!" he shouted. "We have to stop them!"

TWENTY-EIGHT

Mai and Alicia moved in sync, slipping out of the partially opened door and onto the patio beyond. Drake now allowed himself to take in the full spectacle of what lay beyond the windows.

The top half of the immense garden had been turned into an ice rink, its surface glistening under halogen floodlights. All around it trees were decorated with Christmas cheer and illuminated by hanging strings of lights. Artificial snow lay on the ground, scattered loosely and in heaps everywhere. The old men had created a winter wonderland for themselves only, a lonely, crazy vision.

"Freaks," Hayden muttered as she came up alongside Drake, the ever-present Kinimaka looking concerned at her side. "Drake, I'm not buying this. Those guys out there—they're amateurs. And we're being told that they found and massacred the Shadow Elite?"

Drake looked back at Dahl. "Stay with them, please. We need to know what happened here."

Dahl nodded. Drake moved carefully out of the house and into the crisp, cold night. His SAS pals shadowed Mai and Alicia as they skirted the high curb that surrounded the ice rink, heading for tree-cover. Ahead, among the trees, Drake saw a man appear. At first, he looked shocked. Drake took a second to line up a shot and fired, but the man screamed out a warning a split-second before the bullet smashed him off his feet.

Now other men darted fast between the trees, firing hard. Some looked back, and others moved forward and shooting blindly over their shoulders. Drake hit the deck with the rest of his team, shielding their bodies behind the curb, but not one single bullet impacted anywhere near them.

"Go?" Sam checked with Drake.

It was tempting. A strong, fluid team like theirs could rip through a horde of terrorists in seconds. . .but if just one of those wayward bullets struck lucky…

But the eight pieces of Odin were heading for an auction to be attended by the world's richest and deadliest terrorists. Something had to give. A soldier was a soldier because he risked everything for the country and the people that he loved. A hero was a hero because he felt the fear and went in anyway.

"Fuck it," he said. "Hit 'em."

As one they rose and ran in double formation around the circumference of the ice rink, firing precisely and constantly. Two of the fleeing men were hit and went down hard, skidding in the artificial snow. Bullets scudded off tree trunks and through leaves, shattering multi-colored lights and bringing the heavy ropes of trimmings cascading to the floor. Enormous ice sculptures were hit and chipped, some toppling over and smashing to pieces as they landed.

Drake used the excellent tree cover to dart forward without stopping. Quickly he caught sight of the terrorists' rear guard and squeezed off half a dozen shots. Men fell screaming, falling among scattered tree lights and bringing even more heavy trimmings to the floor. Drake quickly sped past them, taking point with Mai, confident his team would mop up and ensure that those who fell but weren't really dead were soon made that way.

He crouched in the snow, breathing lightly, reloading. The flakes crunched as Mai dropped to his side. It was so quiet around them he could hear her low breathing. He peered through the laden branches, pushed a paper lantern aside.

"Like old times?" Mai said.

"You and me?" Drake said. "I guess so. Very old times."

"Still strong and warm in my memory, Matt."

He paused for a second to stare at her. There had been no signs, no warning that she still felt that way. "Whoa, and you're telling me now. Right now."

Mai fired as a head popped up. "We're both soldiers. This is what we do. And well, it's almost Christmas. What better time could there be?"

With that, she sprang up as fresh as if this were her first day of conflict and dashed to the next tree. Drake ducked down as a bullet whistled past surprisingly close and then rose up, firing. A second later, he rejoined Mai.

"My feelings for you never changed," he told her. "Not once through all the years. But seriously, before we look at that, I have to finish all this." He paused.

"For Alyson?" Mai charged again, and now Drake ran with her, half a step behind. Terrorists were fleeing ahead of them, their colorful clothes easy targets, their cries better than homing beacons.

"Yes, for Alyson." Drake panted, firing and talking and scanning for prey. "And for Kennedy. This whole Odin thing is what dragged her in. It's how we met. I want it all behind me before I even try to move on."

"Fair enough." Mai hurdled a fallen terrorist, skipping off his back as he tried to rise, firing between her legs and into his body. "I'll still be here. . ." She shrugged as she landed like a cat. "For a short while."

They had come through the thick of the trees by now and were nearing the rear of the garden. Drake could spy the high stone wall between branches. With quickness born of years of warfare, he spied an enemy muzzle poking around a tree trunk, spun and fired, sending the muzzle flying and the man who held it straight to hell.

Terrorists milled around ahead, gathered at the foot of the wall, some already climbing the half dozen rope ladders that had been thrown over. Mai fell to one knee and started to pot them, like ducks in a shooting gallery, but Drake searched frantically for any signs of the objects they were pursuing.

No, he thought. *A false trail? No way. These people weren't that clever.* And Drake was pretty sure their own presence had come as a surprise to the terrorists. But still. . .

Then, with a thunderous sound that might spell the doom of the world, there came the roar of a powerful engine starting up. Drake knew it immediately for what it was. The getaway vehicle.

They were already escaping with the eight pieces!

"The wall!" he cried. "Hit the wall with everything you've got!"

Hayden and Kinimaka and the SAS team ran together and let loose a wall of lead. Terrorists crumpled to the ground where they stood. Those who tried to return fire died just as quick or were knocked aside by their falling comrades. Men fell backward from the walls, plummeting like empty sacks, crushing those beneath. Deadly chips of rock blasted back as bullets riddled the stonework, stitching ragged lines across the pitch-face blocks.

Drake didn't hesitate. He reached the base of the wall and flung himself at the nearest swinging ladder, grabbed a rung and started climbing. A terrorist climbed above him, just nearing the top of the wall. Drake quickly closed the gap and wrenched the man off the wall, hearing his scream as he cartwheeled through the air and crunched solidly against the ground.

He was vaguely aware of Mai on the rope next to him, keeping pace. He was also faintly surprised that he was in front of her, but then the roar of the terrorists' getaway vehicle and the sight from the top of the wall jolted all other emotion except terror from his body.

The vehicle, a dark colored van with what sounded like a performance engine, shot off down the darkened boulevard that backed on to the mansion. Within a second, it was turning at a junction, skidding a little, and then powering away along an unseen road.

A line of some half-dozen terrorists had been left behind and were pointing their weapons right at Drake and Mai on top of the wall.

Then they opened fire.

TWENTY-NINE

Drake leapt off the wall the instant he saw that the unpitying black eyes of six muzzles were fixed on him. By the time the terrorists opened fire, he was already in free fall. The bullets whizzed over the top of the wall, some catching its top ledge and sending fragments of stone showering down around him.

He let go of the gun. His questing hand reached for and caught the swinging rope ladder. He clutched at it, felt his palms burn, but seized it even harder. Abruptly his fall was arrested; his shoulder muscles complained and his back hurt as he swung into the wall. With a swift kick, he planted his feet on the springy rungs and safely climbed back down to the ground.

Hayden was in his face. "What happened?"

"Twats got away," Drake said. "The pieces are gone."

"And we have no one out there," Hayden hissed. "Because we're all in here! Shit!"

"The secretary, Gates, has been seeking out local assets for days," Kinimaka said. "So has Komodo. They have men prepared to fight. We need them now."

Sam looked at Drake. "The regiment has two teams within an hour's flight," he said.

"Put them on standby," Drake told him and started back toward the house. "Dahl also has plenty of local assets. But first of all, we need to find out where they're going and when they plan to make the sale. This kind of event would be bloody impossible to change."

"Right." Hayden kept pace with him as they tramped through the snow back through the trees to what used to be the Shadow Elite's mansion, now their crypt.

A strained silence surrounded the team as they trudged around the floodlit ice rink and approached the open French doors. The sense of foreboding was strong, as every man and woman imagined what a committed terrorist might do with a doomsday weapon.

Dahl met them at the door. "You failed? Trust a bloody Yorkshireman to fuck it all up."

Drake couldn't even muster the willpower for a retort. He pushed past the Swede and the Norseman, straight up to the still prone Holgate, who was being attended to by Komodo with Ben, Karin and Gates looking on.

"He still conscious?"

"Barely."

"Wake the twat up." Drake growled. "Don't care how. We only need him alive for a minute or two."

The Norseman immediately protested. "Excuse me! There is a lawful—"

Dahl's fist stopped the rest of his tirade. "You keep opening it, I'll keep filling it. No problem."

Within a minute, Holgate was squirming and protesting loudly. Drake nodded in satisfaction. "Good enough." He crouched until he could whisper in the man's ear. "Now, you live or die," he said. "And if you don't care, then we can make you die easy or die hard. It's our choice. You get it? For years, centuries, you people have written and played with the law.

Bended it to your whim. But now. . .*now* we are the law. There's nobody around to help you, Holgate."

Defeated eyes turned toward him. "Aldridge? Grey? Leng?"

"All dead." Drake didn't care. "And they suffered badly, Holgate. How do *you* want to die?"

"The Shadow Elite—" the Norseman began haughtily, but then started choking.

"There is no more Shadow Elite." Drake heard Alicia sigh. "Get it through your thick Viking skull."

Holgate must have heard it too, for tears formed in his eyes. "My fault." He whispered. "All my fault. I led the terrorists here. They were supposed to help me steal the pieces of Odin and transport them to the Czech Republic but, instead, they double-crossed me."

"Shocker," Drake murmured. "Tell me more."

"I was bankrupted, my assets dissolved. But the group would never accept that. It wasn't possible. It wasn't even *considered* possible. Our families have succeeded through even the darkest days of the last thousand years."

"And you bolloxed it all up," Drake said. "I get that. But I don't give a shit, see? What I want to know is where they're staging this bazaar, how many terrorists are involved, and when is it happening? Quickly now, Holgate, before I let my team take turns shooting bits off you."

"An old, deserted town in the Czech Republic. A ghost town. Tomorrow—three p.m. their time.

"And how many?"

Holgate shuddered as, for the first time, he stared Drake right in the eyes.

"Yes?"

"*All of them.*"

THIRTY

With the fight of their lives beckoning the very next day, it seemed only fitting they should spend this night, perhaps their last as a full team, relaxing together. Going up against so many at the same time made the possibility of them all surviving the battle slimmer than a razor's edge.

Belmonte chose a Vienna hotel he was accustomed to and rented out a dozen rooms all on the same floor. The thief was spending money like it didn't matter anymore, and maybe it was partly his way of atoning for Emma's death. Giving up that which he loved the most.

Or—*almost* loved the most.

One thing was clear. Belmonte had suffered a life-changing event and would never be the same. All his priorities had changed forever.

The Hotel Imperial stood in five-star luxury, lit up against the night like a golden treasure at the end of a dark, perilous path. The lobby was an opulent, inviting mix of the deepest colors, rich reds and gilded edges, dark oak frames and a bright, shining chandelier above it all. To the right of the domed revolving door stood a tall, sparkling Christmas tree, adorned with splendid trimmings and sparkling lights. Large, beautifully wrapped presents sat all around its base.

"Oh, how the other half live," Alicia said, stopping and

looking around. Even the snappy Englishwoman pulled her coat tighter to hide her shabby clothes. Whilst Belmonte paid, the rest of the team hung around the lobby, staring at the hotel's well-to-do occupants wheeling hand luggage around and chatting amongst themselves. After a while the master thief signaled them and they climbed a great red-carpeted stairway lined by heavy oak paneling, overseen by another outsized chandelier. At the top they were faced with marble pillars and a warmly backlit statue, above which hung an old, expensive-looking painting.

"This way." Belmonte took off, picking his way down another plushly appointed corridor before stopping and waving his arm. "Down there. Three-oh-five to three-sixteen. Take your pick."

"Just one thing." Alicia wasn't ever one to express her thanks the right way. "My room had better have a pair of those fancy friggin' slippers and a bathrobe."

Belmonte slid his entry card into the lock. "I thought you'd be more interested in the complimentary massage service."

Alicia's eyes widened. "Damn right."

The group began to drift off, looking to chill out for the first time in what seemed, to Drake at least, months. He chose a room, shouted, "Lobby in thirty for anyone who cares," and entered his room alone.

Put his back to the door and closed his eyes.

It was said that when loved ones died, they went up to heaven as angels, there to watch over you. He sent up a silent prayer.

Only trouble was—he didn't know whether he wanted to live or die.

*****

Karin practically dragged Komodo into her room, saving the prim and pedantic image for someone who actually gave a shit. Within seconds, the two were naked and stepping into the hot, powerful shower. Within fifteen minutes, they were still naked, but now under the thick, luxuriant bed covers halfway through round two. Before they finished Karin turned the tables on the big American, straddling him, and shouted, "Jesus Christ you had better find a way not to leave me this time!" before he flipped her over again and put his mouth close to her ear.

"Whatever it takes."

*****

Hayden beckoned Ben into her room as the young man paused awkwardly in the corridor, an unsure expression plastered on his face. When he got her approval, his face lit up. He pushed past her, confidence restored.

"Bloody hell! I know it's only been a few days but it feels like months since we were alone together."

Hayden walked over to the window that was literally surrounded by thick drapes. She pushed aside the net curtain. Outside, she saw a busy pavement and a street choked with traffic. *Nothing changed,* she thought. It might as well be L.A. or Washington D.C. Didn't matter where you were. The architecture might be smarter, the trees older, but the song always remained the same.

"I can't believe we missed the Wall of Sleep's first gig," Ben was saying disconsolately. "Remember? The Festival of

Storms in Leeds. Pretty Reckless and Evanescence. And, of course, the Wall—"

"Stop," Hayden said quietly.

Ben didn't hear. "But I guess I really *rocked* it by finding that tomb underneath Singen, eh?"

Hayden turned her thoughts back through the last few months to the time she had first met Ben and Drake in Washington DC, and had been drawn to the young man's enthusiasm, his intelligence and wit. She had seen the man who was inside. She had felt some kind of urge to bring him out. She had taken on the challenge. . .and felt that she owed him now.

Her mind's eye flicked over Mano Kinimaka, sitting alone in a room down the hall, the ever-present guard at her side, and how he somehow seemed to be on her mind more and more of late. But that was his job—to protect her. It was the care and worry in his eyes that confused her.

She turned back to the room, back to Ben. In his boyish way, he was still appealing. She took a moment to dry swallow twice the amount of painkillers she had been prescribed. The wound in her side throbbed almost as hard as the wound in her heart. The knives that stabbed her seemed like a physical extension of her state of mind.

She was wounded, both physically and mentally.

She sat down on the bed next to Ben, careful not to touch him, but remaining close. Now was not the time for drama.

Tomorrow it might not even matter.

*****

Alicia spent a few minutes in the shower. The water hit her

hard and fast, almost like a soothing massage in itself, but she was not one to dwell on luxuries. She quickly stepped out, toweled off, dried and redressed, took a few solitary minutes to stare at her hotel room and then headed down to the bar. Life was too short to spend it alone, staring at four walls and an empty bed.

The first drink she ordered was a Jack and coke. By the time she was staring at her fourth, a large figure had thudded down into the seat next to her.

"Mano Kinimaka." She eyed him speculatively. "You really are one big bastard, you know that?"

"You heard of the big Kahuna? My mom used to call me the fucking huge Kahuna."

Alicia laughed. "Looking to get shitfaced?"

"Looking for. . .distraction."

"Oh yeah? What you got in mind?"

"Let's get one thing straight from the outset, Myles, you stand no chance with me."

Alicia threw him a little pout. "Her wounds go deeper than the length of a knife blade, mate. She's damaged, that one."

"We're all damaged. You should know. And I really don't know who you're talking about."

"Of course you don't." Alicia slammed the remainder of her glass back in one go. "Maybe we should ask Belmonte. He knows her quite well, or so I'm told."

"Fuck off." Kinimaka half-rose from his chair.

Alicia put a hand on his arm. "Stay. Please." When Kinimaka reluctantly reclaimed his seat, she went on. "I'm an abhorrent bitch. I get that. I don't hold back."

"I can't see why Drake keeps you around to be honest."

"Drake? Well, because he knows exactly what he's getting,

see? These other people—Mai, Gates, even Dahl—they all have their own self-righteous agendas. I mean, look at Mai exchanging that device for her sister. But with me—" She ran the back of her hand from her head down her body to her toes. "What you see is what you get. And what I think is exactly what I will tell you. No secrets, no schemes."

Kinimaka asked the bartender to leave the bottle. He placed it carefully between them. "Hayden's my boss. There can be nothing between us."

"Bollocks. Things change all the time. I've shagged most of my bosses."

Kinimaka shook his head, but couldn't stop the laughter. After a moment he was shaking and snorting. He held up a neat shot, clinked Alicia's glass and downed it in one.

The bartender thoughtfully brought over another bottle.

*****

Torsten Dahl prowled the room that seemed to have become a temporary command center. The SAS boys were talking quietly among themselves at the same time as guarding the Norseman, and Jonathan Gates picked his way delicately through the less trustworthy until he finally reached men he could put faith in on the phone.

Commanders. Generals. Old-school leaders. The stalwart captains of unknown crews, men who did not seek glory but earned it every day. The law of misfortune would not put many of their available men within a day's journey of the Czech Republic, but he was betting anyone lunch at the White House that he'd bag more than a few.

It was too early to start examining who was and who

wasn't part of the Shadow Elite's conspiracy ring. Their limited resources were best employed now in regaining the eight pieces of Odin.

Sam, the leader of the SAS team, had contacted two more teams in Europe, both of whom were willing to make the trip.

Now Dahl paced back and forth, calling in every favor that he'd ever earned in his considerable career. His *Statsminister* was doing the same. Sweden was relatively close to the Czech Republic by plane.

At last, Dahl closed his phone. "Tomorrow," he announced to the room, "we will have a small army."

"The Czechs might not be too happy at the sight of all these foreign soldiers invading their soil," the Norseman barked at him from his small corner of the room.

"Then they shouldn't allow terrorists to host arms bazaars in their country, should they?"

Dahl paused for a moment. His eyes took on a faraway glaze and the makings of a brief smile formed on his lips. He calculated the time back in his homeland. He inspected the room and its security one more time.

A moment, he thought. *Just a moment.* On this night of all nights, he deserved it.

He stepped out into the corridor, found the stairwell and sat down on the top step. Quickly he dialed a number. To his right a big rectangular window looked out over a benighted street where fairy lights glittered like wishes.

The phone was answered immediately. A woman's voice. "Hallå?"

"It's me."

"Torsten. Oh, it's good to hear your voice. Are you coming home?"

She sounded so hopeful, so sure. Dahl kept his voice neutral. "Not yet."

But she was his wife, his life-companion, and he could never keep anything from her. "You come home," she said. "You don't do this. Do you hear?"

Dahl was silent for a moment. His wife knew him better than that. "Are they still awake? Are they there?" He kept his voice soft to keep it from breaking.

The other phone clunked down. After another second he heard a dual squeal, the slapping of bare feet at full pace, and then his two young kids were on the line, tripping over their own words in their eagerness to speak.

He let them talk, drinking in the wonder of them, basking in the delight they took from life and wishing it could always be that way. Childhood flew past in a moment, and each moment he spent sharing it with them left him wanting more. But at the same time, he wanted to protect them with an unquenchable fierceness, in a way they would never hear about. A child sees through the eyes of his parents, so let those eyes be full of pride and happiness, not sorrow or regret or anger.

He sat there, a great soldier with eyes full of tears, and listened to the sound of his children being happy.

*****

Karin climbed out of bed, slipping into a luxurious bathrobe as she padded over to the window. "I've never felt particularly special," she said, not looking at Komodo. "But even when I remember the darkness of my past, I feel beautiful with you."

Komodo knew her now, knew about the shattering event in her childhood that had shaped her as an adult. "You lost your faith," he said. "You nurtured the loss. You'll never have to do that again."

Karin turned quickly, arching an eyebrow. "What are you, Trevor? A shrink or a guru?"

He jumped off the bed and hugged her. "A little of both."

Karin held him tight, staring sightlessly over his shoulder. "And what about tomorrow?"

She felt him shrug. "To part-quote an episode of Buffy, 'Tomorrow, we save the world. Again.'"

"And then?"

"We'll save each other. I'll prove to you that people beyond family can be trusted. You'll think of a way to keep me in bed."

"To keep you with *me*. Somehow."

"Yes. But for now—" He gently disengaged from her and began searching for his cell phone. "I have an army to help build."

One by one he began to search out contact details for his closest comrades.

*****

Alicia didn't hesitate when Belmonte showed his face in the bar. She invited him to join them, and together Kinimaka, the thief and she drank too much, talked too much and stared down the hooded stares of would-be elitists. Alicia coaxed them both out of their shells—Kinimaka over Hayden and Belmonte over Emma. The Hawaiian was dithering, waiting for the right time with his boss—a time that would never come. Belmonte had indeed nurtured and trained Emma to be his shadow and his replacement, but somewhere along the wild path of her tutoring had fallen completely for her sharp wit, her beauty and her fearlessness. He was lost without her.

"An angel with skills, balls and a bloody face." He described her, and Alicia found herself wishing she'd seen more of the thief's assistant. Maybe they could've been friends.

Alicia confessed her need for companionship. She couldn't stand to be alone with her own thoughts. The night terrors overwhelmed her.

Into a dark corner they finally retired, still drinking and talking nonsense, becoming more than colleagues, chatting away the night and any fears it might hold, chasing the dawn towards the new day, comrades in arms and minds.

As one, they were fearless.

*****

Matt Drake watched as the Vienna skyline started to lighten. Dawn was approaching fast—the start of a brand new day that might very well end with the world being a terrifyingly different place.

"Every civilized government in the world should be involved in this," he said, unable to hide his frustration. "But because this bloody Shadow Elite's got their claws into everyone, we can't call on *anyone*. When I was in the regiment, Mai, it seemed a whole lot easier."

"You were a pawn, a robot programmed to follow orders. Now you're a man fighting against the raging machine. It's a harder fight."

"I need sleep." He moved away from the window.

Mai watched him from where she had spent the night, curled across a plush armchair. "Like me, Matt, you'll sleep when you're dead."

That raised a tired smile. "Bon Jovi? I forget sometimes that it was you and I who invented Dinorock."

"And like you and I and the dinosaurs, it appears to be dying out. Everything these days is Gangnam Style."

Another smile. "We won't die today. None of us will. We'll take their armies out and tear the eight pieces from their broken fingers. And we'll do it *Yorkshire* style."

"Or in Alicia's case— *doggy—*"

"Woah. This feud between you two? It has to stop. After a while it tends to grate. We three actually work well together."

Mai shrugged. "Maybe. But however you look at today, it's almost over anyway. We've already neutralized the Shadow Elite. Once the eight pieces are safe, all this ends and those of us who survive...will have some tranquility."

Drake looked at her for a long time, realizing the truth of her words. Ever since he had started the search for the bones of Odin, his life had been like traveling on a hellish rollercoaster, designed by the devil and crewed by his demons. To think, in another day or two it would be all over.

The eight pieces secure. The Shadow Elite gone. Wells out of the picture. The Blood King behind bars that would never officially exist.

That would leave one thing—an assassin called *Coyote*.

But first things first.

"About time we started our charge," he said.

THIRTY-ONE

The quad-engine Boeing C17 Globemaster cargo plane touched down hard and taxied roughly along a patched and potholed runway in a remote corner of the Western Czech Republic. The transport had landed as close to the bazaar's staging area as possible to avoid arousing suspicion, but the soldiers still faced an hour's march at a brisk pace to reach the target area in time.

Dahl and Gates between them had managed to secure the big plane—currently tied to a commercial and civilian release at Vienna International Airport. The money they and their governments offered ensured a swift and quality response from its operators.

In total, about sixty people had made the flight, the majority of them army personnel. Nowhere near as many as Drake wanted, but significantly more than he'd had yesterday. Among them were eleven members of the SAS, a group of Delta soldiers, members of Torsten Dahl's SSG, and a few old friends Gates had somehow dragged in.

The men had been pulled from various operations. Some were on special exercise, others babysitting civilians. One knot had been guarding a company of scientists conducting experiments. Still others had been stuck on extended surveillance posts.

They responded immediately to the desperate call of the men they respected most.

But they still needed a leader. Most had looked to Dahl. But Dahl had looked to Drake.

The Englishman struggled to hide his shock. "Pull the other one, you fruitcake."

"This is your operation, Drake. Always has been."

Not even a second passed before he started talking. The plan lived and breathed inside him anyway, as it did for every mission, always evolving. By the time he had finished, the team wore looks of satisfaction, even if they all did still seem a little worried.

Drake counted himself lucky. The downside to this mission was enormous. They didn't have an aerial view of the topography. They didn't know how many men they were up against. They didn't know exactly where the pieces would be kept. They didn't know the firepower of the enemy. A terrorist was an unknown quantity on a good day, but this. . .the list went on.

But Drake had been winging this since he started back in York, when an Apache helicopter had interrupted a catwalk show. Now it seemed an age ago, but in fact, was a mere few months. He was more than ready to finish with Odin and his bloody bones.

The plane taxied to a halt, bouncing hard. The instant it stopped, a green light came on and the rear loading bay door started to descend. Men ran out into the cold air, moving fast to secure a temporary perimeter. The team leaders checked their compasses to get a bearing. Drake followed Mai and Alicia off the plane, followed by the rest of his team, including all the civilians. They were coming along; every hand would be welcome and needed today.

The icy air hit Drake in the face. Quickly, he tugged his jacket higher, checked his small pack and weapons, and watched as everyone else did the same. Gates and Hayden had secured arms and ammo from a CIA facility at Vienna airport along with some essential extra items—grenades, RPGs, Kevlar vests, communications, water and even some pouches of rations.

Hayden put herself beside Drake as they headed out. "You know I'm really in charge, right?"

Drake saw a half-smile on the American's face. "Oh aye. How's the side?"

"Fuckin' A. If I'd swallowed any more painkillers, I'd be seeing Santa and his fuckin' reindeers arriving behind us."

"Might come in as useful backup." Alicia put in from behind them "Still probably best not to get stabbed again this time."

Drake led them up a steep, grassy slope to the outskirts of a small wood. "Through here for the cover," he said and clicked his mic. "All clear?"

The answer came back, loud with excess static.

"Good," he said. "Let's march."

*****

The teams separated a little as they marched through the dappled forest, each group sticking to their own. It took extraordinary circumstances and even more extraordinary men to bring rival squads like this together and Drake was glad those men were on his side. The circumstances he wasn't too happy with. He cast a quick glance back to assure himself of the Norseman's position, being escorted by two SAS guards. Though the old man had been genuinely shocked at

Holgate's betrayal and his secret group's massacre, he'd still be trying to scheme a way out of this.

They trudged for a while, staying sharp. Drake found his thoughts turning inward. Responsibility for his friends and the team weighed heavy across his shoulders, but no terrorist could ever be allowed to own such a terrible weapon as the one devised by Odin and his equals. To think that the quest for the tombs, the crazy chase after the Blood King, the search for Wells's secrets, had all led him to this- trekking through the bitingly cold and remote Czech countryside with the dark shadows of mountains far ahead being nothing less than the environs of Transylvania.

The com chirped in his ear. He pressed the chest mic. "Yes?"

"Beyond the wood the ground starts to rise," a discordant voice reported. "There are dwellings at the top of the hill."

"The village?"

"If the coordinates are right—yes."

"They're right." Drake thought of Holgate's terror at the end. "Are the houses tightly packed together?"

"Yup. And the village appears to be deserted."

"Good. Wait for us."

The view from the outskirts of the wood struck Drake with a sense of lost hope and desolation. Yellowed, dead grass carpeted the minor hill. Around its potholed summit stood haphazard structures, dilapidated and ruined, with chunks missing from their walls as if a great Transylvanian monster had rampaged through, destroying everything in sight.

And it had, of course. The civilians—the women, the children—were long gone to some unknown fate. The evil men who had wiped out their town had left their mark and simply moved on to the next without even a look back. Men like these would never show remorse.

Drake thought about the kind of men now gathering beyond the rise. Fanatics yes, but worse than that—well-organized fanatics with deep pockets. He clicked his mic. "Move out."

The team moved, at first like a newly made machine that needed oiling and grinding into shape, but these men were the ultimate professionals, and immediately began to adjust to each other. The lead SAS team topped the rise first. Drake saw one of them suddenly lash out, and as he ventured higher saw a lone terrorist fall, his neck broken. The team melted between the buildings. Drake, Mai, Alicia, Dahl and the two CIA agents made up the middle group with the civilians—Ben, Karin, Gates and Belmonte bringing up the rear, now with Komodo and a two-man Delta team as guards.

Drake reached the grassy summit and pressed himself hard against a cold, concrete wall. Its edges were sharp where a grenade had blasted it, its surface pockmarked where bullets had raked it many years before. Whilst he paused, he listened. The sound of men came from somewhere ahead, not near, but conversation and laughter buzzed along with the trembling wind.

Mai tapped his shoulder. "Up." She knotted her hands. Drake used them as a step and waited for her boost. When it came, he propelled his body up and over the edge of the flat roof, landing horizontal and staying absolutely still for a minute. The same thing was happening on houses to left and right and in front. Tiny bits of grit and sharp gravel cut into his hands and scraped a low but harsh protest as he crept cautiously forward, head so low his nose was less than an inch from being cut to ribbons.

He reached the edge of the roof, facing west, and raised his head cautiously above the concrete lip. Immediately below he saw another SAS trooper take out a second wandering guard. The terrorists' perimeter was thin here, but it wouldn't be long before someone made a noise that carried too far.

Ahead, beyond the houses, the ground sloped down to what would have been the center of the village. A paved plaza had been built there, once a meeting place for the villagers, now a market square for extremists. Drake took time to raise a pair of compact Steiner Rangefinder binoculars and not only study their gathered enemy, but also to use the inbuilt laser to accurately distance the various elements he could see.

Several knots of men stood in conversation or wandered around the square. They seemed to be milling around a dozen different spheres of interest. Drake refocused and, between bodies, recognized some stacked crates that bore the imprint *DBA Kinetics* and another that read, simply *Kord*.

They were high-end machine gun companies. Countless crates stuffed to the hilt. Enough weaponry to start and finish a small war.

A small adjustment and he was looking at a consignment of *Vektor* Grenade Launchers. Still another and there was a huge fuss around a pile of anti-aircraft missiles. Each stall was numbered. Drake let the binoculars drift a bit, taking in the view beyond the plaza. The ground sloped away towards the flat plains. A wide, tarmacked road cut an ugly path down to the terrorists' staging area.

Here, Drake saw numerous choppers under heavy guard, several trucks and large drums of what he thought might be oil. Other vehicles—some high-end cars, a military Humvee. And a sizeable tent, more than likely the auction area.

He saw no sign of the eight pieces of Odin. Surely, they had to be in the tent. But, truth be told, he didn't know. And the large mass of men assembled down that slope and among the choppers beyond daunted even him.

Several rows of large containers lined the summit to his right, just where the houses ended. Since the terrorists couldn't have brought the containers with them, he deduced that they must have something to do with the old village, or with whoever moved in afterward and then vanished.

Slowly, he shuffled back and slid down to the ground. Dahl, Hayden and Sam came up to him. "Not good," Hayden reported, her voice higher than usual probably due to the painkillers. "The plaza is not heavily guarded, but the way beyond—that's just batshit crazy."

"More than a hundred," Dahl agreed. "And surprisingly sensible. It's their escape route and the site of the auction. The leaders will be conducting their deals in private on the plaza. Nobody wants a talkative guard eavesdropping on their dealings now, do they?"

Sam looked worried. "Matt, even our team would have trouble getting near that tent."

"Let's look at it another way." Drake shrugged. "The bastards will be over-confident, smug and proud, as terrorist leaders often are. That's our advantage."

"It may be," Dahl said. "But none of that helps us sneak past over a hundred well-placed guards."

Drake met the Swede's eyes. "Who said anything about sneaking?"

It was a moment before Dahl caught on. "Fucking hell, you've got massive balls, mate, I'll give you that."

"Scarily big," Drake agreed.

"Wait, hoaloha." Kinimaka forgot himself in his surprise. "You mean to attack them. *Them?*" He waved a hand in the tent's general direction.

"Not strictly attack," Drake said gently. "More like *storm.*"

"Are you tripping cos you're not getting your daily diet of fish and chips or something?" Kinimaka blustered. "We can't—"

Hayden moved close to Kinimaka and stopped him with a tender hand placed on the shoulder. The Hawaiian almost jumped out of his skin and turned, wide-eyed, to stare at his boss.

"It's alright, Mano," she said quietly. "You should listen to him. He's our leader."

Drake squatted with his back to the wall and looked up, immensely moved to see all the people who he regarded as his "team" gathered round at this last moment. Mai and Alicia sat beside him. Hayden and Kinimaka dropped to their knees to listen. Ben and Karin and the haunted Belmonte had crept to his other side. Komodo—the soldier who had gamely chased down the Blood King with him—sat with Karin. Jonathan Gates stood behind Komodo, grim determination radiating from posture, his face and his eyes.

And Torsten Dahl, the mad Swede, gazed at him with something like utter respect, love and unreserved faith, a hard-earned quality in any man of combat, let alone one as capable as Dahl.

Drake held up an imaginary glass. "We could go home this minute," he said. "The terrorists won't care. The world would never know. Or we could hang around and not back down. Raise a glass to freedom and stuff our way of life down these bastard's throats. We've stuck it out this far together. . ."

Drake met every eye, every concerned flicker. "When our dreams die. . ." He pictured Alyson and Kennedy, but most of all he saw the person he had most wanted to know, but had never known. The person who had lived but never known life—his unborn baby, Emily. "We want to die. Or drink. We realize there are worse things than hell. But I'm still here—and I'm around to tell you this—the last few months have more than hurt us, they've kicked us hard in the bollocks, but they brought us *here*. Together. Right now, with that doomsday weapon less than a mile away." He stood up, hefting his rifle. "So let's go show these terrorist clowns what the term *balls to the wall* really means."

PART 4

DRAKE'S LAST STAND

'...and into the valley of death rode the six hundred...'

'Cannon to right of them,
Cannon to left of them,
Cannon behind them
Volley'd and thunder'd;
Storm'd at with shot and shell,
While horse and hero fell,
They that had fought so well
Came thro' the jaws of Death,
Back from the mouth of Hell,
All that was left of them.'

An excerpt from: 'THE CHARGE OF THE LIGHT BRIGADE' by Alfred Tennyson.

THIRTY-TWO

Among the deserted houses the team crept, just waiting for that moment—the step that proved to be the one too far. It came quickly. They managed to quietly dispatch another three of the terrorists' perimeter guards before it happened, but the fourth's finger squeezed reflexively on the trigger as he died.

Shots rang out, horrendously loud among the grim concrete walls. In that moment every man and woman sprang to life. Guns up, the teams darted between the buildings, spreading out to ensure nobody flanked them. Gunshots rang out as more terrorist guards began to converge. Drake saw a bobbing figure up ahead, fired, and blew a corner of the wall away in a hard, sharp spray. One of the SAS teams had climbed to the rooftops and were keeping pace up there. Every corner posed a new problem, every turn of the street threw shadows and potential hiding places in their faces.

Drake advanced steadily, Mai and Alicia—the two people he would most want at his side in this situation—keeping pace. Every few seconds, more shots rang out. He could only imagine the panic in the plaza, the arms being packed away and the choppers being warmed up. With a quick jab he keyed his chest mic. "Make sure the Norseman's kept handy. If anyone knows who has the pieces, it's him."

The chance was slim, he knew, but they couldn't afford to miss even the slimmest opportunity here today.

"I miss this," Alicia said happily at his side. "Late nights, days of battle and rough sex. My kind of living." She opened fire as a man peered around a corner ahead, blowing a small part of his head away.

More streets, and the attackers spread out even more until their line grew dangerously thin. Drake saw the final few houses ahead where the ground sloped away towards the plaza and hurried forward.

His mic buzzed. *"Problem."*

"What?"

But then he reached the summit of the hill himself and flashed a glance down. A large amount of terrorist guards and what looked like hired mercenaries were running toward them, staying low and firing in sequence so that never a second passed without a bullet in flight. A well-organized force.

Drake cast quickly about. The containers were a few hundred yards to their right, offering advancement and cover. He keyed the mic. "Move right."

They side-stepped quickly, backs to the houses, firing tenaciously and throwing dozens of grenades. Bullets flashed in both directions, hammering against the house walls like thunder, showering those around with mortar, digging up dirt around the advancing terrorists, spinning some around and sending others hurtling back down the bloody slope. Explosions tore up rock and soil, flesh and bone. A desperate melee of death and destruction saw Drake's whole team dodging to the right and digging into positions among the high, steel containers. Drake threw himself to the hard earth, kicking up dust and stones, wasting no time as he sighted on those below and blasted out another barrage of lead.

Then the attackers crested the hill, still firing, and were suddenly among them. Drake fired twice, still prone, taking two men out, then rose and met a head-on assault. He smashed the butt of his rifle into the man's teeth, felt a spray of blood, lifted the weapon and brought it hard down on the top of his head. The man fell to his knees. Drake drew the knife with his other hand and finished it. Another man flung himself at the Englishman. Drake simply stood, unbendable, and met the man's flight with a powerful head-butt to the face. Without sound or movement, his attacker collapsed in a heap.

Gunfire, grunting and screaming, shouts of mercy and cries of bloodlust pierced the day. Mai took a surprise elbow to the face and stumbled back against a metal siding, weapon falling. Drake was almost too stunned to react, to help her, but before he could even move, Alicia drew her pistol, spun and shot the adversary in the time it took him to draw a single breath.

Mai blinked at her. "Thanks."

Alicia just winked before turning her attention back to the man she had by the throat.

Drake shook his head. "This is all just a delay tactic." He could see beyond the edge now, down into the plaza. The terrorist leaders were just finishing up their business as if it were a steady day at the local meat market. They didn't hurry. Barely a single one cast even a glance up the hill to the place where men fought and died on their behalf.

"Damn their arrogance," he whispered furiously. "But it'll cost them."

As the onslaught began to thin out, Drake advanced. He took a quick look around, taking stock. He couldn't see everyone, but saw no fatalities on their side.

"To me," he said into the mic. "To the plaza."

Men emerged from between the containers, weapons ready, steadfastly determined to make the next advance. With high and constant vigilance, they swept down the hill, shooting everything that moved ahead. Now, to Drake's satisfaction, the terrorist leaders and arms dealers were fleeing with abandon, leaving personal bodyguards and crates and boxes of armaments and missiles in their wake.

Beyond the plaza he saw choppers with rotors already whirling and many of the terrorist's security personnel digging into strategic positions. Some of the weapons he saw being readied were more than daunting. The huge tent sat serene, its sides flapping in the breeze, an oasis of calm amidst the storm.

To Drake's left, Hayden appeared in his sight, bounding alongside with the ever-present Kinimaka watching her back. The Hawaiian seemed even more concerned than usual with keeping his boss safe. Probably due to the painkillers, Hayden would be thinking she was invincible. Drake fired at movement ahead, wishing he felt the same way. More gunfire and a stray shot slammed into a box of missiles, sending the lot up in a humongous explosion that rivaled the best New Years Eve firework display.

But these were deadly missiles, exploding fragments and small, deadly warheads. Drake and his team, to a man, threw themselves headlong into the dirt and kept their heads down. When he looked up, Drake saw a fireball whooshing to the sky. Trails of thick, black smoke streamed all around it. He scrambled up. Members of the enemy force, twisted hunks of metal and smoldering timbers now littered the plaza.

Drake advanced onto the square, roughly paved surface, cracking off a shot every now and then when something

The Tomb of the Gods

moved. A man ran at him from behind a fiery hunk of destroyed timbers, but Dahl was quick to meet and stop him dead in his tracks. Literally.

The team hiked across the square, surrounded by flames and destruction, sweeping for any signs of life or enemy snipers. Dahl found an untouched box of RPG launchers and their missiles, which he quickly doled out. Drake saw Ben and Karin and Gates now running down the hill behind them. Belmonte, to his surprise, was already part of the attack team, holding a light machine pistol and a handgun.

So far so good. He wondered again about the eight pieces and experienced a surge of fear. *What if Holgate lied even under extreme regret and duress? What if the pieces were already gone or even on their way to Singen by now?*

God help them all.

Then he crested the final rise and got a first real look at the valley below. *A valley of death,* he thought. On the flatlands, more than a dozen choppers were waiting or being boarded. One lifted off as he watched. The slope down into the valley was heavily covered on both sides of the road by small knots of men holding every weapon imaginable.

They were dug in, and they were waiting, knowing that if Drake's team wanted to advance any more, they'd have to go past them.

Drake's entire team lined up in a staggered formation, two deep along the rim of the valley. At that moment, the big tent's door-flaps were pushed back and out came a small troop of rugged men all wearing *thawbs* — or robes — and *Keffiyeh* — headdress. Behind them came soldiers carrying machine guns, dressed in jeans and jackets and behind *them* came a final group—a scurrying band of European men—probably mercenaries—hefting all eight pieces of Odin between them.

The sale had been completed. The choppers were already warmed up and itching to fly.

Drake saw no other way. He looked across at Dahl and Sam and their men, and thought of the future of their world, of their children, nothing else. *For our children,* he thought. "For our future!" he cried aloud.

The charge was on.

*****

Hard down the grueling slope they flew, feet tugged at by bloodied clumps of dead grass, guns tight against their shoulders, meeting bullet with bullet, battle cry with war cry. And death filled the air. Choppers rose ahead like black birds of prey only to be blown out of the sky by expertly aimed RPG launchers. Fire rained down from the skies. A creeping column of explosions and a deadly wall of lead marched before and among the sixty, the unsung heroes, men eaten by fear but forging ahead despite it all. And even as they fell, they kept firing, even as their dying bodies hit the ground they threw a last grenade or took another bullet for those who still lived and still ran headlong into the face of death.

All across the hill, they were ranged, sweeping down toward the guns. Not one among them wavered, but fought fire with fire and stormed through the deadly onslaught like a wave surging across a reef.

Drake felt more than one bullet sear past his face. A great fiery explosion lit up the hill before him, but he forged through it. Something nicked his ear, probably shrapnel, but he barely felt it. Every stride brought the enemy within reach. Every stride brought the pieces of Odin closer to safety. With precise fire and expert magazine changes, he pounded round after round into their assailants. Bullets, grenades and rockets fired high into the air as men cartwheeled backward, struck at the very moment they pressed their triggers. At one point, a chopper smashed down into the very heart of the terrorists' defense, bursting apart on impact and blasting metal shards, men and terrible tongues of fire outward in a horrific display of absolute mayhem.

That same blast destroyed more enemy fortifications from the rear. Drake's team fell among them, up for blood and battle, offering no quarter. Drake jumped over a high mound, landing amidst a tangle of men and fired three times, three directions, into the chests of his enemy. They fell back with heavy thuds. Mai landed beside him. Belmonte came down on the other side. The thief shot at a masked man emerging from the smoke downslope. Drake lifted his head.

"Keep going." He keyed his mic. "We have the momentum. Don't stop now!"

But at that moment, there was the horrendous sound of heavy gunfire, the kind of sound made by a big caliber weapon that seems to shoot right up from the bowels of hell. They hit the deck as gigantic chunks of earth blasted into the air, chewed up by the huge shells.

"Fuck me!" Mai yelled. "What is *that?*"

"Some kind of heavy machine gun," Drake shouted back. "Bollocks! They have our position. We're pinned."

"No time!" Mai cried, but at that moment the big gun coughed again and a shell exploded beside her, sending her body slamming across the shallow depression.

"*Mai!*" Drake screamed.

Belmonte scrambled over to her. Suddenly a shadow blocked out the sun and Drake looked up to see four enemy soldiers leaping towards him.

The big gun had been used as distraction.

Now Drake, alone, rolled and came up to his knees, blasting one of the men away. But the others were in too close. One knocked his gun away. Another reached for his throat, but too slow. Drake gripped the arm and twisted it down, breaking it at the elbow, then slammed it back up so that the man's body smashed into one of his brethren. Another came at him from the side. Drake fell back, watched an arm holding a wicked knife scythe through the air a millimeter above his nose, and rolled into the body and around until he was behind the man. Then he drew his own blade and buried it into the nape of his neck.

A bullet slammed through the gap between his legs. He looked up. A truly enormous soldier stood before him, grinning, weapon steady, the blood of good men already dripping from his face.

Drake had no way out. He felt a second of regret. . .

. . .the gun fired, but shot wide. An SAS soldier had launched a desperate attack, hitting the giant around the waist. The soldier bounced off. The giant, seven feet of bulging muscle and pure fury, didn't even wobble. He simply re-aimed the gun and ended the other man's life. But now Drake was up and Mai was shaking her head, instantly alert, and diving in from the other side.

Drake struck from the front, three punches and a kick in lightning time. The giant took them all without flinching as he concentrated on Mai, recoiling from her deadly strikes but batting them aside anyway.

Drake struck again. "You'll feel this, you bastard!"

The giant grunted. "I fink you need bigger hands, small man." He kicked Drake in the chest with the force of an elephant, sending him flying back, stunned and winded. Mai dove in again, breaking her enemy's arm but, still dazed, found herself being crushed at the giant's feet.

Then a brief respite came as he stared in confusion at his dangling arm. "It's no bovver." He growled, not even wincing as he prodded the jagged bone back through torn flesh. "I'll mend later."

The enormous man still held a pistol in one oversized hand. His cackle of madness and delight stung even the death-laden afternoon air with frenzied malice.

For the second time in as many minutes, Drake faced death down the sights of a barrel. With no hope he struggled to thrust his body upright. But the giant fired immediately. No speech, no more chatter, just a spark of ignition lighting his eyes firing the thought that he could finish up here and lumber over to his next target.

With the quickness of a bullet, a shadow dove between Drake and Mai and instant death. Then the shattered body of Daniel Belmonte landed beside them, bleeding badly where the neck met the collarbone, eyes hopeful.

"Did I save the day?"

Still running on adrenalin. . . he didn't know quite yet that his wound was fatal.

But the giant just shook his big, shaggy head and raised his gun again. Belmonte noticed and then, against all odds, pushed himself up and grabbed the big man in a hug. Bullets punched through Belmonte's frame, jerking the body terribly with every impact. As Drake watched, he saw the thief's last act in this life—to bring his arm around and bury the knife he had taken from Drake right through the giant's thick neck.

Both men fell in a heap. It still took both Drake and Mai nearly a minute to stand. They both heard Belmonte's final words, no more than a whisper of breath. "Now I will meet her again."

By then the battle had moved on. Drake and Mai checked their wounds, scooped up lost weapons, and continued with a nod to Belmonte's already cooling body.

*****

Hayden obliterated an enemy defense post with Kinimaka, Dahl and several of his Swedish compatriots before looking ahead. Toward the bottom of the slope, the men escaping with the eight pieces had cleared the tent and were heading for an area crowded with helicopters. Hayden cast about. Smoke and fire fogged the area around them. She couldn't rely on anyone else coming to help, so she set off at a run, now starting to feel the return of fire in her side as the painkillers wore off.

"Let me take the lead," Kinimaka urged.

But now wasn't the time to worry about that. Kinimaka had her side, as he always did, and Dahl paced her too. She picked her way down the rest of the slope, stopping briefly as they encountered stiff opposition from behind several stacked barrels ahead. Dahl fired his RPG at the barrels and the opposition went up in flames. Then, with a regretful shake of the head, he threw the weapon away, out of grenades.

Their clothes were torn, their flesh bloody, and their faces set hard with determination and the loss of colleagues along the way, but Hayden and her small contingent forged onward, finally reaching the flat of the valley and facing the field of choppers. The enemy had dug in and some were already shooting.

"See there," Dahl shouted. He pointed out the large group trying to spirit away the pieces. "Hurry. We have no time."

*****

The Norseman welcomed the drifting, cloying smoke with its thick stench of spilled blood and death. When the SAS team that guarded him met harsh opposition and fought hard to survive, he managed to crawl and slither his way through the muck and the mud, a venomous snake slipping through slime, until he managed to outflank the battle. Then, still staying low, he slunk to the base of the hill. Along the way, he even managed to collect a discarded weapon, a fully loaded machine-pistol, which brought a thin smile to those bloodless, melancholy lips. Fortune always landed on the side of the privileged, and none were more privileged than he. He glanced back up the hill and saw the thief, Belmonte, dying. He turned away without a flicker of concern. The pieces of Odin were still within reach, and although the plan had changed, there was still a plan.

The only plan that guaranteed the continued dominance of what remained of the Shadow Elite.

Make Cayman place the blasted things in the right holes and send out a warning to the world. If some small destruction ensued, it mattered little to him. After a few minutes they would stop the process by removing a piece.

But, his mind questioned him, *it might not be that easy. What if you can't stop the process?*

Then so be it. In the true order of things, the death of the Shadow Elite really should spell death for the world. It would be an appropriate and fitting end for this planet.

THIRTY-THREE

As a single unit they attacked the choppers. Dahl ran, firing at a Bell 205 painted jet black, as its occupants desperately tried to slam its doors close and take off. Within seconds, he hit the skids at full pelt and launched his body forward so that he flew into the cockpit, still firing. The windshield and side windows were already shattered. Bloodied men screamed and fell back as he landed among them. Fists and legs thumped against him to no effect. A bullet blasted past his cheek. Dahl wedged himself firmly on the fat stomach of a man's twitching body and sprayed the rest of the cockpit with lead. Within seconds, the interior grew quiet and still.

Dahl peered out of a side window, finding his next target.

Mai and Alicia zigzagged toward another chopper, this one equipped with weapons and looking much like an Apache, but with several modifications. As they neared the chopper, it rose off the ground, skids twitching into the air, rotors at full speed and generating the thrust required to take off. Mai slung her rifle across her shoulder without slowing down and leapt at the rising skid, grabbing hold and twisting her body acrobatically through the air so that she landed on her feet, facing the still-open door of the cockpit.

Alicia landed next to her a second later. Half a dozen shocked and terrified faces greeted them.

"Flight's over, boys."

Alicia shot a guard as he struggled to bring his rifle to bear in the small space. Mai drew her knife and leapt onto the lap of the nearest terrorist, burying the blade in his neck and scurrying across to the next. The chopper lost momentum as the pilot screamed for his life and leapt out of the far door, the machine plunging back down to earth with an almighty crash.

Luckily, it had only had time to rise about ten feet in the air. Alicia leapt clear as it came down, rolling head over heels, then coming up with her rifle sighted on the fleeing pilot. One shot sent him spinning headfirst into a drainage ditch.

Mai jumped from the cockpit a few seconds later. "Nice shot."

"Nice knifework. Now, shall we?"

Their next target, a big black Sikorsky, was already twenty feet in the air and about to swoop into flight.

Both Mai and Alicia lined up the rotors in their sights.

*****

Drake watched as Mai and Alicia played nice and took out the terrorists better than any team in the world. An escaping helicopter they targeted suddenly whirled and plummeted from the skies, crashing to the ground before a massive fireball consumed it. He had to wonder how the hell Mai did it. The Japanese agent was already back in the front line whilst he massaged his back and tried to ignore the tears and bruises that had been inflicted by the giant Belmonte had killed.

Belmonte. The master thief had bowed out with honor and was now somewhere he preferred to be. Drake knew he would never know the full story behind Belmonte and Emma, but thought he owed it to the thief to at least try to find the girl's father and explain. Without Belmonte's expertise and funding, they would never have gotten this far.

If he survived today.

All around, choppers lifted off, four-wheel-drives, and faster, heavier vehicles slewed through the churned grass and blasted toward the road. Drake's team fell to their knees, lining up targets and taking shots. Helicopters lurched a few feet and crash landed. Large Mercedes and Audis flipped onto their roofs or smashed into each other, occupants spilling out and holding wounds or shouting crazily. It was utter mayhem. A military truck bounced and jounced its way to the tarmac and began to pick up speed. In another moment, the loud hiss and searing passage of an RPG foretold the explosion that happened a split-second later. Mangled wreckage and burning rubber blocked the roadway.

With anxious eyes Drake searched among the choppers. It took seconds to spot the running band of terrorists trying to smuggle out the pieces. They were a large group, heading for one of the few military helicopters. He set off at a crazy sprint, signaling the others as best he could. To his right a small chopper roared as it lifted off, its occupants leaning out of the open door, screaming abuse as they loosed a few rounds at his feet. Drake didn't break stride or fire back. The recovery of the pieces was everything now.

With the SAS, Delta and ragtag teams made up of Dahl's and Gates's men covering and mopping up the rear guard, Drake's principal team raced to intercept the eight pieces of Odin. This was it. The whole purpose of their crazy battles over the last few months. Save the artefacts, save the world.

Hayden loped along as best she could, one hand pressed

hard to her old wound. The other held a light machine pistol but, like Drake, she was doing her best to save ammo. Kinimaka jogged at her side, face dirty and bloody, hair plastered with sweat, but eyes as hard and determined as granite. They rushed past an empty chopper, and the Hawaiian tossed a grenade inside and yelled a warning to all. A fortified Range Rover roared ahead, its blacked-out windows hiding its occupants. Kinimaka paused to send a spray of bullets through its engine bay, only moving on when he saw the first lick of flame. The less transport these bastards had available, the less chance they had of leaving this place in one piece.

Hayden met with Drake as they slowed, moving parallel to the fleeing terrorists along an avenue created by an assortment of trucks, four-wheel drives and choppers. She dared a glance behind toward the hill but saw no sign of Ben, his sister or Jonathan Gates.

Eyes to the front she saw the terrorists had reached their transport and were loading Odin's artifacts on board whilst others fanned out to create a protective perimeter.

And with perfect recklessness, Drake cut through a gap between the rear end of a Land Rover and the front of a Dodge RAM and fell among the bad guys. Hayden chased as best she could. The Englishman must have been in contact with Alicia and Mai for they now appeared, wraith-like assassins, tearing through the enemy like a blade through flesh.

As the sun set behind the nearby mountains, fire and hate and determination, fervor and heroism lit up the encroaching dark with all the glory of a colossal firework display.

THIRTY-FOUR

Drake fired twice, then slid beneath a man's return fire and swept his legs. Before that man hit the dirt, Drake shot another and was back on his feet, jabbing stiffened fingers into someone's neck and then leaping feet first toward the next, connecting hard, knocking the man's weapon aside as it bucked and sprayed bullets into the air. Ahead, the pieces were being hastily thrown aboard, the pilot already shuffling the collective. Men leaned out of every available space, rifles poised.

Drake stopped in despair. They were about to spray indiscriminately, killing everything that moved just to safeguard their getaway.

They're terrorists, he thought, as he screamed "Down!" and threw himself headlong just as they opened fire.

Hayden heard Drake's warning, but half a second too late. Her knife wound screamed as she tried to twist violently in a new direction, slowing her movements just enough. That bastard Boudreau would be the death of her yet. The nightmare sound ruptured the air and scything death sped towards her but, in the blink of an eye, something like a mountain stepped between her and obliteration.

Kinimaka! Her partner of three years jerked and spasmed as bullets took him in the chest, knocking him backward into her. His blood sprayed back into her face in a terrible cloud. Hayden collapsed with Kinimaka on top of her and began to scream.

Drake stayed prone, aimed his rifle and potted a couple of terrorist guards. Then he saw the rest being slammed from behind — Torsten Dahl had arrived, hitting hard from the back, throwing them out of the open doors face-first or into the bulkheads with a bone-cracking smash. Soon, the chopper was empty except for the pilot, and Dahl gestured severely at him to close the machine down.

Drake turned immediately to check out the screams he knew were coming from Hayden. At first, he couldn't see her, but then saw Mai and Alicia drop beside a huge bulk and felt his heart sink.

Oh no. It was Mano. Was Gates' CIA liaison underneath him? Had he taken a bullet for Hayden?

He dashed to help, momentarily putting the pieces behind his friends' welfare. Dead terrorist bodies lay all around them. He took hold of Kinimaka with Mai and Alicia and heaved the dead weight to one side. Drake glimpsed the Hawaiian's bloodied face and shredded field-jacket before his eyes fell on Hayden.

The CIA agent held her side in agony, but her eyes were filled with tears of grief and red streaks lined her cheeks.

"He saved me. . ." she blubbered. "M...Mano saved. . ."

Alicia was the first to sink to her knees in the muck around Hayden and place a hand of sympathy and support on her shoulder. "He loved you," she said. "He told me. That man would've done anything for you."

Drake wondered why he'd never seen it. Most likely because he'd been preoccupied with his own terrors of late and not given much thought to the wellbeing of everyone else. Now, across the body of Mano Kinimaka, he locked eyes with Mai and tried to communicate that he wanted to give their connection a chance.

The Japanese girl smiled tiredly, eyes drifting away across the battlefield.

Drake looked too. Plumes of black smoke belched toward the sky to mark downed choppers and demolished cars. A few helicopters managed to escape and hammered toward the last red gold vestiges of the dying sun. The dark shapes of many men lay scattered and heaped across the grass, the nearby road, and the blood-soaked hillside down which he had led the charge. Friend and foe were indistinguishable in the half-light. He saw the distinct figure of Sam and two of the man's SAS comrades trudging toward them, guns resting across their shoulders. The battle, it seemed, was won.

The eight pieces had been captured by the good guys. The world was safe.

It was all over. Two months of blood and hell and it had come to this—the loneliness of a battlefield, the horror and loss of its aftermath, the bittersweet happiness that most of his friends had survived.

Where was Ben? Where were Karin and Gates?

He couldn't see them. But then their familiar shapes emerged from the mist drifting about Sam and his boys, along with at least another half-dozen men.

A deep cough came from nearby, so harsh it sounded to his ears like the cocking of a rifle. He twisted quickly, saw only Dahl still shouting at the pilot to shut down, and frowned. *What had made that coughing sound?*

And then the body of Mano Kinimaka shuddered, and the

big man opened his eyes, staring into the skies and spitting blood from his mouth. "Shit, man." He coughed. "Felt like a Kalua pig hit me at full force."

Drake's mouth dropped open in shock. Alicia was at his side in a heartbeat, ripping the Hawaiian's jacket off.

"The Kevlar took it all." She said in a matter-of-fact way. "He's bleeding from a few small nicks around his arms." She grabbed Kinimaka's face between her small but deadly hands. "You big, lucky, beautiful bastard, you. I don't think I've ever seen a jacket take so many shots."

Drake grinned and rushed to help Hayden—broken and delirious at the sound of her friend's voice—crawl to his side. It felt good to see them embrace and he sat for a moment, spirits rising as the moon emerged from behind a cloud.

It was almost Christmas day, 2012.

Ben and Karin finally arrived, the young man staring down at his girlfriend with a look that said he hadn't the slightest notion of what to do. "I didn't want to mention this before," he said at last, "but today is the twenty-first which, according to the Mayans and some other cultures, was supposed to be the end of the world." He shrugged. "But what did they know?"

Silence followed his words, a silence broken only by Hayden's low chatter with Kinimaka and Alicia's insatiable chatting with the SAS guys.

And then the terrible clatter of a machine pistol on full-auto shattered the stillness, bullets pinging off metal and whizzing through the air. Drake turned in time to see Dahl take a dive off the helicopter, landing alive but dazed, and then saw a figure pull itself up through the far door, still firing at random whilst shouting at the pilot to take off.

"Lift off or I'll blow your fucking head to bits!"

For the second time in five minutes, Drake's mouth literally dropped open. The chopper lifted quickly, the SAS men fastest to react, but unable to shoot it down as it swooped low and flew off rapidly into the clouds.

"The Norseman!" Dahl cried. "I thought you were watching him!"

No one replied. Drake closed his eyes for a brief moment and then dragged his tired body once more to its feet.

"I know exactly where he's going." He ran quickly towards a discarded RPG launcher, but Dahl stopped him with a hard look.

"What?" Drake said. "He needs stopping fast. He's got the pieces of Odin aboard."

"What he needs." Dahl strode past them all, a resolute hatred etched into his features. "Is an Apache Attack Helicopter driven right up his arse."

The mad Swede stopped to open the door of said machine before boosting himself up. "And that's exactly what I'm going to give him."

*****

The Norseman tried to calm his racing heart. The pounding adrenalin made him want to blast the pilot to bits, but he comforted himself with the reality that he could do that later anyway. For now, the man would take him wherever he wanted to go — and that was straight to Singen, where Cayman was waiting.

"Is there a radio in here?" he asked, gesturing with the machine-pistol. His finger jerked reflexively, almost depressing the trigger. The arm of a dead terrorist flopped against his back, making his flesh crawl. One of the pieces of Odin—the carving of the Spear—toppled onto the floor with a thud. The others shifted raggedly, as if testing his resolve. A quiver of fear raced the length of his spine.

The pilot passed him a sat-phone. "Unexpected," the Norseman said in surprise, "but welcome." He quickly keyed in Cayman's number and waited.

*****

Russell Cayman, on any other mission, would long since have tried every avenue to contact his unusually absent bosses. But on this assignment, he had embraced something wholly unfamiliar. A weird feeling had taken hold—the previously unknown emotion of homecoming. Never had he felt so happy, so welcome, or experienced such a sense of belonging.

To the other men, of course, it was just a tomb, a lonely place filled with creepy noises and old bones and dusty coffins. But loneliness had always been his best friend, his happy place, and to know he now shared it with the bodies of the most depraved and powerful beings that had ever existed—much like himself—filled Cayman's empty heart with the nearest thing he would ever know to love and belonging.

As was his habit lately, he had cleared all his men out of the tomb and then climbed eagerly into the crypt of the Goddess, Kali, found his spot among her hard, outsize bones and settled his head. Eyes open he would lie there, imagining her hand creeping around his waist in the dark, her claw-like fingers rubbing the nape of his neck, and those rotted lips whispering into his ear.

"Sleep now," she would whisper. "Sleep, my boy."

His chest would fill with love and he would whisper to the eternal darkness just two words. *"Yes, Momma."*

The breeze blowing past his face was her glorious, fetid breath. The rustling in the darkness was her bones rearranging and adjusting. The faint tickle of spidery feet on his upraised cheek was the fall of her lustrous hair. The distant chatter of rats and other things was the jealous arguments of Gods, begging for their turn with her.

Which they never got. Cayman was Kali's own, her favorite, her best boy.

But Cayman was not so crazy as to think his real-life bosses would leave him to his great dream, no — they would want to shatter it with their expensive hobnailed boots. So he left his mobile phone outside the niche, and when it started to ring just as Kali's soft whisperings were lulling him to sleep, Cayman's head jerked up in guilt and shock and defiance.

Bastards! They would pay for this.

Hurriedly, he exited the crypt and snatched it up. "Yes?"

"This is the Norseman. Where on earth were you?"

So now they rebuked him even when he forced himself out of the perfect dream to take their call. "Tied up."

"Excuse me?"

"I answered as soon as I was able."

"Look, never mind that now. Much has happened. The Shadow Elite are no more."

Cayman was momentarily surprised, his interest piqued. "And what of the tomb?"

"You are allowed to sound a bit despondent about it,

Cayman. It's fine to show your feelings. We made you what you are today. I imagine that makes us some sort of parent figure to you?"

"Yes, sir, it does." Cayman imagined slicing the Norseman's face off with some ancient bits of metal he had found in Kali's tomb.

"Well, I'm sorry to say I'm the only one left. Our friends have perished."

Cayman emitted what he thought amounted to a regretful sigh. "Where are you now? Should we seal the tomb forever?" Joy snared his heart.

"Don't be ridiculous. I'm on my way to you now with the pieces beside me. We'll show the world that we still mean business. *That* is what we will do."

Cayman sensed more. "And?"

"And that tenacious bastard Drake is but a few minutes behind me with some of his cohorts. You must be ready for me, Cayman. Men at arms. Guns prepped. Tomb organized. We won't have long to implement our plan."

Cayman smiled down the phone. "Oh, I'll be ready, sir."

*****

Drake was happy to be behind Dahl as he piloted the big Apache through the oily air. The thudding of the heavy rotors was like music to his ears, Dinorock to the power of ten. The instrument array gleamed and flashed with the promise of unlimited weaponry. Dahl handed him a pair of ear mufflers.

"Fuck that," Drake said. "I'm savoring the sound and every second of being inside this machine."

Dahl laughed and clicked something on the side of his own

headphones. He had pondered for a few moments before deciding to contact Olle Akerman.

"*Ja?*"

"It's me again, Olle."

"Ah. You again. Still not dead? I have my eye on your wife, you know. Such a pretty lady."

"Not quite dead, no. We're chasing the pieces of Odin, my friend. Do you have anything that might help us?"

"I'd say—go faster. Does that help?"

"Olle—"

"*Ja. Ja.* I know. Well, do you see now? Do you remember the words that I spoke? 'The sequence of events will reveal all of the God's secrets and mankind's decision to save or destroy itself.' Odin's much vaunted *Day of Reckoning* has arrived."

"Ragnarok?"

"Yes. Odin avoided his own Ragnarok to fight in a future which he may have seen using the time-travel devices. Now it's up to you to see us through this one."

"Anything about the pieces?" Drake asked.

"I know this," Akerman said. "The pieces are *key*. Not just 'the key.' But *key*. See the difference?"

"Meaning?"

"Whilst trying to translate some of the old *Akkadian*, the so-called God language, I began to wonder why some of the *logograms* referring to the word 'key' were represented not only by pictures of the eight pieces, but also by diagrams showing the center of a great city. I now believe it means the pieces are *the most important part.* Steal, destroy or even break just one piece and the rest won't work. The device itself will never work without them."

Dahl pushed the four-bladed twin-engine attack chopper a little faster. "That's what I wanted to hear."

Akerman's last words were lost in static. "Unless we discover another way to start the weapon. . ."

Drake watched the war-machine in motion, studied the flashing keypads, spinning dials, toggles surrounded by red and black plastic. Dahl flicked several switches to prime the laser-guided *Hellfire* missiles, but essentially, these were back-up. The black shark had more armaments than you could shake an enormous stick at. What Dahl really wanted to use was the IHADSS—the Integrated Helmet and Display Sighting System—the system that could slave the helicopters 30mm chain gun to his helmet display, making the gun track and fire in accord with its wearer's head movements.

Right now Dahl's sights were on the helicopter that held the Norseman.

"Ready to end this?" The Swede brought the Apache swooping nearer, engine roaring, seeming to hover like a giant deadly fly, its "eyes" the weapon pods, its "feet" Stinger and Sidewinder missiles.

Drake sighed. "So, so ready."

Dahl let loose all hell and the Norseman's helicopter exploded in an immense fireball, bits of metal and fragments of ancient artifact and pieces of the Norseman spearing the air in every direction. The boom echoed through the mountains and chased the recently vanished sun below the silver-lit horizon.

THIRTY-FIVE

Russell Cayman heard the loud static crackle as he prepared to end the call. A second before that, he thought he might have heard the Norseman scream.

An interesting sound.

Carefully, he replaced the phone to his ear. He spoke a few words. He waited. Tried again. After ten minutes, he killed the call and redialed.

Nothing but an empty void. Almost as if there was nothing there. Cayman's lips twitched into a smile. The Norseman was dead. Drake, or someone else, had taken the old bastard out. It was over.

Cayman was free!

For now, he thought. If Drake had indeed won the day, then he would send in the wolves to raid the tomb—and soon. It took Cayman just a few moments to realize there was nothing he could do about that. Not even if he kept the Shadow Elite's demise to himself and told the men to keep fighting. The authorities possessed the might to eventually prevail.

Excitement galvanized him. Quickly, he cast about, saw a discarded holdall lying in the middle of the floor below and hurried down to collect it. Within minutes he had hastened back up the stairs to Kali's tomb and was struggling to open the great lid, employing as much force as possible. The heavy concrete slab grinded like the cracking of the earth, but before his strength gave out, he managed to widen the gap a little more.

Within minutes he had filled the holdall with Kali's bones. The larger ones, he had to snap, but he was sure the Goddess wouldn't mind—she'd been dead a long time. With the job done, he stood back from the tomb, taking it all in one last time, and felt the sharp sting of tears at the corners of his eyes.

The home he'd never had.

But he was used to moving on. All his life he'd being shipped from home to home, school to school, agency to agency—just a matter of exchanging one battlefield for the next. And he'd always been ready to kill to protect his temporary sanctuary. He hefted the bones of Kali now and walked out of the tomb of the gods without looking back again. It was time to disappear for a while.

A new chapter in his life had just opened up.

THIRTY-SIX

Mano Kinimaka had already proposed a Hawaiian Christmas, so when the big man decided to spend his recovery time over there, the entire team followed. Only a few days after beating the terrorists and the Norseman in battle, they found themselves put up by a grateful American government at a fancy hotel overlooking Waikiki Beach.

In real life, there were still many tough questions to be asked, traitors to be wheedled out worldwide, and crossed paths to be smoothed over anew, but for one night at least, the hard trials of reality vanished and celebration reigned.

With the festivities slated to begin at five, Drake took a few hours to reflect in his hotel room. With utmost luxury at his fingertips, he walked barefoot across a floor so thickly carpeted it almost felt like walking on feathers. The drapes opened by remote, the air-con operated by voice control. He went to the slightly cracked-open window and watched the waves, the sparkling blue sea and the golden beach for a while, trying to banish all thoughts from his mind.

It didn't work. His life was at a crossroads. Where did he go from here? He certainly couldn't stay living with a lodger and following a career in photography. If Kennedy had survived, then he might've built something with her. If Ben hadn't found Hayden, then maybe they could have worked something out. If Wells hadn't ordered his wife's death, then maybe he could have gotten some fucking peace. . .

His immediate thought was to run, to get as far away from the army and all things associated with it as soon as he could. But he'd tried that already—it didn't work. The army, the SAS—the regiment—was in his blood, as much a part of him as his wife and his unborn baby—Emily Drake.

A light knock sounded at the door. He knew who it would be and walked over to let her in. "Still here?" he asked, intending the double-meaning.

"For now. For tonight."

"And then what? You're gone forever? Back to Japan and undercover work? Can you do that after all this? Will you always be the soldier?"

Mai shrugged. "What choice do I have? To smooth it over with my superiors, I'll probably have to volunteer for the toughest assignment going. But you? Can you let go now?"

"If I have something to fight for. . .I think so."

"And what would you fight for?" Her eyes locked on to his like heat-seeking missiles.

"We just saved the world," Drake told her. "More than once."

"Ach, that was yesterday." Mai kicked off her shoes and ran across the carpet, following unconsciously in Drake's earlier footsteps. "Today—we're ancient history, like Odin."

Drake caught up and wrapped his arms around her waist. "You can't just leave," he told her. "Or we'll never know. Can't you give it a little time?"

"My government demanded I return by tomorrow," Mai said with sadness in her voice. "I'm still their agent. Unless you give me good enough reason to deny them, or—" She spun quickly. "They mentioned something about Gates—his 'pitch.' Know anything about it?"

Drake blinked in confusion. "Nope."

*****

When Ben Blake let himself into Hayden's room, he heard the noise of the shower running at full-force. His thoughts drifted from the horrors and terrors of warfare and the disappointment of being sacked by the band he had created—the Wall of Sleep—and being replaced by an inferior frontman on the day they performed their biggest gig, as back-up to American rock band Halestorm at the O2 Apollo in Manchester.

He'd missed out on everything. This Odin thing had destroyed all his dreams and now even made him seek out his girlfriend by way of her boss to try to make things up to her. But there was still hope. The shower presented a nice place for him to do that.

The bed squealed as he bounced off it into the bathroom. Steam and droplets of water covered every surface. Hayden had been in here for a long time. When his eyes adjusted, he saw that Hayden knelt in the shower room, naked, facing the far corner. Ben stopped in the doorway, at first admiring the curved, tanned body glistening all over with droplets of water and the fall of her hair down the middle of her back. A smile stretched the corners of his mouth, but then another noise came to his ears, loud even above the rushing water of the shower.

Hayden was sobbing terribly, uncontrollably. Her entire body shook with the force of it. Ben ran to her and received an elbow to the ear for his efforts. Hayden swung around, standing over him, fists poised to strike.

"Oh, it's you. Ben. . .there's things we should talk about."

But they didn't need to. Ben could see it all in her face. It would mean facing up to her, facing up to failure, and required more growing up than he was prepared to do right now. He saw their future. He saw their life as it was. They weren't even on the same wavelength. Hayden lifted him to his feet.

"Ben, I'm sorry." She wasn't talking about the elbow and he knew it. His clothes were soaked but he didn't care. He pulled his girlfriend close for the last time. He moved his lips close to her ear.

"I'm sorry too, Hayden. Good luck."

And Ben turned and, even though he stayed on his feet, felt like he crawled out of the shower room, trying hard to block out the sounds of her distress. He put the blame on the shower itself for the water that dripped uncontrollably from his eyes as well as his clothes.

*****

Alicia listened as Dahl called his family, switching instantly from soldier to daddy to loving husband. It reminded her of something she'd seen on the internet, a picture of a rough biker overwritten with the maxim—*doesn't matter how big or bad-ass you are, when a toddler passes you a toy phone, you answer it.*

Dahl was that kind of guy. A loving family man without equal on the field of battle. She admired him, though she'd never say so out loud. For her, feeling respect was a rare and alien occurrence. She could count the number of people she admired in this world on the fingers of one hand.

And, including Dahl, three of them resided in this very hotel. The third, Mai Kitano, had won her over despite a great internal struggle. Alicia still tried to fight it, but had conceded this was one battle she was going to lose.

To her other side, Jonathan Gates was caught in a series of endless phone calls. His smooth talking seemed to win the day more often than not. When he caught her looking curiously at him, he smiled and leaned over conspiratorially. "I have to make the most of this while I can," he said. "As of now, this minute, I have more power than the president. My team saved everyone. Not only that—we unearthed the Shadow Elite and put an end to their machinations. No one will deny me anything for the next few weeks, believe me."

Alicia nodded. "Got it. So what's this 'pitch' I keep hearing you mention? Sounds mysterious."

"Oh, it is." Gates gave her a wide, boyish smile. "I got that passed without any trouble at all after everything that has happened recently. The rest is up to you. All of you."

*****

Karin and Komodo surfaced with barely minutes to go before the party started, literally throwing on a few items of clothing and rushing for the elevators. Karin was breathing heavily, still flushed as she smoothed her skirt down.

"To be continued?" She arched an eyebrow saucily.

"Just try and stop me." Komodo grinned.

Karin draped a Hawaiian *lei* around her neck. "Look okay?"

"Any hotter and they'd have to put out the fire."

Karin swatted him. "Dickhead."

The lift arrived and whooshed open. Karin entered first and waited for the doors to close, ensuring that they were alone.

She turned to Komodo. His eyes went wide, but she shook her head. "No. Not here. Well.. maybe later. But—"

"I know what you're gonna say." The Delta team-leader hung his head. "What happens to us next? I know that look."

"So what *does* happen next, Trevor?"

"We find a way. Worst case? You could live near the barracks. It's a garrison town."

"That's not what I want."

"I got that. Got it loud and clear. I don't have the answer yet, baby. I just don't."

Karin frowned. "Baby?"

"It's American for sweetheart. Or love. Is that how they say it where you come from? *I dun't 'ave th' answer yet, luv.*"

Karin punched him on the shoulder. "You're a right tit, you know that? Look, we're here now. Better scrub up, soldier boy."

"Yes, ma'am."

*****

Little by little the team drifted out into the night. Hawaiian music backed hula dancers as they swayed on stage. Flickering, smoking torches lined the walls that circled their private courtyard. Everyone either took a seat or stood grazing around the buffet, content in each other's company, bonded by shared experiences of action and blood. A girl wearing a grass skirt threaded flowers through each guest's hair or placed them behind ears as each person stepped out. A long table bore the best of a "mainstream" Hawaiian buffet: fresh pineapple, coconut, seafood, pork and spam. Tropical cocktails were placed into every eager hand except Drake's. Pineapple cake, fresh fruit slices and a sweet dipping sauce made dessert.

Hula girls swayed their hips. A fire-knife dance took even Mai's breath away, the men gaining appreciative whistles from Alicia. It was the longest any of them had relaxed with no operation looming that they could remember.

Drake sat alone for a time, drinking in the ambience and watching each and every one of his colleagues in turn. Ben Blake, the rock-singing computer geek, who had started this journey with nothing, gained so much along the way and then ended it with even less than he started. Karin, his sister, who had somehow acquired a purpose and no longer wished to waste her life away. Komodo, the rough-looking Delta team leader who talked to Karin in such a respectful, loving way it made Drake double-take every time he heard the man's voice. Mano Kinimaka, sitting comfortably astride a makeshift bed, so happy that everyone had joined him for his Hawaiian party, now surrounded by Hula dancers, but still making sure Hayden noticed he wasn't interested in even the prettiest of them. And Hayden herself, so worn and wounded, so weary. She had fought the greatest battles of her life and had lived to fight another day. Her eyes might be red-rimmed, but her face was a determined mix of expectation and hope. He passed over Jonathan Gates, not knowing how the politician worked his clever magic, but finding his faith a little restored in the elective system. If someone like Gates could emerge as a future potential presidential candidate, then the world was not lost.

And then to Mai and Alicia—two of the most complex, crazy and ultimately capable people he had ever known. Mai was still a mystery to him, and he had known her the longest. There was no doubt she might hold the key to his future, but he could not hope to commit in one night. No way could he make that decision now. Too many variables were still juggling in the air.

Then he glimpsed Alicia, the girl who wore her heart on her sleeve, never at a loss for words, her harsh tongue her defense mechanism, but still a loyal, if misled, friend.

Finally, he glanced at Torsten Dahl and saw the Swede staring right back at him. Dahl was solid gold in every way. No more needed to be said.

Dahl wandered over. "When I first met you, Drake, back in that cavern where the World Tree grows, I thought at best you were a major prick."

"Likewise."

"I may have been a little off the mark."

Drake smiled, sweeping aside the few unresolved issues and old memories that threatened to spoil the rest of his night. "Likewise."

Dahl held a hand out. "Thanks for the help."

Drake shook it firmly. "Anytime, mate."

The evening wore on. Beyond the low torch-lit walls, the surf pounded against the beach where revelers walked, dipping their toes in the warm, foamy surf. The luau ended and the sound-system began to crank out a few old, mellow tunes as Gates clinked a spoon against a glass and asked for everyone's attention.

"Your countries thank you," he said once everyone acknowledged him. "Though they might never show it. That's my official spiel, and the only time you will ever hear it." He paused. "We're all friends here, right? So fuck that."

The Tomb of the Gods

Drake's eyebrows arched. Gates was becoming more popular by the minute.

"I'm here to say thank you, from the bottom of my heart. If it wasn't for you—all of you—I'd be dead right now. Never mind the state of the rest of the world. So here's to you. For all our sins—we still won." He raised a glass. Everyone drank.

Then he turned to Ben Blake. "Do you remember where all this started?"

Ben nodded. "For you? Yeah, back at the Library of Congress."

"You got it. And it was there, right then, that I first saw the potential for a great team. I watched you all work together and smoothed the road to see how far you could take it."

"You paved the way to keep us in the operational loop." Drake nodded. "We could never have trailed the Blood King without your help."

"I did what was required," Gates said with steel in his voice. "And, thank God, it all paid off. My decisions back then have helped my career now." He paused. "And now the time has come to try something different."

"Never a problem for me," Alicia assured him, sounding more than a little inebriated.

"I want to pitch an idea to you. But of course it's not something you aren't already doing."

"Pitch away," Mai said quietly. "Anything's better than my tomorrow."

Gates spread his arms. "Just this—I've been given the go ahead to assemble a team of specialists—that is military and IT specialists, and foreign, local agency and governmental liaisons, all of which we have assembled here tonight. I'm planning to head up an unmatched new covert agency, a first-class, extreme-team, and I'm offering you all a job."

For a moment there was utter silence, then the questions started firing off.

Drake was first. "A job doing what exactly?"

"Did you not hear the words *extreme team?*" Alicia slurred.

"We write our own charter," Gates told him. "That's just one of the beauties of it. We will choose our own assignments."

"All of us?" Komodo was asking with unrestrained excitement. "Me too? And Karin?"

"Count me in." Hayden was already nodding at her boss. "If Mano will join me?"

Kinimaka's head nodded so vigorously it threatened to roll off. "Sure."

Drake paused only to study Mai's reaction. He could tell immediately that she liked this idea more than the thought of returning to Japan and being put through the wringer once again by her superiors. For him it was a no brainer, with or without her. The difference between action and inaction for him was much more than two letters; it was a good life or a slow death.

That left just a few stragglers. Gates spoke up when he noticed Dahl's deep hesitation. "For you, Dahl, and for anyone else in the future, I propose a working package far better than the one you currently enjoy, which in English means that you'll get to see your family more often."

"How?" The Swede was no pushover.

"Look around you." Gates grinned. "At the caliber of these people and others you could recommend. Everyone will get time off to recuperate or be with their families because we will take fewer jobs than other agencies. We won't overstretch ourselves. I want my people at the top of their game. And one way to ensure that is to extend their happy time."

Dahl visibly wavered.

"But think on it," Gates said forcibly. "I'll take only those who wish to play a major role in this new initiative. I want only the best, for I will have to fight tooth and nail with some of your bosses to retain you. But know this—the funding is already in place."

"Fast mover," Alicia said. "I like it. Oh, and I'm in."

Drake saw Gates's statement a different way. To him it meant the sharks and the snakes would already be gathering at the door—the sharks to feed off the group's successes, the snakes to infiltrate its ranks.

Then Ben was at his side, a human Bassett Hound with his eyes drooping and his face all sad. "What do you think?" Almost as if he was asking permission.

Drake clapped him on the back. "I think it's a damn sight better than singing in a band and shagging groupies, mate."

"Working for the government?"

"Saving lives. Taking down evil. Hey, maybe you could ask Taylor to come and join us. Or that new group you're in to. Halestorm, is it?"

"Nah. Not any more. Lizzy won't respond to me on Twitter."

"No?" Drake tried to sound shocked. "So misguided."

"I like the sound of working with this team," Ben said. "And Karin's in."

"Don't join for Karin, mate. And certainly not for Hayden." Drake had taken off the kid gloves with Ben the moment Kennedy died. He wasn't about to put them back on now. "It won't all be a bed of roses, you know. We could get our arses kicked. If you do join, make sure it's for the team."

"What's our first assignment?" Ben asked eagerly.

Gates eyed him. "You think I'd move that fast?"

Hayden laughed. "I'd be surprised if you didn't."

"Well...there *is* something."

"Let's see what kind of major shit we can get ourselves into." Alicia joined them. "And hey, what's the HQ like? More importantly, what's the armory like? Do we have our own jet? Oh, and that surveillance system that can see through walls? Now, that would be cool..."

Gates was laughing. "Well, I'm not too sure about the jet, but within reason, we should be rather well-equipped."

Alicia grinned back. "That's my kind of talk. Let's drink to it."

Drake grinned and nodded without paying too much attention. He'd already made up his mind and zoned out for a few moments. Memories of Belmonte and Emma spun out of the fog of memory to remind him of their sacrifices. One thing Drake promised himself was that he would seek out Emma's father and explain what had really happened to his daughter. No parent should ever be in the dark about the fate of their child—no worse a torment existed.

And one vile name remained seared into his brain like a loathsome brand, like a wide-open, festering wound. The name *Coyote*—man or woman, near or far, assassin or official...

...one day, Drake would be there to claim much more than his mere pound of flesh from that person. And if the madness of vengeance claimed him afterward—then so be it.

THE END

This is the last book in an initial 4 part series.

Part 1 – 'The Bones of Odin,' Part 2 – 'The Blood King Conspiracy', and Part 3 – 'The Gates of Hell' are available now.

I would love to hear from you! All genuine comments welcome to:
davidleadbeater2011@hotmail.co.uk

Or – through Twitter:
@dleadbeater2011

Printed in Great Britain
by Amazon